Mr. Monk
and the
New Lieutenant

The Monk Series

MR. MONK
AND THE
NEW LIEUTENANT

A NOVEL BY
HY CONRAD
Based on the USA Network
television series created by
ANDY BRECKMAN

AN OBSIDIAN MYSTERY

OBSIDIAN
Published by the Penguin Group
Penguin Group (USA) LLC, 375 Hudson Street,
New York, New York 10014

USA | Canada | UK | Ireland | Australia | New Zealand | India | South Africa | China
penguin.com
A Penguin Random House Company

First published by Obsidian, an imprint of New American Library,
a division of Penguin Group (USA) LLC

First Printing, January 2015

LIBRARY OF CONGRESS CATALOGING-IN-PUBLICATION DATA:

Conrad, Hy.
    Mr. monk and the new lieutenant / Hy Conrad; based on the USA Network television series
created by Andy Breckman.
        pages cm.—(Mr. Monk; 19)
    ISBN 978-0-451-47058-4 (hardback)
    1. Monk, Adrian (Fictitious character)—Fiction. 2. Private investigators—Fiction. 3. Obsessive-
compulsive disorder—Fiction. 4. Murder—Investigation—Fiction. I. Breckman, Andy. II. Monk
(Television program). III.Title.
    PS3553.O5166M67   2015
    813'.54—dc23   2014027548

Printed in the United States of America
10 9 8 7 6 5 4 3 2 1

Set in ITC New Baskerville

To the real Sue Puskedra O'Brien,
whose only request was to be described as a stunning blonde

There has always been a weird phenomenon in my writing career: that strangers call me up out of the blue and offer me wonderful new opportunities. This isn't to say that I'm such a prize or that I'm constantly in demand. In fact, most of my efforts at self-promotion fall flat. But if I stay by the phone—or, in the modern world, my e-mail—someone I'd never heard of will track me down and offer me a great job.

This was true of the TV series *Monk*. And it was true of these books, my four efforts of translating those quirky characters from the screen to the printed page. The people at Penguin got in touch and asked if I would be up for the challenge of taking over the wildly successful series of books, started years ago by my friend Lee Goldberg.

The opportunity caught me at just the right moment. I had finished up my work on *White Collar*, completed a humor book with my partner, and bought a house in Key West, far away from the hiring fields of Los Angeles and New York. One of my life goals had always been to write an ongoing detective series, and there seemed to be no better way than to inherit the enthusiastic—one might say rabid—fans of Adrian Monk.

Unfortunately, all things come to an end. Since I started writing these books, other strangers have called me up out of the blue, and I no longer have the time to create two new adventures a year for Monk and Natalie and the old gang. I will miss them.

Without giving away too much about the plot of *New Lieutenant*, I'd like to think I've left the characters in a good spot to continue with their lives. And I hope, if a new writer takes over, he or she will take inspiration from my stopping point to create a new starting point. Long live Monk!

In my previous three attempts to continue the Monk legacy, I have thanked Tony Shalhoub and Andy Breckman, the two people most responsible for creating the legacy. They stay thanked and remain good friends.

I'd also like to add some appreciation for my agent, Allison Cohen, who is helping guide me into new, exciting frontiers, and my editor, Laura Fazio, who has been a pleasure to work with and whom I will miss.

I'm not very good at saying good-bye. But this is not really good-bye, since I'll be writing other things and you, I assume, will still be able and willing to read. But I do want to thank you all for accepting me into your Monk worlds, if only for a couple of years. Every Monk world is a little different, and I know each reader did some accommodating in order to allow me in.

I appreciate it.

Mr. Monk
and the
New Lieutenant

CHAPTER ONE

Mr. Monk and the Hippies

I have made a slow, sad discovery over the past few months. Brace yourself. You might not want to hear this: Office work is boring.

Okay, maybe that wasn't a shock. But when you fantasize about being a private eye, when you work and plan and visualize yourself opening a real business with real clients walking through the door with exciting, life-and-death problems to solve . . . Well, let's just say there are a lot of hours in the workday.

The red-and-black signage on the front window of our establishment reads MONK & TEEGER, CONSULTING DETECTIVES. I would be the Teeger. Natalie Teeger, single mom, ex-bartender, ex–blackjack dealer, ex-assistant to a brilliant and dysfunctional crime consultant. The Monk would be Adrian Monk, ex-cop and my ex-boss. We're in this thing together now, trying to share our modest office space in a mini-mall without annoying each other to death.

Even though my name is listed second, I'm the official boss. I'm the one who took the time and effort to get my investigator's license. But Monk is the one with the genius for solving any possible or impossible case—except his own case of OCD. You probably know all of this. Right? As I said, I've been bored and I'm starting to repeat myself.

Lately we've taken to splitting our hours, just to give each other a break. At first I was nervous about it. But Monk surprised me with his ability to open up the shop by himself and deal with the demands of a storefront and not scare away too many clients. He does have this habit of making mortal enemies with the other fine businesses facing onto our communal parking lot. But we're working on that. Baby steps.

It was exactly one o'clock on a cloudy afternoon when I pulled my Subaru into an empty spot just as Monk and Luther Washington were coming out the door.

As long as I'm saying things you probably already know, I'll mention Luther. He's Monk's driver. Not really a driver. But a year or so ago, Monk met Luther and bought his car service company. Luther stayed on to manage the business and give Monk a free ride whenever he needs one. I'm sure Monk could have avoided the expense of buying a company and simply paid for his rides. But that would have provided Luther with an exit strategy he doesn't have now. Luther is financially forced to be Monk's friend. And, except for a few hiccups along the way, I think it's working.

It seemed to be working on that afternoon when I pulled up. The two of them were acting like a couple of schoolboys, scurrying around the side of the black Town Car. Luther held open the passenger door for Monk, then put on his cap and got behind the wheel. They were almost giggling.

"How was your morning?" I asked through the open window, trying to keep things professional. "Any exciting business I should be aware of?"

"Exciting," Monk echoed, then seemed to change his mind. "Uh, no. Nothing exciting. We got an inquiry about a child custody case, which I turned down. The landlord came by with a plumber to check out that smell in the bathroom. They said it's my imagination, but my imagination doesn't smell like that. I'll call them again in an hour. Oh, and the hippies next door are still making a racket. You don't even have to press your ear to the wall to hear their antiestablishment music. It's practically blaring."

"Yeah," said Luther with half a grin. "They're really causing pain."

Monk answered that with half a chortle. "Causing pain. Good one."

Hmm. I wasn't aware that Luther had even met the hippies. "Okay," I said, stretching out the word. "What's up with you two?"

"Nothing, boss," said Monk, and he rolled up the window. "Go, go," I could hear from behind the tinted glass as Luther scooted back out of the space.

I watched them drive off, make a right onto Divisadero, and blend in with the downtown traffic. Okay, I thought, heaving a deep sigh. Time to visit the hippies and apologize. For whatever.

The hippies, as Monk called them, owned Paisley Printing, the shop just to the right of ours as you face the parking lot. Peter and Wendy Gerber were probably still in their twenties, thin and scruffy. Back in the seventies, they might have been labeled hippies. Since then, other labels have come and gone to describe their look: granola, new age, sixties retro—or, to quote my father, old-school San Franciscans.

Peter and Wendy were sweet and good-natured, struggling to make ends meet in a business dominated by the likes of Kinko's and Office Depot, not to mention the surge in desktop publishing. They certainly didn't deserve to have Adrian Monk holding his nose every time he smelled a whiff of incense, or his pounding on the thin walls every time he heard the music of the old guitar that Peter plucked on during the spells between their printing jobs.

"Natalie," Wendy called out warmly through the open door. At least she still considered us on speaking terms.

"Wendy. How is everything? I hope Adrian hasn't been bothering you."

"Adrian? What a sweet old soul he has. No, I haven't seen him." Wendy was a long-haired brunette, but with the kind of frizzy, flyaway hair you might expect on someone my age. She swept back a long strand. "I expected to see him pacing out front, you know, spooking away customers, only we don't have any customers."

"Natalie." Peter was toward the back of the shop, looking up from a laptop. He sported a scruffy three-day growth that always looked the same. "I love it when Adrian pounds the wall. He can't help but keep time, so it's like I've got my own drum section. Freakin' cool."

"My bad. We did have a customer," Wendy recalled. "Clyde. I forget his last name. African-American dude with a very centered aura." She held up her hands as if holding the aura for me to examine. "Teeny tiny order but super weird. We wasted all morning getting it right."

"Time is never a waste," Peter corrected her. "It's an artificial construct reflecting the circular flow of the universe. We're all part of it, you know."

"Don't mind him." Wendy laughed. "You can decide for yourself if it was a waste." And with that, she led me behind the counter to the monitor on top of the main, white-laminate work space. "I guess it's for a clinic or a medical supply business?" She phrased it as a question.

Wendy used her mouse to bring up the image of a poster. The letters were big, almost magenta on a multicolored background, in a kind of retro-forties font. There was no illustration to speak of, just four oddly spaced words filling the lower part of the sign, plus an arrow.

HIP
CAUSING YOU PAIN?
⟶

"I guess it's a window ad," I suggested. "For a hip replacement facility? You're right. It is super weird. How big was the final product?"

"Clyde was very specific," said Peter as he joined us at the worktable. "It had to be exactly two feet two inches by three feet seven and a half inches. He kept looking at a photo, but real James Bond secret-like. He kept fiddling with the color and spacing. It must have taken us an hour plus."

"And after all that, he only wanted one copy," said Wendy,

shaking her frizz. "We kept telling him a dozen would be almost as cheap, but he said he only needed one. Matte finish on a self-adhesive plastic-peel backing. All-natural inks, too."

"Did he pay cash?" I asked. I had a sinking feeling about this story. "Did he wait and take it with him?"

"Whoa," said Peter. "Both of those. It's like you're tapping into his spirit."

"Unfortunately, I think I am." From the start there had been something familiar about the font and the colors—and, now that I thought about it, about the African-American man . . . and the phrase "causing pain," which I'd run into more than once in the past few minutes. Just call me Sherlock.

"Natalie, where are you going?"

Peter and Wendy followed me out of the shop and to the right. I couldn't stop them, not that I wanted to. If I was right, they deserved to see it.

And there it was, plastered on the stucco wall that separated Paisley Printing from the third shop in the row, the Farmers' Natural Market, a pricey, overly quaint food store. Gracing the wall space—as recently as an hour ago—had been two side-by-side paintings, both done in an old-fashioned style, brightly colored and reminiscent of fruit crate labels. The first announced the presence of "Fresh Baked PIES" while the second celebrated the shop's "Fair Trade COFFEES."

"Freakish mystery solved," I said.

At the moment, the coffee painting was completely obscured by Peter and Wendy's newly printed hip ad. I had to hand it to Luther; it was a perfect fit. It covered the coffee ad perfectly. And the letters, with a nearly identical font, lined up with those of the pie painting next to it. "Not cool," said Peter, staring at it and tugging at his stubble. "Who would do this?"

The "this" in question was the following:

FRESH

BAKED

HIP PIES

CAUSING YOU PAIN?

$\longrightarrow$

The bold red arrow pointed directly to the Paisley Printing storefront. "Fresh baked hippies." I moaned as I read.

"It was Adrian, wasn't it?" said Wendy. "Why would he . . . I know he has his issues going on. But I thought he at least respected us."

"It wasn't Adrian," I stammered. "I mean, it was. Obviously. But he doesn't do practical jokes. Clyde, your African-American dude? His name is Luther and he's Adrian's friend. Luther must have been the force behind it."

"It is kind of funny," Peter admitted, getting over his initial shock. "We worked so hard making it just right. And the whole point was to prank us with our own work. Good job."

"I'm so sorry," I said. "I'll go talk to the market people. I'm sure they can peel it off without harming the wall."

"It's totally harmless and peelable and biodegradable," said Peter. "The dude paid extra to make sure." He stretched to his full height, grabbed the top two corners and slowly pulled down the fake hip ad. It came off in one piece, and he just stood there, holding it, staring at it, his eyes drooping at the edges. "We like to take pride in our work, you know? Make the client happy."

"I'm sure they were happy," I said lamely.

A few minutes and several more apologies later, I was back in my office, at my desk, on the phone, doing my best to yell at Luther Washington. Or should I say Clyde?

"It was Mr. Monk's idea," he said smoothly, refusing to raise his voice in response. "I acted as the facilitator, you might say."

"That is so not true. I know Adrian a lot better than you do. He would never even think of pulling a prank like that. He can be unthinking and self-centered and a dozen other things. But the man is not cruel."

"Well, maybe I did go proactive," Luther admitted. "But I had to do something to stop his whining about the hippies. I figured he needed to feel some control over the situation."

"And hurting their feelings made him feel in control?"

"Hey, the poster was his brainstorm. He went through the whole morning smiling and focused and not worried about a thing."

"I know. That's how he gets when he's in the middle of a case. But a case is a lot more productive than insulting a couple of sweet people we have to work next door to every day."

"So we punked the hippies. Big deal." Luther lowered his voice to a growl. "We all got our ways of dealing with Mr. Monk. You use your psychology and I use mine. It's as simple as that."

It wasn't as simple as that. Being a caretaker for Monk is a delicate proposition. In the past I never had to worry about some stranger coming in and leading our little genius astray. For one thing, it takes a rare character to put up with him. For another, Monk has a moral compass of magnetized iron. He won't even warn me about a lurking patrol car on a freeway when I'm going a few miles over the speed limit. "Yes, I saw him, but I'm not a radar detector," he would say as the officer would be busy writing me a ticket on the side of the road. "That would have been cheating."

But there are always gray areas, chinks in Monk's armor. One of those chinks is his need for friendship. Luther is Monk's employee and has a vested interest in at least pretending to be a friend. And Luther, I was discovering, had ways of working outside the box.

I don't know which happened first—Luther hanging up on me or Daniela Grace walking through the door. Let's say they happened at about the same time. "Daniela," I said, putting down my phone and breaking into a big smile. "Good to see you."

"Don't get too excited, dear. I don't come bearing a new case."

Daniela is a senior partner in a white-shoe law firm, although with her, the preppy white oxfords had been replaced by black Manolo Blahnik heels. She was skirting the upper reaches of middle age, thin and stylish and reminiscent of my mother. It takes a village to keep these women looking so spectacular.

I tried to hide my disappointment. "You don't have to have a case to come and visit. It's always a pleasure. Do you want some tea?"

"No, thanks. Just a quick question." She stood in the doorway as if expecting me to get up and go over to greet her—which I did, of course. "The last time I was here, I noticed that printing company next door. Have you ever availed yourself of their services?"

"Yes, as a matter of fact." I don't know why I say half the things I do. "Just availed ourselves this morning. They did a project for Adrian." I was telling the truth. And I suppose I was feeling a little guilty and sorry.

"Was Adrian happy with their work?"

"Happy?" I replied. "He was practically giddy."

Despite the years of expertly injected Botox, Daniela managed to raise her eyebrows. "High praise indeed. My firm is putting together a series of IPO documents for one of our clients. All very hush-hush. We would do it in-house, but frankly our people get paid too much by the hour and don't have the time. You say these printers do high-quality work? Are they reliable?"

"Very reliable and great quality. They did a color match on a sign that was incredible."

"Good," said Daniela. "Personal recommendations are always the best." She took a step out the door and examined the hanging sign. "Paisley Printing."

"They're good people," I insisted. "They won't overcharge and they seem very careful and honest."

"Done," said Daniela, and made a right turn out the door without ever coming fully inside. "I'll say you recommended them."

"Please do," I called out after her, then turned back to face my empty office.

At least someone was getting a job today.

CHAPTER TWO

Mr. Monk Celebrates a Birthday

It turns out we got a job, too. Peter and Wendy might have considered this the result of my good karma, but only if they ignored Monk and Luther's bad karma.

Less than five minutes after Daniela went over to introduce herself, my phone rang. It was Captain Stottlemeyer with a consulting gig. We hadn't had a police case in months, not since that infamous triple homicide in that warehouse on Stockton Street. I guess that's the curse of specializing in weird, unsolved murders and living in a relatively safe city.

Once or twice during this dry spell we'd run into the captain. But neither of us had seen Lieutenant Amy Devlin in ages. She was the captain's number two and I was eager to see how she was doing. Even though it had all worked out, I knew the triple homicide had been hard on Amy, both professionally and personally.

As soon as I hung up, I called Monk's apartment. When he didn't answer, I swallowed my pride and called Luther. "Yep, he's with me," Luther reported. "We're shopping for apples."

"How's it going?"

"We found eight, so I'm thinking another fifteen minutes."

I told Luther about the job and gave him the address, a stately single-family home on El Camino del Mar, just a five-iron shot from the Lincoln Park Golf Club.

When I pulled up, they were already on the scene. Luther was leaning against his Town Car, munching around the core of what looked like a red Gala. He didn't like going into crime scenes—squeamish, I guess—which was fine with me. "Sorry about the prank," he said, not looking at all sorry. "How did the hippies take it?"

"They were amazed and shocked and hurt," I said. "But they'll get over it."

"Good. Tell Mr. Monk the cars are all booked this evening and all day tomorrow, so I won't be able to drive him."

"That's fine. You shouldn't have to do it anyway. Just because he's your boss . . ."

"I don't mind it in small doses. It's kind of like a social experiment." Luther handed me a brown paper bag filled with small, flawless apples, then got into his Town Car. "By the way . . ." He started rolling up the driver's side window. "There are nine left."

"Nine? What's he going to do with nine apples?" Luther just smiled and pulled away, leaving me holding the bag.

I was still standing there when Monk came storming out of the house, wearing blue booties and plastic gloves. "Natalie, Natalie, Natalie." He was almost screaming.

"It wasn't me," I instantly tattled. "Luther ate one. I couldn't stop him."

"What? Apples? Who cares about apples? Devlin's gone. And that's not the worst part."

"How can she be gone?"

By the time I got him somewhat coherent, Captain Stot-tlemeyer had come out to join us. He was also in booties and gloves and didn't look pleased that his investigation had been interrupted. "What happened to Devlin?" I demanded.

"She took an administrative leave," said the captain. "But between you, me, and the fence post, I think she's quitting."

"And that's not the worst part," Monk repeated.

I didn't know which was more disturbing, the fact that Amy was thinking of quitting or the fact that she hadn't told me. "Quitting? Why didn't she tell me?" I said, covering both bases.

"Wait till you hear the worst part."

"All right, Adrian. Tell me the worst part."

It was at precisely that moment that the worst part came out of the doorway, looking as smug as you can in plastic booties and gloves. "Are you girls coming inside or not?"

His name was A.J. Thurman. Lieutenant Thurman. His father, Arnold Senior, had been a captain on the force—a well-respected, stand-up guy who'd retired just a few years back. No one knows how Arny Junior became a lieutenant. It certainly wasn't due to his social skills. Monk and I had known A.J. for years. Even as a rookie, he'd been a rude loudmouth with no respect for anyone.

"The worst part is Lieutenant Thurman," said Monk.

"I realize that," I whispered out of the corner of my mouth.

"Then why did you ask?"

A.J. shook his head. He has a look that just screams "cop": intimidatingly large with a sandy crew cut and enough sub-stance around his middle to let you know he means business. His laugh, right at the moment, was mean and condescending. "There's no love lost on either side of this, Nattie girl. But since the captain is determined to waste taxpayer money on you . . . what do you say? Anyone up for fresh booties?"

"Lieutenant Thurman is my new partner," said Stottlemeyer, lowering his voice to a growl. "And since we're all professionals, I expect you to get along."

"You replaced Amy with him?" I had to ask. "Him?"

"That's not what I meant by getting along."

From then on we tried to keep it civilized. I deposited the bag of apples in my car. Then the captain joined us in donning new footgear and hand gear. Seconds later we were in a huge Arts and Crafts living room that looked like it hadn't been touched in a century, with a beamed ceiling, dark wood wainscoting that came up to my shoulders, and a stacked stone fireplace you could roast an ox in.

Two CSIs were working the room, one of them dusting for prints, the other taking scrapings from under the fingernails of the body on the hardwood floor beside the grand piano. He finished with the second hand, bagged the results, then stepped back and let Monk in there to do his thing.

The victim was an elderly woman dressed in a sky blue bathrobe and matching slippers. The presumed weapon was at her side—a carved stone doorstop, probably used to hold open the substantial front door during the month or two of hospitable weather we get every year. Monk examined the bloodstains on the stone and the gaping wound on her left temple where a section of her skull had been caved in.

"The name is Margery Burns," said A.J., referring to a small spiral notebook. "She lived alone. No one else came or went on a regular basis except the weekly cleaning service.

Today was their day. Around one p.m. they found her like this. The body was a few hours old, ten a.m. or thereabouts. The ironic thing is . . ." He paused to chuckle.

"Today was her birthday," said Monk, barely looking up from the body.

"How did you know?" The lieutenant glared at Monk the way a Puritan might have glared at a witch.

"The piano is covered with unopened birthday presents and cards," Monk pointed out, "meaning that her birthday was coming up but hadn't yet arrived. She didn't open things until her birthday, apparently. I approve of that."

"So what?" said A.J. "Tomorrow could be her birthday. Ever think of that? Or the day after."

"No," countered Monk. "Ms. Burns has a ring of pearl and alexandrite on her right ring finger. Those are both stones for June and today is June thirtieth, last day of the month. Alexandrite is a fairly rare stone and combined with a pearl, it practically screams birthstone ring. Plus, you just said the word 'ironic' with that mean little laugh of yours. What was I supposed to think?"

"Today's her birthday," A.J. confirmed, and went back to his notes. "Our reconstruction is that a burglar broke in through the kitchen pantry door. When the victim heard the noise and came downstairs, she confronted the intruder and was attacked with the doorstop. On her birthday. The burglar then ran upstairs, took a jewelry box and cash from the victim's bedroom, and fled the scene."

"Why didn't he take the rings from her fingers?" I asked. This was a standard question.

"Because he'd just killed an old lady and wasn't cold

enough to pry them off," said the lieutenant. "Besides, any-one who watches TV knows that handling a corpse can leave tracers—fingerprints, skin fragments."

"And why did he use the doorstop?" Monk asked. This was not a standard question.

"What do you mean?" asked the captain.

Monk stood up from the body. "I mean there are heavy objects all around." He pointed. "There's what looks like a Roman bust on the piano, a heavy crystal vase in that niche by the stairs, two matching Chinese pots on the tables under the window. Sharp objects and blunt objects everywhere. Yet the killer walks over to the front door and bends down to pick up a doorstop. Why?"

"Why do you think, Monk?" asked A.J. Monk rolled his shoulders but didn't answer.

"Captain?" The dusting CSI had finished the room and was ready to give a preliminary briefing. "We'll need to take elimination prints from the body and the cleaning service. But it looks like the perp did some wiping down. There are wipe streaks on the doorstop and the doorknob. Also the coffee table top and one of the chairs; chair arms and back." He pointed to a pair of wood and leather chairs in front of the coffee table.

"Could that have been done by the cleaning service?" asked Stottlemeyer.

"I think not," said the CSI. His name was Ted and we'd worked with him before. A smart guy. "They were last here a week ago today, so there's a slight dust layer on most things—except the doorstop and chair, et cetera, which, as I said, have been wiped down."

"Are there prints on the other chair?" asked Monk.

"Yes, sir. My guess is they're old prints from the victim, but we'll have to wait until we get to the lab to be sure."

"So our burglar-murderer wiped down a chairback," I said. "Why would he do that?"

"Plenty of reasons," said Lieutenant Thurman. "After killing her, he sat down to think things over. Or he touched the chair during the commission of the crime, maybe knocked it over and had to pick it up."

"Pick it up?" The captain shifted his gaze to the chaos of the blood and the corpse not five feet away. "That was very tidy of him."

"Or the bad guy took a seat and waited for Mrs. Burns to come down the stairs this morning, which goes against your theory of a burglary gone wrong." That was my opinion.

Ted had no opinion of his own. That wasn't his job. With the room now clear, he excused himself to go upstairs to work on the bedroom, where the jewelry box was missing. A.J. waited until he was gone. "Enough of the fancy questions, Monk. It was a burglar, plain and simple. Come back to the point of entry and see for yourself."

"I don't need to. You go," said Monk to the rest of us. Then he raised his hands in his patented style, as if framing the scene, and began focusing on the grand piano.

The kitchen pantry was at the back of the old house, beyond the parlor and the dining room and the kitchen. On the door to the rear yard, a pane of glass had been broken just above the lock mechanism. A trail of muddy footprints was staggered across the white tile.

There are several ways to tell if a bad guy broke into a

house or just faked a break-in. And all these ways are known to anyone who has ever read or watched a mystery. For example, glass shards outside the window would indicate it had been broken from inside. A shard caught in the trough would prove the window had already been open. The lack of footprints on the outside . . . etc. Any of these clues is a red flag and easily avoidable by anyone with half a brain and half a minute.

In this case, there were none of these indicators, which proved nothing. But it was enough to make A.J. adopt a smug I-told-you-so grin. Meticulously, he led us through the lack of evidence, then actually said it: "I told you so."

"Maybe." The captain shrugged. "It's a decent theory, don't get me wrong. But let's get Monk's opinion."

A.J. bristled. "I should have known. What you're saying is you trust Monk's opinion more than you trust mine."

"No, Lieutenant, that's what I'm trying very hard not to say."

CHAPTER THREE

Mr. Monk and the Family Values

On our way back to Monk and the grand piano, we passed the dining room again, and for the first time, I noticed two middle-aged women sitting patiently, their hands folded, as if waiting for dinner to be served. "Is she still out there?" the taller, more pulled-together one asked meekly. I could barely hear her.

"Yes, ma'am," said A.J. "The coroner's people should have her bagged and removed within the next fifteen."

A.J. would have just left them there and moved on. But the captain decided we could spare a few humanizing moments. We joined him at the table as he sat down to explain what was happening and to express his condolences.

These women were not the cleaning service, as I had assumed from their outfits and their attitude. They were, in fact, two of the five daughters-in-law—Julia Burns and Louisa Burns—who had been informed of the matriarch's death and had come over to do what they could to help out. It was a telling detail that none of the five sons had yet arrived, and only two of the daughters-in-law were there.

A.J. seemed anxious to get back to what he considered the real investigation. But Stottlemeyer behaved like a regular human, taking time with the relatives of the deceased, prodding them with a few sympathetic words. He seemed eager to listen.

The Burns family, we learned, was a dysfunctional mess, with five underachieving sons, no daughters, and the widow Margery, who had just turned eighty-two today. Happy birthday.

According to the daughters-in-law, Margery had never been a pleasant woman, and her sons had inherited many of her traits. According to the women who knew them best, all five were greedy and cheap, with very little sentimentality about the family, especially Mom.

"What about all the cards and presents on the piano?" I asked. From what I'd seen, there had been at least one red and gold Cartier box gracing the piano top.

"Pure fear," said Louisa. "Mother Burns was always changing her will or threatening to. None of her boys had any money. One of them runs a bookstore, another does landscape lighting. My Jimmy works part-time as a mechanic."

Julia sighed in agreement. "The wives call it the inheritance curse, this kind of underachieving attitude. If a man gets promised millions, enough to set him up for life . . . Well, it takes a certain strength of character to forge your own way in the world. The money could come any day, as my Eddie keeps saying. Or it could be twenty more years."

"They thought they would get some on their father's death," said Louisa. "But he'd left everything to Mother Burns. They hated him for that. Her, too, for keeping it all."

"Still think it was a burglar?" I whispered out of the side of my mouth. The lieutenant grunted but didn't answer.

"Did Mrs. Burns know her sons felt this way?" asked Stottlemeyer.

Julia nodded. "She was hurt. Called them ghouls. She stopped asking them to visit, which was fine with them. But the woman still expected her presents and cards. The boys would scrimp and save. And heaven forbid if they bought something on sale. She would somehow always know, like a sixth sense."

"Are all the sons currently in the will?" I asked.

"As far as we know, yes," said Louisa. "But that can change at any moment."

"Actually, it can't." Monk was standing in the doorway. I don't know how much he'd overheard, but it was probably enough. "The will can't change, now that she's dead."

"You're right," said Julia. "Are you a policeman, too?"

"Not quite," I said, and I took this chance to introduce ourselves—Monk and Teeger, consulting detectives. I expressed my condolences, although it seemed like no one in the family needed consoling.

"We took their statements before you got here," Stottlemeyer said. "Both Mrs. Burns teach at the Bay School in the Presidio. They were in classes all day until the lieutenant started making his calls to the next of kin."

"The ME's office just removed the body," Monk informed the rest of us. The women looked relieved. "Why don't we go back to the living room?" he suggested. "I want to open the presents."

Before anyone could ask why, Monk was leading us back to the mansion's imposing main room. "Normally I would need your permission as family members," he explained. "But since this is a crime scene, I don't."

"Go ahead," said Julia. "It's not as if you're ruining the surprise for her."

"Just be careful," said Louisa. "I know my Jimmy. I'm sure he'll want to return whatever he bought."

Monk started with the birthday present closest to him, the small red-and-gold Cartier box. The gift tag said it was from Carl, the eldest. "Did the mail come today?" Monk asked as he carefully untied the ribbon, pressed it flat, folded it neatly, and put it to one side.

"It did," said A.J. "It was on the floor when the cleaning staff came. No cards or presents, if that's what you're thinking. Just a catalog and the PG and E bill."

"Got it," said Monk. A second later, he had opened the box, riffled through the tissue paper, and held up a small gold mesh bracelet. Very elegant. I'm embarrassed to say all three women in the room said "ooh" pretty much in unison.

Monk set the bracelet aside and went on to the box shaped suspiciously like a picture frame. He worked on the ribbon while the rest of us stood there and practiced the art of patience. "Would you care to know why the killer used the doorstop as a weapon?" Monk asked the air in front of him. "Just for your information."

"Enlighten us," said Stottlemeyer.

"Because it was cheap and heavy," said Monk. "The killer didn't want to damage anything that was part of the estate. The Roman bust or the Chinese vases are valuable. Breaking them would have hurt the killer's inheritance."

"Inheritance?" said Louisa, looking a little insulted. "Are you saying one of her own sons did this? One of our husbands?"

"Picture frame," answered Monk. He held up a designer frame. Offhand, I'd say antique platinum with a thin edge of mother-of-pearl. Inside was a photo, almost as old as the frame, of Margery and her five young sons, all smiling, unaware of what the future would bring them.

"That's from Eddie," said Julia. "I picked it out myself."

"Lovely. Where did you get it?" I had to ask.

"At Gump's on Post Street. They have some great things."

"I know," I said. "My parents used to shop there."

"Is this chitchat part of the investigation?" asked the lieutenant. He had a point, although he could have phrased it nicer.

Meanwhile, Monk had gone on to the ribbon on the next box. "Does anyone know why Mrs. Burns was killed on her birthday?" he asked the air again. "Any opinions?" I could tell he was goading A.J. And A.J. was just dense enough to take the bait.

"A coincidence," he answered. "Or maybe the burglar did his homework. He knew there'd be presents worth taking. Or maybe he figured she'd be sleeping late on her birthday."

"Maybe," said the captain, meaning *I doubt it very much.* "Monk, why don't you tell us? This is why we're paying you the medium-sized bucks."

Monk's mouth turned up into a thin smile. Everyone likes being appreciated. "The difference between Ms. Burns' birthday and any other day was that she opened her presents. So, we're opening the presents." He had already untied, pressed, and folded a third ribbon.

It was an unimposing gift box, the kind you could buy at any Walmart. Instead of fancy tissue paper, it was lined with crumpled newspaper. Inside the layer of newspaper was a simple glass bowl, like a little fishbowl. Monk held it up. And this time no one said "ooh."

"What the hell?" said Louisa. "How did that get here?"

"Do you recognize it?" Monk asked.

"Yes. It's usually on a shelf in our pantry. I think flowers came in it originally. You know how it is with cheap vases. You always keep them somewhere, just in case."

Monk checked the card on the piano. " 'From your adoring son, Jimmy.' "

"Whoa," said A.J. "Jimmy really dropped the ball on this one."

"Not just the ball," said Monk. "He dropped the doorstop, too."

CHAPTER FOUR

Mr. Monk and the Minimum Wage

Two days later, I was doing the morning shift.

Business had picked up slightly. Through a personal connection—namely, my daughter, Julie—our firm had been hired to do a few background checks for a software company in Berkeley that had been founded by a few of her ex-classmates. It wasn't something Adrian and I liked doing, and frankly, there were a lot of security companies that did this sort of thing better. But it helped pay the rent.

I was determined to finish up one of the checks before lunch, but I got sidetracked by a call I had to make to Lieutenant A.J. Yesterday I'd sent him an invoice for the Burns case and had just received an authorization for only a fraction of our usual fee. With anyone else, I might have thought it was a mistake. With A.J., I knew it was trouble.

"I'm paying you for two hours," A.J. said when I asked. "And I was generous enough to include travel time. You and the Monkster were there for an hour, max. Your boy wanders around the house, opening birthday presents and making mysterious pronouncements. Then he spits out a name and expects to get paid for a full day?"

"But it was the right name," I argued. "You were looking for some fictitious burglar, if I might remind you."

"We would have checked all the angles."

"The captain would have checked the angles."

"I would have, too. It's procedure. The sons had a motive, which was something I didn't know to start with. And if Jimmy ever tried to sell the jewelry he stole from her bedroom . . ."

"Blah, blah, blah. You would have spent days tracking down all the brothers, checking their alibis. The presents on the piano would have been returned unopened, and the one crucial lead in the case never would have seen the light of day. That cheap little bowl would be back on a shelf in Jimmy's pantry. No questions asked."

Monk had been right, of course. Margery Burns had been murdered by her one son who'd simply grown tired of waiting. Another birthday, Jimmy Burns must have thought. Another obligation to buy something criminally expensive for a sour old woman who kept threatening to disinherit him. This eighty-two-year-old who refused to die.

So Jimmy refused to buy one more thing. Instead, he sent a gift-wrapped decoy. Then he broke in on the morning of her birthday, sat in the living room, and waited for her to come downstairs. When she did, he grabbed the doorstop and gave his mother the one gift that keeps on giving.

Jimmy's wife, Louisa, hadn't known anything. That's what she said. And that's what Jimmy said. When Captain Stottlemeyer and Lieutenant Thurman brought him into an interview room and turned on the heat and brought out the glass bowl . . . That was all it took.

"Adrian got you the thing that got you the confession," I pointed out, trying to keep my temper in check. "He saved you days of work and a dozen false leads."

"I'm not arguing about that. Look, an electrician saves me days of work. That's his job. But if an electrician takes an hour to replace some wiring, I'm not going to pay him for a full day. No way."

"Yes way," I said with great eloquence. "We don't do hourly fees. On a case like this, Lieutenant Devlin used to pay a two-day fee or more—until the DA came through with the indictment. That's been our understanding for years."

"Well, the understanding just changed," said A.J. "Now, if you'll excuse me, I have police business to take care of."

In response, I probably said something sarcastic and clever, but I don't remember. I do remember slamming down the phone. And I remember stepping outside and pacing the parking lot, trying to calm myself. If I'd had a cigarette, I would have lit up and smoked the damn thing. Well, maybe an e-cigarette.

I was going to have to have a talk with Adrian about solving cases so quickly. I knew it was a matter of pride with him, like a magician popping up at the back of the audience seconds after he's locked into a box onstage. But the magician isn't being paid by how long it takes him to get out of the box.

When my pace slowed and I could finally see straight, I noticed her. She was a woman about my age, also a blonde. But she kept her hair a little longer, a little wavy, and had highlights of auburn in it, while mine had highlights of mousy brown. Other than that, we were fairly similar, which was probably what made me instantly sympathetic. "Excuse me," I said. "Can I help you?"

The woman was standing at the curb, not far from the pawn-shop entrance. But she wasn't focused on the rings in the window. She was focused on the Monk & Teeger sign. She seemed indecisive, trying not to stare but not ready to walk away, either. I could empathize. It must not be easy to come in off the street and entrust your problems to a complete stranger. "I don't mean to intrude," I said, "but do you need a detective? I know that's an odd question. But the way you're looking, you either need a detective or a color copy or a fresh baked pie."

The woman chuckled. "You're right. I do need a detective. I've been standing here for the longest time, trying to get up the nerve. Are you Monk or Teeger?"

I invited her inside, made a new pot of coffee, and informed her that I was Teeger. She was Sue O'Brien.

It took Sue a while to get to her point, but I didn't press her. We just sat in the two client chairs, nothing too business-like, and chatted—about life and children (she didn't have any) and husbands (I no longer had one) and careers and friends and how her colorist knew how to get just the right auburn hints into her hair with just a touch-up every two weeks. She had a warm, infectious laugh and after a few minutes, I felt as if I'd known her forever.

I did notice that when the subject veered toward her husband, she tensed a little. The third time this happened, I ventured a guess. It might have been rude of me, but . . . "Sue." I bit my lower lip. "We don't do divorce work."

"Oh." She looked disappointed. "That's too bad. I was hoping you might be able to help me."

"I would love to. Truly. But my partner, Adrian Monk, he's our primary investigator. He won't do divorces. You see, he had a wonderful marriage to a woman who died. He looks at divorce as a kind of betrayal of marriage. Nothing personal," I assured her. "Of course, murdering your wife is also a betrayal, and we've worked on plenty of spouse-murdering cases. Don't ask me for the logic here."

"No," said Sue with a nod. "I'm a practicing Catholic. I understand his objections. There is something sordid about skulking around looking for affairs and hidden bank accounts."

"Is your husband having an affair?"

"He is," she said. "With someone at his company. But I have no proof. And I'm pretty sure Timothy is hiding money in a secret account somewhere."

"Why?"

"Because . . ." Sue covered her mouth and cleared her throat. "Because at some point soon Timothy is going to ask for a divorce. I can feel it. And when he does, I want to have my ducks in a row. I don't want him shafting me in the settlement. Pardon my French."

"What makes you think he's planning to shaft you?"

"You tell me, Natalie. Let's say your husband is a top-tier divorce attorney who's fooling around with a coworker who happens to be another top-tier divorce attorney. Wouldn't you want to be prepared?"

"Your husband and his girlfriend are both divorce lawyers?"

"Two of the biggest sharks in the city. Over many a dinner, he's told me tales about hiding assets for his male clients. That's why I need a good private investigator."

"What you need is a good lawyer," I suggested.

Sue shook her highlighted locks. "The second I go to a lawyer, Timothy will find out, believe me. Even going to one of the big private investigators could be a stupid move. Timothy uses private investigators all the time. And the second Timothy knows that I suspect him, it'll be over. He'll see that I get next to nothing. A divorce lawyer's divorce? Please. It will be like a living billboard for him. A matter of pride."

Speaking of pride, mine was now hurt. "So that's why you're hanging out in strip malls. You're trolling for some insignificant, off-the-radar PI. Is that it?"

"Sorry." Her checks flushed. "Not insignificant. But you have no connection to Timothy. The only chance I have is to be ready when he comes after me. Are you sure you can't help me?"

"I told you. Adrian won't touch it."

"What about you? You're a private investigator. Mr. Monk doesn't have to be involved. You're the head of the company. He can't tell you not to take a case."

"It's not that straightforward, Sue. We're partners."

We went back and forth like this. She was a nice woman in need. She had no career of her own and no other source of income, which made her feel even more vulnerable. But at least there were no children to complicate matters. Sue O'Brien had done nothing worse than to be married to a cheating divorce lawyer. It was hard to keep saying no to her.

"Adrian's going to be here any minute," I finally pleaded, checking my watch. "He's never late, and . . ."

"And you don't want him asking questions and getting all

excited about a divorce case. I get it. I just hope you can change your mind. It would mean so much."

Sue O'Brien gave me her card and I gave her mine. Even though there was no reason to, it seemed polite.

I had just returned from washing the coffee cups in the bathroom, eradicating as much evidence of her visit as I could, when I looked out the front window and saw him approaching in that smooth but awkward stride he had when avoiding the perilous cracks in the sidewalk.

"Did you change perfumes?" he asked. Those were the very first words out of his mouth.

"Yes," I lied. "And I just had a cup of coffee and washed out the cup, in case you're wondering."

Monk seemed to accept this at face value. He wiped his private peg on the wall and hung up his jacket. "Lieutenant Thurman is only paying us for two hours," I informed him.

"But I solved the case." He was still centering his jacket on the peg.

"But it only took an hour. How many times do I have to tell you to take your time?"

Monk looked aghast at the thought. "Taking extra time would be cheating."

"Cheating? How is it cheating?"

"Because the bad guys would think they're smarter than they are. It sends a wrong message—like throwing softballs so that your kid can hit a few and not feel so bad."

"First of all, that's not cheating—that's good parenting. And second, it's not the same thing at all."

"Plus it's dereliction of duty. If I'd taken an extra day, I wouldn't be doing my best work. And who knows what kind of new mischief Jimmy might have done in the meantime?"

"Really? You think he might have killed another eighty-two-year-old relative if you hadn't so instantly pointed him out? Admit it, Adrian, you were showing off."

"I do things at my own speed," Monk said, still arranging his jacket on the peg. "Not because I might get paid more."

"Well, something had better change, because if the department starts paying us by the hour, we're going to be out of business."

"You should talk to the captain." The jacket was finally perfectly centered. If only he spent this much time on the details of solving each case.

"I will talk to him," I promised. "But consulting expenses are under the control of the lieutenant."

"Then we need to get rid of the lieutenant."

"I'll talk to the captain," I promised again. "Meanwhile, we need new cases, ones that you can't solve in an hour. I realize the money is my part of the business, but you need to start being more flexible."

"I am not working on a divorce, so you can tell her no thanks."

"Tell who?"

"The woman who was just here. It's not your perfume. It's not Daniela's. There's a second coffee cup on the shelf, uncentered, meaning she was here long enough to discuss something over coffee. And since you didn't mention the possibility of a new case, you must have turned it down, meaning a divorce. I don't do divorces."

"Great. Then I guess we'll just starve."

Monk laughed. "We won't starve. I have enough canned goods in my kitchen for a month."

I managed to stay civil and calm—one might say unnaturally calm. I let Monk settle in behind his desk, then said good-bye and left him in charge for the rest of the day.

I was barely behind the wheel of my old Subaru when I pulled out Sue O'Brien's card and dialed the number.

CHAPTER FIVE

Mr. Monk and the Fingernails

The next time I got a chance to talk to Captain Stottlemeyer was at a funeral in a side chapel of a small Episcopal church in my neighborhood of Noe Valley.

Judge Nathaniel Oberlin served for decades on the California State Superior Court. Monk and I had both testified in front of him, and from what I'd seen, he'd been a by-the-book jurist, but a fair one, with a slightly wicked sense of humor. He and Captain Stottlemeyer had been friends from way back, which was the main reason Monk and I had been invited to the viewing and the ceremony directly following, to lend the captain some moral support.

According to what I could piece together, the judge, a widower, had recently been in Thailand visiting his daughter, Bethany. She worked as a teacher at an American-sponsored school in some jungle province, an adventurous girl barely out of college.

The judge had been careful to get all the appropriate vaccinations before leaving, but that didn't stop him from returning to San Francisco two weeks later with what looked like a classic bout of gastroenteritis, otherwise known as travelers' diarrhea.

Like most returning travelers, Oberlin didn't seek medical attention. His symptoms seemed to be responding to a few days of self-imposed rest. But then, on a blustery, rainy morning, after too much time alone in an empty house, the judge felt well enough to join the living and walk his usual fifteen minutes into work. He collapsed on the courthouse steps, his umbrella tumbling down the street in a gust of wind.

The doctors at San Francisco General immediately tested him for every tropical disease known to man. A blood test determined that Oberlin had contracted dengue fever, a viral disease that can be painful but is usually not fatal. In this case, it had been. His Honor Judge Nathaniel Oberlin's condition had continued to worsen and he'd died two weeks later in the hospital from cardiac arrest.

Young Bethany, an only child, flew in for the funeral. She was now in a straight-backed chair in a corner of the viewing room, looking thin and frail, staying about as far from the open coffin as a person could get. Captain Stottlemeyer had been hovering by her side, like a bodyguard in black. When a fresh batch of mourners walked through the door, he slipped away and joined me by the table of cheese and crackers.

"Where's Monk?" he asked. I nodded toward the coffin, where my partner stood gazing down at the judge's body. The sight bore an uncomfortable resemblance to a hundred-plus crime scenes where he'd been staring down at a corpse, except this time the body was unmutilated, embalmed, and dead from natural causes.

"Captain, we need to talk at some point. I know this isn't the best time."

"This is about A.J., right?"

"Yes," I said. "And the fact that you know it's about A.J. tells me you know he's a problem."

The captain scowled. "You're going to have to get used to him, Natalie. I handpicked him to be Devlin's replacement. He's a good man."

"He doesn't seem like a good man. He's rude and disruptive. And he pretty much hates us. He's trying to pay us by the hour. Did you know that? The Burns case. Adrian wrapped that up in record time, and now the lieutenant is trying to pay us one-quarter of our day rate."

I expected Stottlemeyer to be surprised by this tidbit. But he wasn't. "You'll have to tell Monk to slow down his crime solving. Stretch the next one out for a day or two."

"You knew about this?" I asked, raising my voice. "You're okay with this?"

"I'm not okay." The captain kept his voice low. "But the lieutenant's in charge of the case-by-case allocation of resources. I can't undermine him. Maybe in a few weeks I can have a talk with him."

"What do you mean, in a few weeks? That's not like you."

"Natalie, this isn't about A.J. It's about his dad."

"His dad? Captain Thurman?" I was instantly outraged. "Are you saying you took on A.J. Thurman because Arnold Thurman asked you to? That's wrong."

Stottlemeyer looked like I had just slapped him in the face, which saved me the trouble. Not that I would have. "Arny would never ask me that, and I would never agree. But Arny is sick. Heart disease. No one knows how long he has."

"Oh," I said. "I'm sorry. I didn't know."

"Arny and I were fraternity brothers. A whole group of us got very close during those four years. Struggling through classes, and girls and pranks and parties. Guys can bond a lot at that age. Arny and I wound up in the academy together. I'm A.J.'s godfather, for Pete's sake. The boy was always a disappointment to his dad, from the start."

"I don't like to say this about another human being." I said it anyway. "Lieutenant Thurman is a bumbler and a bully. No one likes him."

The captain couldn't argue with that. "I think it's mainly insecurity," he said. "A.J. never really had a chance, you know, following in his old man's footsteps. I wanted to do it for Arny, take the kid under my wing and help him along while his dad is still with us."

Okay, I felt bad. You would have, too. "Isn't there another way to help? Making him your number two can be dangerous if he's not up to it. There are convictions at stake and evidence that can get screwed up. Not to mention the health and welfare of Monk and Teeger."

"I'll have a talk with A.J.," the captain promised. "And you have a talk with Monk. On the next case, make him take his time. He can hold up his hands and twirl for four hours instead of one."

"Four hours? How do you think A.J. would react to four hours of Monk twirling?"

"I can only imagine."

"Exactly."

In the midst of all of our deep discussion, with dozens of people milling around, I hadn't even noticed A.J. Perhaps he had just arrived. Like most of the men, he was in a black suit.

Monk was the exception, of course. His wardrobe for a funeral was the same as for lounging in front of the TV, a light checkered shirt under a dark brown jacket.

Speaking of Adrian Monk, he had now managed to remove Judge Oberlin's memorial photo from a tripod by the podium and had propped up the awkwardly sized frame on the lower, closed section of the black coffin. I could see his eyes darting from the photo to the judge's remains and back again. His expression was serious and focused. People were starting to notice. A few were pointing curiously at the man in the brown jacket and the propped-up photo.

My first reaction, based on many years of experience, was, *Oh, no. Please don't let him announce to the gathering of loved ones that the judge had been murdered. Please don't let him say this man in the coffin isn't the real judge at all but an impostor. Please don't let him say the judge was a transgendered woman who had lived her whole life as a man. Please don't let him say the body in the coffin is really a dummy. . . .*

"Monk! What the hell are you doing?" This was A.J. speaking. He had marched directly up to my partner, their noses separated by mere inches, as confrontational as you could get. "Don't you know how to behave in public? Put that picture back. This is a funeral."

"The funeral of a murdered man," Monk muttered. Believe it or not, I was relieved. It could have been so much worse.

A.J. shook his head in disgust. "Typical. Trying to steal the spotlight from a dead man. You're an embarrassment of a human being, you know that?"

"You're right," Monk agreed, with a pitiful nod. "I am an

embarrassment. I wish I was less embarrassing, believe me. But that doesn't change the fact that Judge Oberlin was murdered."

"He wasn't murdered, you self-important little freak."

Captain Stottlemeyer was on this in a second. I was right on his heels. Between the two of us, we managed to get them away from each other's throats and into a corner. People were looking, but I hoped we still had it under control.

"My hearing may be going, Monk," the captain whispered, "but I can still hear you say *murder* across a crowded room. Are you sure, old friend?"

"He was poisoned. A heavy metal. Arsenic. Maybe thallium."

"He died of dengue fever," I said, making the obvious objection.

"No," countered Monk. "The judge had contracted dengue fever, which is often asymptomatic, sometimes painful, and only rarely develops into a deadly hemorrhagic fever."

A.J. laughed. "Hemorrhagic? What are you, some sort of expert of everything that causes death?"

"I am," said Monk. "I have a list if you want to see. I've been compiling it since I was six. Fifty-two pages long, single-spaced, and I'm adding to it all the time. But that's not my point. What the judge died from was cardiac arrest. Quite a few things can make the heart stop. In this particular case it was poison."

A.J. was about to respond, but Stottlemeyer stopped him with one of his patented looks. A second later the captain's gaze shifted to the body in the casket and the photo propped up on top. "Are you talking about Mees' lines?" he asked.

"See for yourself," said Monk. And as subtly as possible, the four of us inched our way back to the open casket. It probably wasn't that subtle.

For those of you unfamiliar with Mees' lines, also called Aldrich-Mees' lines, also called leukonychia striata (I confess, I had to look that one up), they're the white bumpy ridges that run across the fingernails and are a clear indication of heavy-metal poisoning.

We all stared down at the corpse with its hands folded reverently across its chest. "That's why I wanted to compare his nails with the ones in the photo," said Monk. "You see the difference?"

The difference was obvious, but only when you have a genius right there pointing it out to you. In the formal portrait, the smiling judge had his hands cradled over his gavel. The nails showed no milky white ridges. In real life—or I should say real death—the lines were there in the pink portion of the nail, the same color as the white half-moons we all have at the bottom of our nails. Those half-moons are called lunules, by the way. I also had to look that up.

"From their position and intensity, I'd say he was exposed to a heavy dose a couple of weeks before his death." Monk shrugged a shoulder. "Of course, I'm no poison expert, but I do have a list."

"Two weeks," Stottlemeyer mused. "That's around the time he collapsed on the street, heading into work."

"Exactly," said Monk. "There may have been additional doses afterward. But the initial one is probably what caused his collapse."

"Let me get this straight," said Lieutenant A.J. Thurman.

"You're saying that when the judge was in the hospital being treated for dengue fever—"

"Dengue is a virus," Monk interrupted. "There is no treatment except to relieve the pain and wait it out."

"Whatever. So you're saying that all this time he was being poisoned and no one in the hospital knew? Unbelievable."

"Very believable," said Monk. "A heavy metal won't show up in your standard blood test. And the doctors already knew what was wrong with him: dengue fever. I assume the family didn't request an autopsy."

The captain glanced over to the far corner, where Bethany Oberlin was seated in her straight-backed chair. An Episcopal priest was bending close, gently preparing her for the short service that would take place in a few minutes, right before the casket would be closed and the long journey to the Colma cemetery would begin. "She's the only immediate family," said Stottlemeyer. "There was no reason for her or anyone to request an autopsy."

"There is now," said Monk.

"Wait a minute." Lieutenant A.J. shook his head in disbelief. "You're really going to interrupt a funeral? You're going to tell that poor girl her father was murdered and that you have to take his body out of the coffin, put it on a cold slab, cut it open, and then have another funeral in a week? Put her through the whole thing again? All because you see a few weird ridges? For all we know, the embalmer might have done something to make it look like that."

"It's not the embalmer," said Monk. "It's the poison."

"So, you're going to go up to her now and tell her this?"

"No, I'm not," said Monk. "You are. You're a homicide officer."

"He's right," agreed the captain. "Do your job, A.J."

"Me?" A.J. recoiled. "Why me? Why not you, Captain?"

"Because the judge was an old friend and I'd rather not."

"The judge was my friend, too. My dad and him were tight from the old days." A.J. dug into his pocket. "Tell you what. I'll flip you for it."

"We are not flipping coins in the middle of a funeral," said Stottlemeyer. "Go over to Ms. Oberlin and inform her, as sympathetically as possible, that the service is being postponed while the SFPD gets a court order and takes custody of her father's remains in a criminal death investigation. Do it."

The junior officer really had no choice. He stared daggers back at Monk as he slowly lumbered across to the girl in the straight-backed chair.

As I watched him go, I couldn't help thinking that this was not a positive step forward in our relationship with the new lieutenant.

CHAPTER SIX

Mr. Monk Takes His Time

The autopsy results came back two days later.

Despite the embalming fluid and all the other post-mortem indignities, the medical examiner had been able to isolate enough tissue and blood and nail samples to confirm Monk's diagnosis. The poison turned out to be thallium, element 81 on the periodic table. In the good old days it had been commonly used in rat poisons and ant killers, despite its amazing toxicity. Thallium is still fairly available, if you know where to look.

The initial dose had been large, probably administered shortly before the judge's collapse—shortly, as in less than an hour, perhaps mere minutes. Other doses had been administered in the following few weeks, right in the hospital, until the weakened man had succumbed to a heart attack.

The judge's symptoms had been similar enough to those for dengue fever—nausea, seizures, severe headaches, and severe joint pain. No one was blaming the hospital staff. The killer—whoever it was—obviously knew the judge had come back with some exotic ailment and was hoping his death would be blamed on whatever it was. If it hadn't been for Monk and the fingernails, he probably would have succeeded.

On her return to the States, Bethany Oberlin had been staying at the family home on Hyde Street. After the interrupted funeral, she was taken directly to the SF General and given blood and urine tests for heavy metals. Not a trace, thank God. Then she drove across the bay to stay with an old school friend while the house on Hyde Street was sealed on Captain Stottlemeyer's orders.

The first people allowed in were a forensics team in hazmat suits. After a day of vacuuming, sample taking, and checking the garbage cans, they proceeded to lab analysis. Nothing. Not the faintest residue, even though the deadly poison could be as fine as dust and leave traces everywhere. On the third day, the homicide team was granted entry, including the paid-by-the-hour consultants.

"How's he going to find anything the poison guys couldn't find?" A.J. complained as Monk wandered his way through the two-story house, his hands raised in his usual method. I couldn't tell if Monk was doing this any slower than usual, but I hoped so.

"You'd be surprised what Monk can find," said the captain.

A.J. snickered and shook his head. "This is a dead end. If such a high dose of poison had been administered in the house, there should be some small trace—in the kitchen or a medicine cabinet."

"Not necessarily," said Monk. "It could have been in something individually wrapped, like a stick of gum or a cough drop."

"Then where's the wrapper?"

"I'm working on it, Lieutenant," said Monk. "It takes time. It could take days."

It was at this unfortunate moment that I happened to glance at my watch. A.J. caught me looking. "Are you guys trying to pad the bill? Is that what this is about? If you know something, Monk, you need to tell us. Those are the rules."

"I'm not aware of that rule," I said. "But no, we're not trying to pad the bill. I checked my watch because I happen to have a lunch date with my daughter. Is that all right, Lieutenant? Or are you going to dock me for leaving early?"

The lieutenant said he didn't object, as long as Monk stayed behind and kept his hands up. The captain volunteered to get Monk back to his apartment, then followed me out to the front porch. "Say hello to Julie for me. How's she doing?"

"She's doing great," I said. "She still wants to be an intern for the firm of Monk and Teeger. But I think that's just her way of not facing the future, whatever it is."

"Most moms would be happy to have their girl stick around a little longer."

"True. But most moms don't chase down bad guys or sniff out poisons."

"You got a point," said the captain. "I wouldn't want my kid in law enforcement, either." He eased himself down onto the edge of a sturdy stone umbrella stand, a body-language signal that he had something more to say.

"What is it?" I asked.

"Do you think Monk's padding the bill? Honestly?"

"Isn't that what you told him to do? Take four days to give you the answer?"

"I know what I said. But if he knows how the judge was poisoned, that's pretty important. Once the judge was admitted to the hospital, it's a different story. The killer had plenty of access. Doctors, nurses, orderlies. Visiting hours. But the initial dose, the one that made him collapse on the court-house steps, that's our mystery."

"What about motive?" I asked. "Someone must have wanted Nathaniel Oberlin dead."

"I have a team working that angle, two of my best. But Nate was a widower. No romantic connections. No enemies. No heirs, except Bethany, who was in Thailand at the time. His murder could be connected to an old criminal case, I guess. That's what we're checking into."

"Are you sure the judge was alone that morning?"

"As sure as we can be. A neighbor saw him leaving the house alone. The courthouse is a fifteen-minute walk. There were no injection sites on the body, we're pretty sure of that. So it had to have been ingested."

"It's been weeks, you know. There's a good possibility we'll never find the source."

"I know," agreed Stottlemeyer. "That's why I need to know if Monk is stalling."

I paused to give it some thought. "I know Adrian pretty well. And he's a terrible liar, even when it comes to body language. I don't think he's stalling or padding the bill. He's as confused as the rest of us."

"That's too bad," said the captain. "Nate was an old friend. You don't get many old friends. I'd hate to see this bastard get away with it."

"We'll do our best. No stalling."

"Thanks," he said, pulling himself up to his feet. "And I'll make sure you get paid."

*   *   *

My lunch that day wasn't with Julie. I'd lied. And it wasn't even a lunch. It was a progress report to Sue O'Brien.

I had taken her case. I'd taken it against Monk's unwritten rule about divorces and perhaps my own better judgment. In my defense, Sue was a sweet woman who really needed help, help that other investigators couldn't supply. And, don't forget, her plea had come at a moment when we had just been paid a two-hour rate for solving a complicated homicide.

During the last few days, while the lab and the guys in the hazmat suits were busy at work, I was skulking around on two fronts, trying to gather as much evidence as possible against Sue's wayward husband while desperately trying to keep my activities off Monk's radar, which probably rivals the radar capabilities of O'Hare International.

When I arrived at the mini-mall, my honey-blond client was waiting on the bench outside the door. I quickly ushered her in and we settled in a far back corner, just in case Monk's radar was working in high gear.

"Any news?" she asked right off the bat.

"Precious little," I had to admit. Then I went on to explain.

Her husband, Timothy O'Brien, had been easy to find. He was a named partner at Smith, Willard & O'Brien in a high-rise in the Financial District. He did not have a Facebook page or much other Internet presence, except for a few photos of him giving lectures at the San Francisco Law Library. For two days, I had followed him from the O'Brien manse in Pacific Heights to the office and back again.

"He does spend a lot of time with Gayle Greenwald." Gayle, to bring you up-to-date, was the woman Sue had identified as the coworker and mistress. "They leave the office within five or ten minutes of each other. Then they go around the corner and meet at Jezebel's Tavern. It's one of those super-trendy bars that try to look like dingy dive joints but charge you fifteen dollars for a weak cocktail."

"I know Jezebel's," said Sue with a wry smile. "And it's a very fitting name."

"Yesterday I managed to get the booth right behind them. I have a little recorder with a directional mic. It's no good in court, of course, but it's more reliable than taking notes."

"And what were they talking about?" Sue asked. "Their plans for the future?"

"Business, mainly," I had to admit. "They seemed very friendly. Pet names, that sort of thing, but nothing detailed. They were focused on some high-stakes divorce case they're working on together."

"You mean my divorce case?"

"You don't have a divorce case," I reminded her. "Not yet. If you want to listen to the tape yourself . . ."

Sue took a deep breath. "I would like that, yes."

I retrieved the micro-recorder from my top drawer and slid it across to her, feeling pretty sleazy as I did so. This was one of the downsides of a traditional PI firm, the part that Monk hates: the spying and the sex and the raw emotions. Of course, the other part involves bloody corpses and grieving relatives. That part doesn't bother him.

"It's about twenty-five minutes long," I said. "To my ears,

there's nothing incriminating, no talk of bank accounts or hidden assets. It doesn't sound like they're discussing you. But you may have a better insight into it."

"I may indeed." In slow motion, Sue took the recorder, gently placing it in her left palm and poising her right index finger over the play button. "Do you mind if I listen to this alone?"

"Not at all." I was actually relieved. "Do you want some tea? I think we're out of tea, so it gives me an excuse to go to the market a few doors down. They have some great teas. I'll be sure to take my time. Make yourself at home."

And that's how I left her, looking vulnerable in the back corner of my office, her finger motionless over the button.

I took my time, as promised, roaming the crowded aisles of the cutesy little market. When I came back half an hour later with three selections of overpriced tea, Sue had already finished. She was sitting primly, stone-faced, exactly where I'd left her, her hands folded over the micro-recorder.

"So?" I asked, pointing to the recorder.

"You're right. Nothing incriminating. Maybe they're not having an affair." There was a note of optimism in her voice. "Is there any way to find out for sure?"

"You could go on a trip," I said. The idea had just occurred to me.

"On a trip? Why?"

"I can't follow your husband everywhere. I don't have the resources, and it's too easy to get caught. But if you go away to visit a sick aunt or some old classmate, I can concentrate on your house."

"No." Sue gasped and covered her mouth. "You think they would do it in my house? In our own bed?"

"Yes," I said. "From my limited experience, there's nothing a mistress likes more than shacking up in what may become her future home. You can stay at a local hotel, someplace with a spa. I don't think Timothy and Gayle will be able to resist spending a night together. If we're wrong, that's even better."

"But if Gayle shows up?"

"Then we'll go to phase two. We'll get some assets transferred into your name and look for secret accounts. My daughter has some very savvy tech friends. We can bring them on board without raising any red flags."

"I don't know." Suddenly she wasn't so sure of herself. "Timothy is unpredictable. If he finds out I'm spying on him, I don't know what he'll do."

"What do you mean? Are you saying he can be physically dangerous?"

"Maybe," she confessed. "He has a temper. And he doesn't like to be fooled or to lose control."

"All the more reason to get out of the marriage."

"I know. I shouldn't be having second thoughts. But if I suddenly disappear, you'll know . . ."

"Disappear? Don't say things like that."

In the end, Sue agreed. She would tell him tonight. An aunt of hers in San Diego had taken ill and she would be gone for at least two days. Poor Tim would have to fend for himself. Then she borrowed my office phone and made a reservation at the Fairmont on Nob Hill, using her maiden name.

"Your maiden name is what?" It had sounded like a sneeze.

"Puskedra," she enunciated. "It's easy. You spell it the way it sounds."

"Are you sure you didn't make that up? No offense, but it sounds like just a bunch of letters strung together."

Sue laughed. "The world had better get used to it, because I think Susan Puskedra is going to be my name again. My new old name."

"Maybe you ought to stick with O'Brien. For humanity's sake."

"Not a chance."

CHAPTER SEVEN

Mr. Monk and the Vanishing Act

The next morning was my shift at the mini-mall.

Sue Puskedra O'Brien and I had our plan in place. She would be leaving home on her fictitious trip around two p.m., checking into the Fairmont for her two-day hideaway. By that time, her husband would be at his downtown office and I would be staking out the parking structure next door. I had even called his assistant, pretending to be an enormously wealthy dot-com socialite in need of a consultation with the famous Timothy O'Brien, only to be told that Mr. O'Brien was busy with back-to-back meetings in the office until six p.m. "Would I be available at six?" she asked. No, I replied, and quickly hung up. This left me fairly certain of Timothy's whereabouts until six, although I still intended to spend my afternoon stalking him.

I was at my desk that morning, on the phone and the computer, doing another background check for Julie's friends, the ones with the software company. Did you know that you can find out just about anyone's real age and other general details by typing a total of five, maybe six words into your search engine? It's true. I won't tell you what those five words are, just in case you're tempted to go and figure out my real age.

It was a warm, breezy day, even though rain was being predicted for the evening hours. I had the office door propped open and looked up to see Daniela Grace just as she was getting out of her car and heading next door. She saw me seeing her and made a detour to say hello.

"How is Paisley Printing working out?" I kept my tone cheery even though a little knot was forming in my stomach. "I know Peter and Wendy are a bit unorthodox."

"Working out well," Daniela replied, still standing in the doorway. "Although they're not very fond of your Mr. Monk."

"There is some history there," I said, trying to be vague and diplomatic.

"So I gather. As soon as I said you recommended them, they became quite paranoid. Peter kept asking if this was some sort of prank. He made me show them my business card and my driver's license. It's the first time I've been carded in decades."

"Monk has pulled pranks on them in the past."

"Really? He doesn't seem like a prankster."

"He's been hanging with a bad influence. Kids. What can you do?"

"Well, Peter and Wendy seem to be darling people. They're very imaginative, with a great color sense. And I think they're very trustworthy, which is exactly what I need for this job. Don't look surprised."

"I wasn't surprised," I lied. "I just thought they might be a little laid-back for your tastes."

"They are," she admitted. "But they remind me of myself back in the day. I was living in a free-love commune in the

Haight during the Summer of Love, you know. I had my moments." And she shook her hips, or what was left of them.

I didn't know how to respond. I would have guessed Daniela had spent the summer of '67 hosting teas for the Junior League. "Well, I'm glad Peter and Wendy are doing well."

"They're a little disorganized. But I'm giving them firm deadlines and it seems to be working. Please thank Adrian again for his recommendation. Well . . ." She threw me a little wave. "Gotta go crack the whip. Have a good day, dear."

By the time Monk arrived for his shift, I had completed one more background check and was both anticipating and dreading this afternoon's stakeout. I didn't even think to ask about the poisoning case, not until Monk brought it up.

"I put in a full six hours yesterday." I wasn't sure if this was a boast or a confession. "The lieutenant was ready to strangle me. But he couldn't say I wasn't working. I was working."

I watched as he centered his jacket on his private peg and arranged his umbrella in the office umbrella stand. "Did you really come up with nothing?" I asked. "I know we talked about stalling, but . . ."

"I'm not stalling," Monk said. Finally satisfied with his jacket, he closed the door. "The forensics team did a thorough job and so did I. My opinion? The thallium was never in the house, not unless the killer came back and cleaned up, which is doubtful. The judge had a state-of-the-art security system and he seemed to use it diligently. Even his own daughter didn't know the code."

"So you're saying the victim ingested the poison on his walk to work?"

"I don't know what I'm saying." And then he paused, his eyes unfocused. For a second, I thought he'd had one of his revelations. Until . . . "Holy Mother-of-pearl. What is that racket?"

"What racket?" Other than a little muffled street noise, I heard nothing. But as soon as Monk headed for the left-hand wall, I knew. "Peter's playing his guitar."

"Why is he so loud? It's like a rock-and-roll concert."

"He's not loud. We just have thin walls."

"I think I need to put up another poster about fresh baked hippies."

"You are not putting up another poster," I said firmly. "What you and Luther did was mean. You should be ashamed."

"Me? I'm not the one carrying on like Woodstock."

This was an argument I couldn't win. If Adrian Monk can see details that no one else can, then he can hear them, too. No amount of protesting about gentle, barely audible guitar strums was going to convince him. "Adrian," I pleaded. "We have a year and nine months on our lease. It would be nice if you could avoid alienating everyone on the block."

"Okay. I'll try."

Two hours later, I was parked in a rare legal space in the Financial District, with a view of the main exit of Timothy O'Brien's building and the only exit of his parking garage. I settled in beside a plastic bag of quarters to feed the hungry, expensive meter and made a final call to Sue's cell. "Are you at the Fairmont?" I asked.

"I'm on my way," she said. "I called Timothy to say goodbye, so I know he's at the office. This is going to be a long day for you, Natalie."

"Don't worry about me. I haven't had any liquids since this morning and I've got a full playlist of the Stones on my phone. What more does a girl need?"

"I don't know about Gayle, but Timothy's not leaving the office until six."

"I just want to be sure," I said. "Now get to the hotel and have a spa day. Tim's treat."

Sue was wrong about nothing happening before six. At five thirty-seven, just as I was stretching my legs and getting ready to feed a few more quarters, Gayle Greenwald came out, stood by the curb, and raised her hand for a taxi. One stopped for her almost immediately and they headed west, in the general direction of Pacific Heights.

At five fifty-two, Timothy O'Brien made his own exit, briefcase in hand, and strode up the ramp into the parking structure. I started my engine and waited for his charcoal Mercedes to pull out onto the one-way street. It had just started to rain.

It was kind of a nonevent, to be honest, and probably the easiest tail job I've ever done. The Mercedes was driven at a respectable speed, didn't run any stop signs or lights, and wound up right where I'd expected it to, in the garage attached to the O'Briens' faux Tudor mansion, one of those long, one-room-deep structures meant to impress. All curb appeal and no depth.

At a few minutes after six, it was dark enough to require indoor lighting, and I watched as the house gradually came alive, room after room. No one else seemed to be home. I was more than a little disappointed. Maybe the man wasn't a cheat, after all, I thought. And then the yellow taxi pulled up.

The person who paid the driver and got out of the cab was not the person I'd expected. It wasn't Gayle—not unless it was the male version, without the *y*, like the actor Gale Gordon from *The Lucy Show*. But I doubted it in this case.

It was a man in his mid-thirties, pencil thin and dressed to show it off, with skinny black jeans and a formfitting teal dress shirt. He dodged the rain to the covered porch and brushed himself off. When he knocked, the door flew open almost instantly. It was still wide-open when Timothy O'Brien and the man who wasn't Gayle fell into each other's arms and shared a passionate kiss.

Okay. This was interesting.

If this had been the only surprise of the evening, it wouldn't have been that big of a deal. Many women have suspected their husbands of infidelity, only to discover that the man they were married to was gay. Even in this day and age. Even in San Francisco.

The bigger surprise came a few minutes later, after I had pulled around the corner and called Sue on her cell. After just two rings, an electronic voice informed me that the phone was no longer in service.

It had to be a mistake, of course. I dialed again and got the same message. Next I called the Fairmont Hotel and asked to be put through to Sue O'Brien's room. I was informed that there was no Sue or Susan O'Brien staying there. Nor was there a Sue or Susan Puskedra. Or a Sue or Susan Puskedra O'Brien.

It took nearly forty-five minutes of rush-hour traffic to get from the curb appeal of Pacific Heights to the Fairmont on Nob Hill. The determined look in my eyes got me taken seriously by the head person on the desk that evening, a petite Asian girl not much older than my daughter.

We stepped into an inner office where she checked and rechecked, first with her computer, then with everyone who had been on the front desk since two p.m. No woman even remotely fitting Sue Puskedra O'Brien's description had made a reservation.

"But I heard her make it," I protested. "She used my office phone."

"We have no record of the reservation," the desk manager told me. "I'm sorry."

It was at that moment that I recalled what Sue had said about her husband and if she suddenly disappeared. I didn't know what was going on, but it definitely wasn't good.

CHAPTER EIGHT

Mr. Monk vs. the Rainy Night

Right away I knew I had to tell Monk and beg for his help. It would be embarrassing, yes, and he would be raging mad. Or else he would be hurt and disappointed, which would be worse.

In the past, I might have tried to solve the case myself. I might have trudged forward and tried to deduce what had happened to my client. But even I can learn from experience. The sooner I gave Monk all the facts and let him do his magic, the less damage there would be. And I suspected there would be damage somewhere. There usually is with a mystery like this.

I drove directly from the hotel to the Pine Street apartment. The rain was coming down more heavily, not just the annoying drizzle we're all so accustomed to here. I used the doorbell, not my key. The key might have sent a more desperate signal than I wanted, so I stood out in the rain until he buzzed me into the building.

As soon as he opened his door, he lurched back. "Why are you so wet?" It was like I was threatening him with a water balloon.

"Because it's raining."

"Then you should have used your key. Stay in the hall and I'll get you some towels."

I stood there, uncomplaining, while he retrieved four fluffy towels and handed them out the door. "If you're planning to step inside, take off your shoes."

"I need to talk to you about something," I said as I started to towel off.

"Obviously."

"I'm telling you in advance, you're not going to like it."

"Does it involve you bringing water and mud into my house?"

"Worse, I'm afraid."

"What could be worse?" He continued to block the doorway. Then his phone rang. "Stay there," he warned. And he retreated into his inner sanctum to answer it. "Trudy. Hello. What's the matter?"

I know I haven't mentioned Trudy much. Not this Trudy. The original Trudy, the one I know I've mentioned, was Monk's wife, the love of his life who was killed in the late 1990s by a car bomb. This Trudy is Leland Stottlemeyer's wife. She's a brunette with longish, wavy hair and an enviably full figure. They met several years ago and got married two months later. For a while, the captain called her T.K., thinking Monk might be uncomfortable with having another Trudy around. But Monk turned out to be fine with it. "Everyone should have a Trudy in their life," he had said.

Trudy Stottlemeyer has done her best to stay away from our dangerous world. I think she's fooled herself into thinking that Leland is a plumber who just keeps odd hours. So when Trudy does make contact, it's almost always something important.

Monk listened for a few seconds, then covered the receiver. "Don't take off your shoes," he shouted in my direction. That didn't mean he'd changed his mind and I could wear them inside. It meant we were going out. This time we had the advantage of umbrellas—Monk's primary umbrella and any one of his three identical backups.

The Stottlemeyers lived in a neighborhood known as Dogpatch, not far from the bay, in a cozy, newish bungalow meant to look a hundred years older than it was. Trudy was on the porch waiting as we shook out our umbrellas and joined her. "I can't convince him to go to the hospital," she said.

"What happened exactly?" I asked.

"He was out walking the dog. Teddy hates the rain, so it's always a challenge making him do his business. When they came back, Leland was fine for a while. Then he started shaking and feeling nauseous. He said it was just a chill. But then right before I called you, he threw up."

"What do you think it is?" asked Monk.

"I don't know." Trudy shrugged helplessly. "But you know how nervous I get about his work. Judge Oberlin was poisoned and everyone thought it was just a virus. Convince Leland to go to the hospital. He won't listen to me."

"Let me talk to him," said Monk. He stuffed his umbrella into a huge clay pot by the door and I did the same. Before entering, he wiped his shoes on the mat, but I noticed he didn't take them off. Hypocrite.

"Hey, Monk. Natalie." The captain was on the couch in front of the blank-faced TV, wrapped in a blanket and looking miserable. "I don't see what all the fuss is about. If I'm not feeling better by morning . . ."

I don't know if it was just instinct or something specific about the captain's state. But Monk kept his distance and motioned for the rest of us to do the same. "What did you eat, Leland? Anything different from what Trudy had tonight?"

"What are you talking about, Monk?"

"Your color, your tremors, the fact that you haven't taken a sick day in two years and seven months, plus the coincidence of both you and the judge collapsing during rainstorms."

"Rainstorms? What does that mean?"

"I don't know, but I hate coincidences."

Trudy's hand went to her heart. "We ate the same food. I bought a lasagna at the market. And a salad. We shared a beer from the same bottle. Do you really think . . ."

"No chewing gum or mints or mouthwash since he got home? Dessert?"

"No," she replied.

"I'm not poisoned," growled the captain. "Trudy, honey, you worry too much."

All three of us ignored him. "How about visitors?" asked Monk. "Has anyone been in the house? I don't care how innocent or friendly."

"Not for days, no," said Trudy. "And I always lock the doors and windows. I'm very careful."

"And you're okay?" I asked her. "You're not feeling any symptoms?"

"Nothing."

"I have the sniffles," said Leland. "No big deal."

"And how is Teddy?" asked Monk. "Your monstrous mutt of a dog. I can smell his wet fur from here. How is Teddy feeling?"

"Teddy?" Stottlemeyer's eyes went cold. "I don't know. Teddy!" With some effort, he pulled himself up. Apparently it was okay for him to ignore any danger he might be in, but when it came to his dog . . . "I haven't seen him since we came back. Teddy Bear. Come here, boy!"

The dog didn't come right away, which seemed unusual behavior, from the way Stottlemeyer reacted. "Teddy? Where are you?" He began to go from room to room in the one-level house. Then he started over. "Teddy?"

Monk was the first to hear the whimpering. It came from under the bed in the guest room/office, soft and pitiful and steady. The captain and I stuck our heads under and saw the long-haired, medium-sized dog. The poor thing stared back at us in guilt and pain, squeezed in under the box springs, staying as far away as he could from a puddle of green vomit in the corner.

"Oh, my God," said Stottlemeyer. "We gotta get him to the vet." He reached under and began to gently pull Teddy out. "Come on, big boy."

"You're not going to the vet," Trudy informed him. "You're going to the hospital. Now."

"Did you and Teddy run into anyone during your walk?" asked Monk. "Anyone at all? Think."

"No," the captain said. "It was raining. No one was out."

"Did the mongrel pick up anything off the street? Did you both touch anything?" Monk shivered. "Did you pick up the dog's poop in some unsanitary way? Not that there is a sanitary way."

"Teddy didn't poop and I didn't touch anything."

Trudy took her husband by the hand and started leading

him toward the door. "We're going to the emergency room. Natalie, there's a number on the fridge for the emergency vet. Also the address. It might be quicker. . . ."

"I'll take care of Teddy," I said, and I rushed off to get the information. Then the captain let me take Teddy out of his arms. I could feel the poor thing shivering through his fur.

Monk and I hadn't bothered to take off our coats, so we were on the porch, ready when Leland and his wife emerged wearing theirs. The rain hadn't let up in the least. "Adrian, you go with the captain. I'll drop off Teddy and join you as soon as I can. What do I tell the vet?"

"Tell him to check for heavy metals. Probably thallium."

"Is there an antidote to thallium poisoning?"

"Prussian blue," said Monk.

"Prussian blue?" I asked. "What is that, a color?"

"It's a pigment. The Germans used it in their uniforms for centuries. It's lighter than cobalt but darker than sky blue. It's close to the classic Levi's blue in color. If the vet happens to be a painter, he might have some on hand. Obviously, if you're poisoned, you're not supposed to just wear the color; that would be silly. You have to eat the pigment."

I had to ask. "How do you know these things?"

"How do you not? It's basic survival."

"Just save Teddy, okay?" the captain said, then reached for his black golf umbrella. "Let's go." But Monk had already grabbed the captain's hand, pulling him off-balance. He almost fell. "Monk? This is no time for sentiment."

"Don't." Monk took a second, his hand still clutching his friend's hand, his eyes focused on the three umbrellas dripping in the clay pot. "It must be in your umbrella."

"What?"

"Thallium powder. That's why Teddy's sick. That's why Trudy isn't sick. That's why there wasn't a trace in Judge Oberlin's house. That's why you and the judge both collapsed on rainy days."

"In the umbrella?" I asked.

Monk almost smiled. "It's a brilliant plan. The killer wouldn't need access to your house, just your umbrella. The second you opened it . . ."

"Adrian, thank you, but shut up," said Trudy. Then she beeped open her husband's car and began to drag him out into the rain.

CHAPTER NINE

Mr. Monk and the Visiting Hours

As Monk had said, it was brilliant—a heavy dusting of thallium powder inside the folds of a closed umbrella. When the umbrella was opened, the powder would be released and be either inhaled or absorbed by the skin. If the killer had been careful enough to keep the powder in the outside folds, the rain would wash away the remaining evidence into the street. As for timing, the poison could have been put in place weeks ago, anytime after the last good downpour. The murderer wouldn't need to have access to the house.

"It could have killed Trudy," the captain said over and over. He was in a hospital bed at SF General, barely wheezing out the words.

"Does she ever use your umbrella?" I asked.

"A big, black golf umbrella? No," he admitted. "She has her own. But they were side by side in the damn pot. What kind of coward endangers a man's wife?"

We were talking about her as if she weren't there. But Trudy was in the room with us—physically, at least.

"I don't think he was concerned about collateral damage," Monk said calmly. "He was after you. Not your wife. Not your dog."

"Really, Monk? You're going to school me in keeping things logical? In a situation like this?" The captain didn't have to say any more, not with a wife named Trudy who could have been killed.

"You're right, Leland. I'm sorry."

Everyone had survived that rainy night in Dogpatch. The emergency room staff had done an immediate blood test. When they found a dose of thallium in the captain's system, a nurse went running to the drug dispensary, where they kept a poison control cupboard, complete with an airtight canister of Prussian blue. They fed four of the Levi's-hued pills to Stottlemeyer, twenty milligrams, then sent a messenger in an ambulance to the Paw and Claw Vet Clinic on Indiana Street, where I was waiting at the door. Teddy didn't feel like eating, of course. But a calm, highly skilled vet managed to pry apart his teeth, get a single pill into the dog's mouth, and massage his throat until it slid down.

The rest of us tried not to overreact. We had a lot to be thankful for. The captain was alive. Teddy was alive and spending the night at the vet's. A forensics team had taken the umbrella pot and its contents to the lab. Unfortunately, that left Monk with only two backup umbrellas, but he could deal with that. It was probably our refusal to overreact that sent Trudy over the edge. She stayed at Stottlemeyer's side all night, holding his hand, shivering almost as much as the dog had been. When I returned to the hospital at nine a.m., I had to practically drag her out and drive her home for a few hours of rest. Captain's orders.

On my way back to the hospital, I stopped to pick up Monk. He had been up all night, too, vacuuming his apartment and making waffles. I could tell how disturbed he felt about the captain and his Trudy. It must have brought back all sorts of memories. But we didn't talk about it. Instead, I sat down at his kitchen counter and shared in some waffle therapy, with a dollop of syrup centered in every square. When it comes to making square food, he's actually a pretty good cook.

An hour or so later, when we walked back into the captain's private room, we were thrilled to see Lieutenant Amy Devlin sitting by his bed, looking as buff and hard as ever. "Hey, guys. Long time." It was as if nothing had happened, as if she hadn't taken an administrative leave and dropped off the face of the earth, not even bothering to call. "Did you hear that his poop is blue now? Not that I've personally seen it."

"It's true," confirmed the captain. "That blue stuff absorbs the thallium and flushes it out. Literally."

"No more poop talk," said Monk. "Isn't it enough that we have to put up with cold-blooded killers?"

Amy got to her feet. "Well, Leland, now that my replacements are here, I can go." She almost never called him Leland. It seemed both too personal and too distant. "It was great to see you. We shouldn't wait until the next attempt on your life to be in touch."

"You know where to find me." The captain spread his arms. "At least for the next few days."

"You're leaving?" I said. "But we just got here. We haven't seen you in ages."

"We'll catch up," Amy promised. "But you guys are in the middle of an investigation. I don't want to interfere."

I didn't know how to respond. "Let me walk you out," I

said, hoping the right response might come to me along the way.

"I spoke to the doctor right before you came," whispered Amy as we headed down the hall side by side.

"And?"

"Leland will be fine. A day or two more of the blue stuff, just to make sure. Then he'll be released."

"That's good. Are you really quitting the force?" It was something I had to ask. Straight out.

"I am quitting, yes."

We had arrived at the elevator bank and I faked pushing the down button, hoping she wouldn't notice. "How can you leave? You can't."

"My uncle and cousins are officers in Boston. The force there is actively recruiting women for the major crimes division. I know I seem tough, Natalie." She ran a hand through her spiky black hair. "But the ordeal I went through with the warehouse shootings, it made me think about family. I miss them. I would have come through something like that better if I'd had some family around."

"I understand that," I said. "I meant, how can you leave now? With the captain in the hospital and someone trying to kill him?"

"I'm on leave," said Devlin. "I couldn't help if I wanted to."

"Don't you care about him?"

"Of course I care. He's been a great mentor, like a dad. And more patient than my real dad, believe me. But he has you and Monk and the whole department. Look, if you need me for anything, I'll be around for another week. Call me. But the captain's in good hands. Don't sell yourself short."

When the elevator dinged, it startled me. I still hadn't pushed the button.

"Natalie. Devlin. How's the old man doing?" It was Lieutenant A.J. Thurman. Amy's replacement stepped out of the elevator, holding forth a grocery store bouquet.

"Another reason for you not to leave," I whispered in Devlin's ear. She shot me a sympathetic grin before stepping past him into the elevator. Would I ever see her again? Of course, I told myself.

"Take care of yourself," Amy said just before the doors closed.

I escorted A.J. back to the room, all the while thinking how the captain's ex-partner had come to visit before his current partner. "I didn't find out until I showed up at the station," A.J. said, almost reading my mind.

"I guess you got left out of the loop." I didn't mean for it to sound quite that dismissive.

The captain seemed genuinely glad to see A.J. walk in. I busied myself arranging the tiny bouquet in a milk glass while Monk went back and forth between the two windows getting the venetian blinds to line up just right.

"How is your dad doing?" asked Stottlemeyer. He had more interest in talking about other people's health than his own.

"Hanging in there," said A.J. "It's just a matter of time. We've talked to the doctors about a heart transplant. But the waiting list is so long. And he probably wouldn't survive the operation."

"I'll come by the house as soon as they let me out."

"Good," said A.J. "Dad would like that. He keeps talking

about the old days, you know, about the fraternity. How your father owned a bar and how you all used to sneak in and drink the hard stuff and refill the bottles with colored water. Is that true?"

Stottlemeyer smiled. "We just fiddled with the cheap stuff. My pop was a real connoisseur, not just a bartender. The man knew his whisky. We'd do summer vacations visiting the best distilleries. Even to Inverness, Scotland, one year. So I knew better than to go near the good liquor."

"Sounds like a character, your pop. And you guys never got caught?"

"I think he knew. His customers must have figured it out. But I think that was his way of keeping tabs on our drinking, checking the bottles the next day and not saying anything. The year we all turned twenty-one, Pop threw us a party. Nothing but cheap stuff. We all had such hangovers the next day, we swore we'd never drink again. Not that the resolution lasted, mind you, but it was a good lesson."

"The lesson was don't drink the cheap stuff," said A.J. with a charming smile. I still didn't like the man. He was still an incompetent bully, but I could see how the captain might have a soft spot for him. And A.J. must have sensed that the last thing the captain wanted to talk about right now was his own situation. "Oh, I almost forgot. Captain, this came for you at the station. Someone left it on your desk." And out of his jacket pocket, the lieutenant pulled a folded letter-sized envelope.

"On my desk?" He took the envelope and unfolded it. "Captain Leland Stottlemeyer" was hand printed in block letters, the three words underlined.

Whatever Monk and I had been doing before, we were suddenly on alert. So was the captain. It was experience that taught us this, but also common sense. If you're a police captain and someone just made an attempt on your life, and the next morning there's a hand-delivered envelope on your desk . . . What kind of idiot wouldn't be suspicious?

Monk was at the bedside before me. Out of nowhere, like a magician, he produced a ziplock baggie. Without a word, the captain slipped the envelope inside and sealed it shut. "Lieutenant? What the hell?"

Monk was just as furious. "The second you saw it, you should have bagged it with tweezers. What is wrong with you?"

"What?" said A.J. "Is something wrong? I thought it was a get-well card."

"A get-well card?" said Stottlemeyer. "On my desk? After a murder attempt? It's not even the same size as a get-well card."

"You want gloves?" Monk asked the captain. "I've got gloves."

Stottlemeyer mulled this over. "What the hell, sure. I'm already in a hospital."

A pair of clear vinyl gloves, size large, came out of Monk's inner jacket, probably from the same reservoir that had held the baggie. As Stottlemeyer put them on and unzipped the baggie, we all instinctively took a step back.

He used a knife from his set-aside food tray to slice open the bottom of the envelope, just in case there might be any DNA on the glued flap. He pulled out a single sheet of paper, carefully unfolding it. All our eyes were focused. If there was any dusting of gray powder, we didn't see it. The captain cleared his throat and read aloud the two handwritten sentences.

"You and Oberlin stole seven years of my life. Next time you won't be so lucky."

CHAPTER TEN

Mr. Monk Loses a Client

It's funny how killers, even smart ones, can't resist helping you out. After "the night of the umbrellas," as I call it, we suspected the motive might be revenge for some case Stottlemeyer and the judge had been involved with. What other connection could there be? Not only did this note confirm that, but it gave us a time frame. Seven years.

"It doesn't have to be seven years ago," said Monk. "It could be ten years ago and the killer has been postponing it for three."

"Postponing it," I asked. "Why would you postpone revenge?"

"Maybe he's been planning it carefully. Or he's been sick."

This was Monk, as logical as ever. He was at his desk, the mirror image of mine except that he'd removed his computer from the desktop and packed it away in triple plastic wrap in a closet. I'd been surprised by this offense against the laws of symmetry. But I think my partner had grown annoyed that this mysterious, unusable machine was taking up so much space. His desk now looked like it had been time-traveled from somewhere in the forties, with a blotter in the center—remember blotters?—two holders, one for pens, one for pencils, an in-basket, and a matching out-basket, both of them empty.

It was a day later and the captain was still in the hospital. The doctors had revised his prognosis down slightly. They were concerned about the possibility of heart damage and had connected him up to a cardiac monitor. A patrol officer was assigned to his door, which was probably unnecessary since Trudy Stottlemeyer had returned and taken command of the room like a mother grizzly.

As for the note, the department's forensics unit had come up empty. Lieutenant A.J. was investigating what civilians might have had access to the captain's desk during the time in question. And since the firm of Monk and Teeger had been involved in most of the captain's big cases in the past ten years, we had been retained to check into those cases— and our memory banks—for leads.

I had just cross-referenced a list of trials involving Judge Oberlin of the California State Superior Court and Captain Stottlemeyer of the SFPD. I tried to be generous with the dates, not to let any possibility slip through. There were nine cases that could fit the time frame, some of them with multiple defendants. I printed out a brief summation of each case, slipped them into a manila folder, and centered the folder in Monk's in-basket.

"Why isn't he trying to kill us, Natalie?"

"Excuse me?" I actually knew what he was talking about, but I guess I wanted him to lay it out.

"Our thallium killer didn't mention us. If it was a case we were part of, wouldn't he want to kill us, too?"

"What's the matter? Are you feeling left out?"

"Just curious."

"Maybe he does intend to kill us but doesn't want to give us advance warning. Feel better?"

"Or maybe it was a case we weren't involved in. The killer said seven years. Didn't we go to Germany seven years ago?"

"Was that only seven years?" I wondered out loud. "Seems like a lifetime."

In some ways it was a lifetime ago. That was back when Monk's first psychiatrist, Dr. Kroger, was alive, long before Monk had solved his own Trudy's murder. Back then he was still dependent on his sessions with Charles Kroger—three times a week on a good week. So when the doctor left to go to a medical conference in Germany, Monk felt he had no choice. He drugged himself on antianxiety meds and booked us on the next flight. Between solving a few murders in Germany and a few more in Paris, it wasn't what you'd call a vacation. But the adventure did take us away from the San Francisco criminal court system. That month or so for us was a blank spot.

"Did the captain testify in any cases in front of Judge Oberlin while we were gone?" Monk had already picked up the folder. He flipped through the pages and found the dates quickly enough. "Huh," he said, examining the few paragraphs of sketchy detail. "Two cases. Both with the captain as lead investigator, both pleaded in front of Judge Nathaniel Oberlin, and both ending up in convictions. Who knew?"

I smiled. "It seems the captain is capable of making arrests and getting convictions without you."

"I never doubted it. Leland is a competent professional,

one of the very best." Monk rotated his shoulders in a little shrug. "But you're right, Natalie. I'm surprised."

"So these are the cases we focus on," I suggested. "I'll call Lieutenant Thurman and get the complete files."

"Thurman?" Monk shuddered. "What a moronic jerk. And I say that with full apologies to all the moronic jerks who maybe aren't quite as bad."

"Don't work yourself up, Adrian."

"I'm not working myself up."

"Like it or not, we have to get used to him. The captain is going home for some bed rest. Until he's back at full capacity, A.J. is in charge."

"In charge?" Monk moaned. "No, that's unacceptable. What about Lieutenant Devlin? She can come back, at least until the captain is safe."

"I already asked her. She said no."

"What about Randy Disher? He can come back."

Randy had been the captain's number two for years, until he'd found a better job on the other side of the country. "Randy's a police chief in New Jersey. He's not coming back."

"You don't know that. Okay, what about Lieutenant Devlin?"

"I just told you."

"Okay, what about Randy Disher? I'm giving you all these options."

"Adrian, stop it."

My phone buzzed in the pocket of my cardigan. I pulled it out and checked the display. It was Timothy O'Brien's office, returning my call.

"What about you, Natalie? You could be a temporary lieutenant. I'll talk to the commissioner."

"I have to take this," I said, and headed out the door. "Meanwhile, breathe deeply and count to one hundred. We'll figure a way to work with A.J."

I didn't want to walk out with Monk still in that state, but I had no choice. I made my way down the sidewalk past the door to Paisley Printing. I followed my own advice and took a deep breath.

"Hello? Yes, this is Mrs. Teeger. Thanks for getting back to me. Is it possible to get an appointment with Mr. O'Brien today? I know it's late notice. I'm filing for a divorce and one of my girlfriends at the Metropolitan Club . . ."

I think it was mentioning the Metropolitan Club that did the trick. Places don't get much richer or snootier than this Waspy bastion on Union Square. O'Brien's assistant managed to squeeze me in for a consultation that afternoon at two.

The call couldn't have taken more than three minutes. I spent an extra minute or two standing there, thinking about Sue. She had come to me in her hour of need and I'd reassured her, made her believe I knew what I was doing. Now I had to go back inside and tell Monk what I should have told him yesterday.

Disappearances shouldn't be taken lightly. I had already driven by the O'Brien house twice, once last night after dropping off Trudy and once this morning. In both cases, Sue's BMW had not been in the driveway. She wasn't registered in any local hotels or hospitals. And her cell phone was still out of service. I didn't know where else to check. If I could just get Monk to join me in my meeting with O'Brien . . .

When I walked back into the office, he was on the phone.

"The captain needs you, Randy. Someone's trying to kill him and you're the only one. You can take a leave of absence. And Natalie has a spare bedroom."

I dove for my phone, pushed an extension button, and got in on the call. "Randy. Hi, it's Natalie."

"Natalie." The last time I'd spoken to Randy Disher, he'd been in bad shape. This was after he'd falsely accused his local mayor of murder and become the town's laughingstock. His own officers had taken to making crank calls and luring him to nonexistent crime scenes. At the time, Randy was talking seriously about coming home to San Francisco, a move I was totally against. "I hear the captain needs me," he said.

"No," I said. "I mean, it's nothing Adrian and I can't handle."

"If someone's trying to kill Leland and I can help, of course I'm going to be there. You couldn't keep me away."

"Randy, you have your own town to keep safe. And Sharona. We don't want to take you away from Sharona."

Sharona Fleming, for those who don't know, had once been Monk's nurse, back when he needed a full-time nurse in order to survive the chaos of this world. She was now back in her home state of New Jersey, working in a hospital and sharing her life with Randy.

"Sharona will be glad to get rid of me for a week or so. I haven't been very good company." He lowered his voice. "And I think she's getting a cold. I don't want to catch her cold."

"You don't want to be there to take care of her?" I asked.

"Have you ever been around Sharona when she's sick?" It was a rhetorical question.

"I told Randy about the cases from seven years ago," said

Monk, who couldn't help smiling. "He remembers them both. He'll be an invaluable asset."

It didn't take a genius to see what Monk was up to. "The captain is safe," I assured the ex-lieutenant. "We have all the notes from the investigations and the trials. There's no reason—"

"But that can't substitute for someone who was there. I helped put these scumbags away, remember? What are their names again? Monk said, but I didn't write it down."

"He wants to do it for Leland," my partner emphasized.

"It'll be like old times," said Randy. "I'll be on the first flight I can get. See you tomorrow." And he hung up.

"I know what you're up to." This time I said the words out loud. Very loud. "So, you're willing to disrupt Randy's life and lure him back just so you don't have to deal with A.J.? Are you really that selfish?"

"Randy wants to move back. We just have to make it easy. Once he's at Captain Stottlemeyer's side again, he'll realize—"

"You want Randy to give up his dreams and everything he's achieved just so you can feel more comfortable."

"Sure, you can make anything seem bad when you sneer like that."

"And what about Sharona?"

"She'll give up her job and move back with him. She can be our office assistant."

"I'm calling Randy right now. I'm telling him your plan."

"No, don't," pleaded Monk, his palms pressed together. "We really need him. Honest. If this is connected to a case, one that happened while we were away in Germany . . ."

He had a point. Under any other circumstances, I would have welcomed a professional visit from Randy. "Okay. But just temporary. As soon as this guy is caught and the captain is safe . . ."

"It's a deal. You're my hero, Natalie."

"You don't have to say that."

"No, I mean it. That's what being partners is all about, helping out the other person even when you think he's wrong."

"I'm glad to hear you say it, Adrian, about helping each other. That makes this next part a lot easier."

Monk still managed to be furious with me. Even after I reminded him that partners help each other out, he still pouted and threatened to leave me on my own. "We don't handle divorces," he whispered again, as we sat in the polished waiting area of Smith, Willard & O'Brien.

"Well, it's not a divorce now. It's a missing person."

"You still shouldn't have done it."

"I know, Adrian. And you're my hero."

It was a few minutes after two when the phone on the receptionist's desk buzzed. She reluctantly put down her sudoku puzzle, said a few words into the receiver, and guided us down the hall to the closed door of a corner office. She knocked gently, then opened it.

I don't think I've described Timothy O'Brien yet. He was a large man—not particularly overweight, just large and imposing—with the remains of a head of Irish red hair around the rear and sides, cut short in a stylish way. When he smiled,

I imagined his face could look quite handsome. But he wasn't smiling.

"Mrs. Teeger?" He made it all the way around his mahogany desk to shake my hand. "I was led to believe this would be a private consultation. About a family matter, I was told."

"Mr. O'Brien, this is my associate, Adrian Monk."

"I've heard of Adrian Monk, of course," said Timothy. He didn't reach out to shake Monk's hand, which was just as well. "Unless my assistant has become unforgivably sloppy, I take it this appointment was made under false pretenses. You are not in the market for a divorce, am I right?"

"I apologize," I said. "I needed to see you right away."

"And without my knowing the purpose of your visit."

"Mr. O'Brien," said Monk, "I see that you're not wearing a wedding ring. Do you have any idea where your wife is?"

"My wife?"

"Your wife, Susan, has been missing for almost two days. One day and twenty hours to be precise. I know she told you about having a sick aunt in San Diego. That was a canard fabricated by Mrs. O'Brien and Natalie here."

"Mr. Monk, I'm gay."

"That's what Natalie tells me. Do you think your wife suspected?"

"Suspected?" O'Brien stared at Monk over the top of his rimless half reading glasses. He pressed a button on his phone console. "Gayle, can you come in here?"

Her office must have been right next door, since it took Gayle Greenwald less than thirty seconds to arrive in his doorway. This was the first time I'd seen her close-up and in office lighting. She was older than I'd originally thought—almost Sue's age, attractive with highlighted brown hair. Not quite the husband bait I'd imagined.

"Gayle, this is the brilliant detective Adrian Monk. He wants to know where my wife is."

"Your wife?" Gayle laughed. "You were never married, were you? I've known you since law school. I was there when you met your first boyfriend, Frank. Kind of a pretentious jerk, although I never said so."

"Agreed. He preferred to be called Francis, which should have been a clue."

O'Brien was nodding his head while I shook mine. "No, that can't be right. A woman came into my office. Susan Puskedra O'Brien. She told me her life story. She said she was your wife and that you were having an affair. The two of you."

"You mean Timothy and me?" asked Gayle. She laughed. "Maybe we should have. It would have saved me from a bad marriage."

"Yes," Timothy agreed. "Then you would have had two bad marriages." They were both treating this as a joke. Maybe it was.

Monk turned to me, scowling. "Did anyone meet this Sue, besides you?"

"I don't think so, but . . ."

"Did she show any ID? Do you have a photograph of her? An e-mail address? A business card?"

"Yes, a card," I said, and began to rummage through my bag. "When we first met." I pulled out the card triumphantly and handed it to O'Brien.

"Susan O'Brien," he said. "With a phone number only."

Monk leaned my way. "You didn't have her fill out a client form or sign a contract?"

"No. I didn't want you finding out."

"Did she pay you, at least?"

"I was going to bill her at the end of the week."

"Great, just great. Thank you, Natalie. You're my hero."

It seemed that Monk was getting better at sarcasm every day.

CHAPTER ELEVEN

Mr. Monk and the Clean Sweep

Puskedra. I should have known when she gave me that name.

"How could you not know?" Monk demanded.

"I don't know," I moaned. "I take things at face value. A sympathetic woman walks through the door and talks about her cheating husband. Why would she invent a story like that?"

"She didn't walk through the door," he corrected me. "She was on the street, casing the joint. You're the one who pulled her inside and got her talking about her quote, husband, unquote. You made it easy for her."

On our drive back to the mini-mall, I told him everything, every detail I could remember about our nonexistent client. "Made what easy? What did she do?"

"There are three possibilities." He released one hand from the strap of his seat belt and raised an index finger. "One, she needed your professional attention distracted while she did something nefarious. This doesn't make the most sense. If she needed to distract someone smart and important, it would have been me."

"Distracting you can be done with a crooked sign in a window."

"There's a crooked sign?"

"Proves my point. What's the second possibility?"

He raised a second finger. "She needed some information about Timothy O'Brien but needed to do it secretly. That recording you made between O'Brien and his coworker . . ."

"It seemed pretty innocent. You'll listen to it, of course. But anyone could have sat in the booth behind them and heard the same conversation."

"Maybe." Finger number three. "Or maybe she needed you out of the way for a few hours—while you were surveilling O'Brien's house."

"But you were at the office during those hours. I assume you locked up tight and put on the alarm?"

"I did. There's also possibility three-A." He raised his pinkie, then bent it at the joint. "She needed to be alone in our office, and she did it by using the excuse of listening to the tape privately. How long was she in there?"

I thought back to that afternoon when I'd left her and went off to buy some pricey teas, an expense that just added more insult to injury. "Half an hour," I said. "She wanted to be alone, so I left her alone."

"Well, that's it. Ms. Unknown Puskedra O'Brien did something in our office. I told you offices were bad. All the rest— her story, the case, your stalking of a homosexual lawyer—was just window dressing. Speaking of window dressing . . ."

"Our signs are straight, Adrian. Don't worry."

As I pulled into my parking space, Monk had already taken a mini level out of his jacket. I don't know who else in the world would need a level small enough to fit into a pocket, but apparently there's a market for this. Five minutes later, satisfied that all our signage was still perfect, he joined me inside.

"I think the whole mini-mall is off by an inch or so, but the signs are straight. There's only so much one man can do."

Nine times out of ten, Monk's attention to detail drives me crazy. But this was time number ten. I swept my arm over the office. "Okay, Adrian. Focus. What did Ms. Unknown O'Brien do in here?"

My OCD-gifted partner began his routine, framing the scene, dropping his hands to open a drawer, then lifting them again, then closing the drawer. Three times he took tweezers from his pocket and stored things in baggies, also from his pocket. When he finished, we met in the center of the space, between the desks.

"I couldn't find any bugs or electronic devices," he reported. "But I'd have someone sweep the place to make sure. I don't mean physically. I can sweep physically."

"Julie and some college friend are coming over," I said. "He's an electronics security expert."

"Good. You should have him check your computer. Also mine in the closet. After she left, did your computer seem different? The height or direction of the chair? The angle of the screen? The position of the mouse?"

"I don't think so."

"Good." He held up a baggie. "I found a blond hair that's not yours. It's a little thicker, wavier, no split end. The color's a little brighter."

"Yes, Adrian. That's from her."

"We could do a DNA test, but since there's nothing to compare it to, it's pretty useless." He held up the second baggie with something barely visible in it. "Also the cut end of a fingernail. Even though it has your shade of polish on it, I know it's not yours, since I strictly forbid anyone in this office from cutting fingernails except over a wastebasket on top of a double-ply tarp."

"That's mine," I said, and took the baggie.

"I know. I'm just making a point. Speaking of wastebaskets, I found this in yours." In the third baggie was a slip of paper. "I'm no geologist, but from the layers of trash and the depth, I estimate it's from that same day, early afternoon. It doesn't match the notepad on your desk, so she brought it with her."

I took the baggie and held it up to the light. There were eighteen rows of numbers or letters. The first row said "0-0," the second row "1-2," the third row "A-B," the fourth "P-W," the fifth "1-A," the sixth "A-1." I forget the others, but they all seemed like gibberish. All were written in pen and all were crossed out in the same kind of ink.

"I have no idea," I said. "Is it some kind of code or secret writing?"

"I don't know," Monk admitted. "But it can't be too important if she left it in your wastebasket." Monk took back the baggie and slipped it into his jacket. "At least we have something."

"And that's it?" I couldn't hide my disappointment. "You did your whole Monk thing and came up with one piece of paper?"

"Natalie, it's been days. If I'd been in the loop from the beginning, this woman wouldn't have done whatever she did. Probably. I'm not a magician. You can't hide things from me, then expect me to solve it all instantly."

"You're right." He was totally right. "I'm sorry, Adrian."

He shrugged, accepting my apology. "There are times when you're right and I'm wrong. There are killers who would still be free if you weren't part of team Monk. But on the whole, I think we'd be better off if you just read the rule book and obeyed the rules."

"What rule book?"

"The one I'm going to write this evening. We definitely need a rule book. And the first rule, no divorce cases."

"Got it," I said. "Do you need a ride home?"

"I'll walk. You need to stay for Julie and her friend. Besides, it's not raining for once and I need the exercise."

"If it does rain, be sure to check your umbrella."

"I always do," he said, and was out the door.

Julie and Trevor arrived a short time later. I hadn't told them the whole embarrassing story, merely that our offices might be electronically compromised. Trevor—a tall boy, impossibly young and thin, with some remnants of acne on his chin—took some mysterious black boxes out of his backpack and began with my desktop computer. He didn't ask questions, but treated it as he would any school project. Julie, on the other hand . . . "How did your office get compromised?"

"*Might* be compromised. It's a long story," I said, even though it wasn't.

"I'll bet if I was your intern, this wouldn't have happened."

Julie has gotten it into her head that after she obtains her degree from Berkeley this spring, she should throw it all away by becoming an unpaid intern at the flourishing firm of Monk and Teeger. This is instead of going to law school, which used to be my daughter's dream. So far, I've managed to say no and make it stick. "No," I said again, for good measure.

"Does this have anything to do with the poison attack on the captain?" Julie and the captain were good friends, dating back to when they met. She'd been eleven and involved in her first murder case.

"No," I repeated. "It's a different case."

"Two cases? Mom, you need an intern—that's all I have to say."

"I wish, but I'm sure you're going to say more."

Trevor poked his head up over my monitor. "Your Wi-Fi is password protected. That's good. How about your computer?"

"Also password protected and I change it every week."

"Hm, you should really change passwords every day."

"That's not going to happen."

He shrugged in the same way parents shrug at their clueless kids. "Any other devices in the office?"

"There's an identical computer in the closet, but I'm not sure it's ever been turned on."

"Your phone?"

"I keep it with me."

It didn't take Trevor long to sweep through my system, or whatever the process is called. Meanwhile, Julie and I unwrapped Monk's computer from the closet and set it up. "It's never even been initiated," announced Trevor after a few clicks. And we wrapped it back up.

Using another mysterious black box, Trevor toured the office slowly, listening on a headset for something. "All clear, Mrs. T.," he finally reported. "You're good to go."

I didn't know whether to be relieved or annoyed. "So you're saying there are no bugs, no cameras, nothing funny on our computers. Nothing missing or added to the office."

"I don't know about the missing or added part," he said.

"Mom, what's up?"

"Nothing, sweetie. Nothing Adrian and I can't handle." I clasped my hands and put on a happy face. "Thank you so much, Trevor. I owe you and Julie a fancy dinner somewhere."

"Sweet," said Trevor.

"Mom," said Julie in a tone that suggested having dinner with Trevor would not count as a reward.

A minute later, I watched from the doorway as the thin young man opened the car door for Julie. Then I waved them on their way, all smiles until they disappeared.

Who the hell was Sue Puskedra? I had to ask myself. If I knew who she was, I'd have a fighting chance of figuring out her game. If I knew her game, I'd have a chance of figuring out who she was. As it was, I knew nothing except that I had trusted her.

That was the most galling part, I guess. She had made me care. I had listened to her dilemma, felt a real connection, and sat in my Subaru for hours waiting for a man to walk up to a mansion in Pacific Heights and kiss another man. I'd even fretted over how to break the news to her that her husband was gay.

I'd been had. And I did not like the feeling.

CHAPTER TWELVE

Mr. Monk and the Old Lieutenant

Police Chief Disher dragged in his suitcase and dropped a carry-on duffel bag off his shoulder. He looked just as boyish as he had the first time I'd met him standing over a corpse in my living room all those years ago. Even though Monk had been the one to insist that Randy work with us in San Francisco, of course Randy was staying at my house.

Randy glanced around the Julie shrine and smiled. "Jonas Brothers," he said, pointing to an old poster taped above the bed. "How did you know I was a fan?"

"Who isn't a Jonas Brothers fan?" I said, and left it at that.

"You're making me feel very welcome. But I just have to warn you, this is temporary."

"Of course it's temporary," I said. "I'm not about to have a roommate."

"I mean, I'm not taking back my old job. I could tell from the way Monk was talking on the phone . . ."

"Adrian isn't the most subtle person."

"I know I complain about being chief, but I'm going to make it work, Natalie."

"Your life is out there now," I agreed. "You have a house. And Sharona . . . Oh, how is her cold? I forgot to ask."

"Her cold is doing great. But my baby girl is cranky times ten. It's good to be away."

"Well, at least her family is nearby. And all her friends in Summit."

"Oh, Sharona hates Summit. She's constantly talking about moving back here. And the house is a rental."

"This is only temporary," I reminded him.

"Absolutely. As soon as we solve the captain's case . . . Look at this." He unzipped his duffel. "I keep a journal, ever since I started on the force. I brought the one from two thousand eight. It's got both cases fully outlined. I think it'll be a great help." He pulled out a thick blankbook with "2008" handwritten on the cover and doodles of what looked like dinosaurs surrounding the numbers.

"Great," I said, and handed him the armload of fresh towels I'd been holding. "I'll let you get settled."

Randy and I had an early lunch of PB&J sandwiches in my—make that our—kitchen and we caught each other up on all the gossip. I knew many of the players in Summit politics, having worked there for a short time as a police officer. It was hard to believe they were still giving him such a hard time about arresting the mayor, although if they ever caught a glimpse at his journals, it wouldn't help his credibility.

We picked up my partner on Pine Street in front of his building. "Good to see you, Lieutenant," said Monk as they automatically changed seats. Monk will only ride shotgun, which Randy knew, of course. It was just like old times.

"Police chief," Randy corrected him. Okay, not quite like old times.

I was glad not to see Trudy at the captain's bedside. She

had been on duty almost nonstop and was taking the afternoon off to go home, treat herself to a shower, and take the other male in her life on a long walk to the park.

I was not glad to see A.J. The bulky lieutenant had a folder full of papers strewn over the bed and together, with the captain raised to a sitting position, they were reviewing something or other. I didn't ask.

"My God, Randy." Stottlemeyer nearly jumped to his feet. With everything that had been happening, neither Monk nor I had thought to inform him. "What the hell are you doing here?"

"I came to help track down your killer." Randy stammered, "No, I didn't mean that. I mean your would-be killer. Not that I wouldn't come back to track your real killer. I'd do that in a heartbeat. Next time."

"Good old Randy." The captain laughed and this time did get out of bed, hugging his old partner to the front of his hospital gown. There were no wires connecting Leland to a heart monitor and he no longer looked like he needed one. "Police Chief Disher, I'd like you to meet my partner, Lieutenant A.J. Thurman."

The two men shook hands and I couldn't help noticing the difference—Randy's sweet, open expression going face-to-face with the lieutenant's pinched and suspicious one. "Good to meet you, Chief. I joined the force the year after you left. But I've certainly heard enough stories about Randy Disher." There was a hint of ridicule in his tone that I'm not sure Randy caught.

"You're a sight for sore eyes, buddy." Stottlemeyer eased himself back down. "But what makes you think you can help?"

This is where Monk took over, explaining his theory that the killer must have been referring to one of the two cases that happened during our extended European jaunt. "I worked on all the other cases involving the captain and Judge Oberlin. And since no one is sending any death threats my way . . ."

"Hey, what about me?" said Randy. He looked genuinely hurt.

"What about you?" asked the captain.

"What about my death threats? I know I wasn't the officer in charge. But all the same, you'd think they'd want to kill me, too."

"Maybe they do," said Stottlemeyer. "They just haven't gotten around to it yet."

"You're just saying that."

"No. You're all the way out in New Jersey. I'm sure you'll be next on their list. Just wait your turn."

Randy looked reassured. "Well, I hope not, honestly. Because that would mean you'd be dead. Hey, you want to look through my journal?" And he held up the volume from 2008.

"Sure," said Stottlemeyer, and brushed aside a section of A.J.'s papers. "I've missed those journals. That was the year of the dinosaur, I see."

For the next few minutes they huddled over the handwritten pages: Monk, Randy, and the captain sitting on his bed. Randy had already shown me the entries over our PB&J lunch. So I took advantage of the break to stand back and focus on Lieutenant Thurman, pressed into a corner of the room, arms crossed. The man did not look happy.

"I'm not sure this guy's a suspect. He's in prison," said Stottlemeyer. "Or should be. It was second-degree murder."

"He's in San Quentin," Monk acknowledged. "But he could have friends on the outside. And let's face it, being in prison's a pretty good alibi."

"I remember him," said Randy. "Kept going on about how a jury couldn't convict him without a murder weapon."

"But they did," said the captain. "And he wasn't too pleased about it."

"It's worth checking out," said Monk. His gaze turned serious. "What's this fingerprint in the margin?"

Randy took a look at the red smudge at the top of the page. "Raspberry jam from lunch with Natalie. Sorry."

By late that afternoon, the four of us had made our way over the Golden Gate Bridge into Marin County, taking the 101 to the Richmond Bridge exit. Instead of going over this second bridge, we turned onto Sir Francis Drake Boulevard, toward a scenic spit of land overlooking the San Francisco Bay, just east of the little town of San Quentin.

It had taken an hour or two to get the captain checked out. The doctor's okay was the easy part. It was Trudy Stottlemeyer's okay that was problematic. I finally was handed the phone and assured her that Monk, Randy, and I would be taking good care of him and would drop him off at home as soon as we did one little errand. I didn't mention the errand included a trip into the depths of the California state penal system.

Lieutenant Thurman had been almost as hard to placate, but not out of concern for the captain's health. "A.J., there are four of us," explained Stottlemeyer. "That should be enough to interview one inmate. Your resources can be better used working other angles—the note, and who could have dropped it on my desk."

A.J. didn't totally buy that, and he was right not to. The captain did little to hide his excitement. He might not have been at one hundred percent, health-wise, but the adrenaline rush of being with his old partner was carrying him through.

"The lieutenant seems like a nice guy," said Randy from the backseat of the Subaru.

"He's okay," I answered from the driver's seat, and felt I was being generous.

The man we were visiting, Jasper Coleman, had been arrested a little over seven years ago, coincidentally on the very same day Monk and I were winging our way to Frankfurt, Germany, in pursuit of Dr. Kroger.

Jasper and his wife, Celia, had lived in Bernal Heights, in a ramshackle cottage lodged between two vacant lots. According to Jasper's statement, they had been in bed that night and were awakened by noises somewhere in the house. Jasper got up and told Celia to stay in the bedroom and lock the door. When he walked into the living room, he found a tall black man wearing gloves trying to pry their flat-screen TV off the wall mounts with a crowbar. According to Jasper, he and the intruder struggled until Jasper slipped and fell and was knocked unconscious with the aforementioned crowbar. A nasty bruise on the side of his head was the only physical evidence of the struggle.

When he came to, Jasper claimed that he found the door to the bedroom broken down and his wife dead on the floor, also bludgeoned with what was probably the same crowbar. Metallic traces were found in one of Celia's gaping wounds. But the weapon was never found, a fact that was the basis of much of Jasper's defense.

"Well, well, what a surprise," said the large, fleshy man as an armed guard led him into one of the prison's interview rooms. "Captain Stottlemeyer." I'm not sure how many convicted felons could instantly remember the officer in charge of putting them away. Jasper Coleman could and did.

"I'm here, too," said Randy. "Lieutenant Disher. Remember?"

"Yeah," said the inmate, looking unimpressed. "Dumb and dumber. When are you two going to find Celia's real killer?"

"We found him seven years ago," said Stottlemeyer.

The four of us were lined up in chairs on the opposite side of the bolted-down steel table, like a small jury facing the accused—in this case, the convicted. Monk was on the far right, dividing his attention between Coleman and the pages of Randy's journal from 2008. He seemed mesmerized by the combination of hard facts and random observations, not to mention the sketches and doodles in the margins of almost every page. Monk and I introduced ourselves, but Coleman couldn't have cared less.

"What do you know about Judge Nathaniel Oberlin?" asked the captain.

"I know that the two of you were in cahoots, that you scumbags railroaded me. I know that I've been wasting away for seven years due to you." Coleman allowed himself a thin grin. "I also know Oberlin got poisoned and you yahoos thought it was a tropical disease."

"We know better now," said Monk. "It was someone with a grudge against the judge and the captain."

"Really? I guess I'm not the only innocent guy you screwed

over. Does that mean you're next, Captain? Are you coming down with a tropical disease?"

"Not yet," said Stottlemeyer. "That's why we're here."

The convict's laugh was low and mean. "You trying to pin this on me, too? A guy in prison?" He leaned forward. "Just between us, I hope he gets you. I'm rooting for him."

"What friends do you have on the outside, Coleman? Anyone who might help you get revenge?"

"I'm not a killer. My wife's killer is still out there, thanks to you."

"No, he's in here," replied the captain. "There was no evidence of an intruder. No neighbors reported seeing anything. There was no DNA except yours and Celia's, no fingerprints."

"It was freaking three a.m. and the guy wore gloves."

"Wearing gloves to jack a TV off your wall? And this thing about three a.m. when the two of you were fast asleep?" The captain had the SFPD report file in front of him, which might have been slightly more reliable than Randy's journal entry. "There was food in Celia's stomach. According to the ME, she had eaten a good-sized snack somewhere after two a.m., when, according to your statement, you were both sound asleep."

"Maybe she got up without me hearing," said Jasper Coleman. "Or the medical examiner made a mistake."

"Or maybe, after years of late-night fights and Celia's calls to the police about spousal abuse, you finally killed her. That's the conclusion a jury of your peers came to."

"That was your doing." Jasper's wrists were shackled to the steel table, but he still managed to point both index fingers at the captain. "You and the judge and Bloomquist, the assistant DA. The three of you cherry-picked the evidence. You glossed over the lack of a murder weapon, which made the jury gloss over it. From the second you showed up, you had it in for me."

"I suppose you know," I said. "Edgar Bloomquist died in a skiing accident five years ago."

"In Switzerland. I celebrated with a piece of cake. I had another piece of cake when Oberlin died."

"Leaving just me," said the captain. "Don't start baking that cake."

"Hey, what about me?" said Randy. "I had it in for you, too."

Stottlemeyer scowled. "Randy, no one had it in for Jasper Coleman. We checked all avenues of the investigation. Impartially. As for the crowbar, Jasper had plenty of opportunities to dispose of it before the first responders arrived. According to them, he was in the bathroom washing his hands."

"I'd been attacked. I was putting a cold, wet towel on my head."

"Randy, what is this?" Monk asked. He was pointing to something in the ex-lieutenant's journal.

"What's what?" Randy went to look over Monk's shoulder at the page in question. So did the rest of us.

"It's a doodle," said Stottlemeyer. The little sketch was squeezed in just below Randy's journal entry for that day: all about the weather, what he had for lunch, his interview with the dead woman's husband.

"It's a doodle," Randy repeated. "You know doodles. They come to you out of the blue, no thinking necessary."

I refrained from any wisecracking about Randy and his nonthinking process. It wasn't the time or place.

The doodle in question was in the lower right corner, a thin dirty hand, wearing a wedding ring, picking up nails, carpenter nails, off the floor. Randy was a decent artist. In high school, I believe his ambition had been to draw comic book heroes.

"Why did you draw that?" asked the captain curiously.

"I don't know," said Randy. "It was seven years ago and . . . I don't know."

Monk raised a finger and thought out loud. "The other two doodles on the page have something to do with Mr. Coleman—his face, him sitting in a chair. But this one's different. A man's hand picking up . . ." My partner scrunched his brow and turned to Jasper Coleman. "Were you picking your fingernails during your interview with Randy?"

"Doing what?" said Jasper. There was an instantly defensive tone in his voice. "I wasn't picking my nails."

"Interesting," said the captain. He began leafing through several pages in the SFPD file. "Randy didn't mention anything about nails in his interview report."

"Maybe not," said Monk. "But my bet is that he noticed it, at least subconsciously. Later that day, when he was writing in his journal . . ."

The captain wasn't convinced. "Randy draws dragons. That doesn't mean he's arrested a dragon."

"Hold on, Leland. Wow." Randy threw his elbows onto the table and pressed his head between his fists. "Monk's right. Jasper was picking his fingernails. Somehow it must have registered, but I didn't write it down."

"I was not picking my nails," growled Coleman, leaving even less doubt than before.

"Let me check on that." The captain cleared his throat

and flipped another page in the official report. "By the time Mr. Coleman was taken into custody and was swabbed, there was nothing under his nails. Of course that was hours later."

"What does that mean?" asked Randy, turning to Monk. "You think it was blood or skin tissue? I can't believe I let a suspect pick his nails during an interview."

"He wasn't a suspect at the time," I pointed out. "He was a victim and a witness."

"Still, I should have had a swab done right then. What was I thinking?"

"Don't beat yourself up," said Randy's old partner. "We put the guy away without the swab, that's what counts."

Monk looked up again from Randy's old journal. "By the way, Mr. Coleman, when did you get married?"

We all followed Monk's gaze to the gold band on the convict's left ring finger. "Celia and I got married in two thousand and four," said Jasper. "Why?"

Stottlemeyer made a face. "He wore that ring all through the trial, trying to get jury sympathy. I'm surprised he's still wearing it."

"He's not," said Monk. "Mr. Coleman has put on a fair amount of weight since his conviction. I'd say sixty pounds, no offense. Prison food can do that. Randy's doodle shows a skinny man with a bruise on his head. Yet the ring he's wearing now fits perfectly. Hence, it's a new ring."

Stottlemeyer looked up to the guard standing by the door. "Is this true?"

The guard was smiling. "It's true, sir. Jasper got himself a fan. They were married in the prison chapel about a month ago."

We were all taken aback by the news, except Monk, of

course. I mean, you hear stories about gullible women be-coming romantically obsessed with famous killers. But I'd always thought of it as a kind of urban myth.

"She came here interested in getting justice for me. We wound up falling in love. What's wrong with that?"

"Seems like a very sweet girl," volunteered the guard.

"Mrs. Kristen Jones-Coleman," said Jasper with some pride. "The name was a compromise. We had a long discussion about keeping her maiden name."

Stottlemeyer brushed his mustache. "You mean she had reservations about taking the name of a wife killer?"

"Just the opposite," said Jasper. "She wanted my name. I had to talk her into using both, at least until you guys wise up and catch the real guy."

"Yeah," said the captain. "We'll get right on that."

CHAPTER THIRTEEN

Mr. Monk and the Planted Evidence

Despite the remnants of rush-hour traffic, we got the captain home in time for dinner. On the curb in front of the bungalow in Dogpatch sat an SFPD cruiser with a familiar face behind the wheel. Officer Joe Nazio often pulled this kind of duty. I parked the Subaru right behind him and we all got out to say hello.

Like almost everyone, Joe was glad to see our friend from New Jersey. He teased Randy about being a big-deal police chief. And Randy teased him about getting stuck as a glorified babysitter. "Actually, every officer in the precinct wanted this job," said Joe. "Protecting Captain Stottlemeyer? That's an honor."

The captain is pretty old-school and doesn't take praise very well. "For the sake of your career, I'll try my best not to get murdered."

"Please do that, sir."

A second later, the door to the bungalow flew open and the real bodyguard emerged, all smiles and wearing an apron. If an assassin ever did manage to get past Joe Nazio, he would have to contend with Trudy Stottlemeyer. And with

Teddy. From somewhere in the house, we could hear him howling with anticipation.

The next morning Trudy called, bright and early. "Leland isn't going into work, doctor's orders. I know how excited he was to see Randy. But the excitement has worn off and he needs his rest. I hope you can get along without him."

Trudy had always tried to ignore the danger of Leland's job. But this time he had been doing the most domestic of chores, taking the dog out for a walk. They'd both come back with a near deadly dose of thallium coursing through their systems. That was hard to ignore.

"No problem," I said. "Tell the captain we're off to meet the wife. We'll drop by later to report in—unless you think he really needs total rest."

"No, Leland wants to be kept in the loop. Just call before you show up."

Before leaving San Quentin, we had stopped by to see the warden. He informed us that, except for his ongoing anger issues about his conviction, Jasper Coleman had been a model prisoner. There had been no reason for the state to deny visiting rights to Kristen Jones, a twenty-something paralegal who had read an article and become fascinated with his case. And there had been no reason, a year or so later, to deny the couple the right to get married.

"It's the law," said the warden. "Even if it seems like an unworkable marriage, some people make it work."

I telephoned Jasper's bride from the prison's razor-wired parking lot and said we were private investigators looking into her husband's case. She seemed eager to set up an appointment for the following day and gave me the address.

I was surprised to see that Mrs. Kristen Jones-Coleman had taken up residence in the old Coleman house. Was she actually sleeping in that bedroom, where Jasper had bludgeoned Celia to death? Were there still stains on the floor? Even if Kristen totally believed in his innocence, what kind of woman would do this?

In stark contrast to the rest of the block, the Coleman house was awash in flowering plants: morning glory vines on the fence; beds of roses and lilies; a row of hydrangea bushes nearly blocking the curb in front; pots of violets on either side of the front door. The lush setting might have felt cheerier if it didn't remind me so much of the flowers at a funeral.

"Every house has seen its share of tragedy," said Kristen shortly after we walked in. No one had asked the question, but she knew we were thinking it.

Kristen had just made a fresh pot of coffee. I took a bottle of Fiji Water out of my tote for Monk and the four of us settled around the coffee table by the front window—three coffees and water in a glass that Monk had personally washed out, no ice—not far from the spot where her husband had hit himself with a crowbar before getting rid of it somehow and calling 911.

"Sometimes I do think about that horrible night," she went on. "But Jasper won't sell. And I want it to be here for him when he's released."

"Your husband still has a lot of anger with the police," said Randy, getting right to the point. "There was a captain and a lieutenant on his case."

"I don't know about a lieutenant," said Kristen. Randy's face fell. "But Jasper told me all about a Captain Stottlemeyer and a Judge Oberlin. They were the ones responsible for this travesty. The judge died, that's what Jasper said. We celebrated with a cake I brought in on visitors' day."

"You celebrate people's deaths?" I had to ask.

Kristen shrugged. She didn't care. "You mentioned on the phone that you were private detectives."

"Yes," I confirmed, speaking for the majority. "We're looking into the death of Judge Oberlin. There is a possibility that he was murdered in connection with an old case."

"Oh." She looked disappointed. "I thought you might have some evidence to help Jasper."

"Not per se, no." Not anywhere near per se.

"Then why are you here? You don't think . . ." She opened her mouth and drew in a little gasp. "You think Jasper might be behind the judge's death? That's ridiculous."

"We have to check all possibilities," I said. "Does your husband ever talk about getting even with the system?"

"Jasper's in prison. How could he kill a judge?"

"Someone on the outside could be helping him," Randy pointed out.

"Who on the outside? Jasper doesn't have any friends. . . . You mean me?"

"We sort of do," said Randy. "I mean, that's why we're here. We're checking out the possibility."

"That I would kill someone? How would that help? Neither one of us is a murderer."

Kristen struck me as a sweet-natured girl, petite but not particularly pretty. Smart, but perhaps naive and easily manipulated. She wanted to believe she was part of a bigger cause, working to right a wrong and free the man she'd fallen in love with. "Jasper wants to clear his name. That's all."

"And you really believe he's innocent?" asked Monk.

"I do. The police combed the house looking for the weapon. They took a metal detector to the backyard and the front. Also the lots next door. It would have been impossible for my Jasper to do anything like that, given the injury he sustained."

I don't know when Monk started focusing out the front window, but I noticed it now. He was sitting straight in his chair, maybe even rising slightly to get a better view. "Are you a gardener, Mrs. Coleman?"

"Yes," she said, looking a bit confused by the change of subject. "I never got to grow things in my little apartment, except a few geraniums on my balcony."

"And you've been living here for a while, since before you got married."

"Yes," she said, more guardedly now. "How did you know?"

"I'd say at least six months," Monk observed, "from the way the plants have taken root and spread out. Jasper Coleman's been in prison, so I assumed it was you."

Kristen nodded. "He asked me to move in. The house was empty and it's still his property. There's nothing wrong with that."

"Nothing wrong at all," said Monk. "A house needs someone to look after it."

"Monk, what's up?" Randy stretched his tall frame to look out the window. "Does this have something to do with the fingernails? Dirt under his fingernails?"

I'd had the same thought. "Did Coleman bury the

weapon? How? Where? The police ran a metal detector over everything."

Monk ignored us. "Those hydrangeas out by the street-lamp. Did you put those in?"

"I did," admitted Kristen. "It's public property, I know, but other people do it. I think it adds a nice touch."

"Very nice," said Monk. We were all standing now, turning from the coffee table to get a better look out the window. "Randy, are crowbars ever made of aluminum? It doesn't have to be a crowbar, but something similar. A tire iron?"

"Sure," said Randy, happy to know something Monk didn't. "Cast aluminum is used for crowbars and tire irons. What does that have to do with gardening?"

"A lot. Mrs. Coleman, you seem like a healthy, symmetrical person, everything in its place. I assume you planted all pink hydrangeas. No sane person would mix blue and pink."

"I think they were all pink, yes."

"And yet the flowers on one of the bushes are starting to come in blue. Curious."

Without another word of explanation, Monk led the way out the front, followed by a curious parade of three. The houses in this neighborhood were fairly close to the street. In fewer than five strides we reached the strip of garden by the curb, perhaps three feet wide and thirty feet long, with the lamppost in the middle.

The hydrangea bushes were small but well manicured, spread out enough to give them room. In a year or two they would probably outgrow the space and need to be replanted.

"If you sweep a metal detector around the base of this streetlamp, it's going to go off," said Monk.

"Sure," said Randy. "It's galvanized steel."

"So a clever killer could step out the door at three a.m., stuff an aluminum crowbar tip-first into the ground, and go back inside. The police would get pings but they probably wouldn't dig. What would be the point?"

"Are you saying it's buried here?" asked Randy, pointing to a bush just to the right of the post.

"No." Monk pointed to the bush on the left. "It's here, under the bush with the blue flowers."

From the second we pulled up, my partner had been distracted by the asymmetry of the puffy balls of color. I, too, had noticed the difference but didn't think twice about it. As is often the case with Monk, the annoying little detail had turned out to be important.

"Hydrangeas are sensitive to acidity in the soil, like aluminum. It can change their color. You see? This whole row, pink except here, on this one side of the lamppost. So . . ." Monk paused for effect. "Why is this one small patch of dirt more acidic? It's not rust from the lamppost."

"Not if the lamppost is galvanized steel," said Randy. "It wouldn't rust."

"There's only one way to find out. Mrs. Coleman?" I asked, pointing to the blue bush.

"No," she spat out instantly. "You do not have my permission to dig. You're just trying to get more evidence against my Jasper. Planted evidence," she added, seemingly unaware of the pun.

There were so many things wrong with her logic. I gently attacked her points one by one. "First, we don't need your permission to dig since, as you pointed out, this is public land. Second, we don't need more evidence against your husband. He's been convicted. Third, you planted these bushes yourself. They look pretty undisturbed, so I don't know how we could have planted evidence. Mrs. Coleman, what we need from you is a shovel. May we please borrow a shovel? It will save us some time."

The poor woman finally gave in. I think she was holding out hope that Monk might be wrong. But she didn't seem surprised—after Randy dug around the root ball and pried out the hydrangea and set it to one side and started digging a little deeper—to hear the clink of metal on metal.

It was an aluminum crowbar that Randy pulled out of the hole and showed off. He was wearing plastic gloves, courtesy of Monk, and dropped the crowbar into a large plastic baggie, courtesy of my PBS tote. It wasn't evidence in an ongoing case, but we would turn it over to the DA's office just to be safe. It always pays to be safe.

"That proves nothing," said Kristen, her voice cracking just a little. "The real killer could have put it there."

"Why?" asked Monk.

"Why?" she repeated. "To get rid of it."

"Why?" Monk asked again. "Why would a killer remove a murder weapon from the scene, then stop outside and take the time—and the risk—to push it into the ground by a streetlamp?"

Mrs. Kristen Jones-Coleman desperately wanted to have an answer for this. But she didn't. "Jasper's a good man," she protested. "He didn't kill anyone. That crowbar doesn't prove a thing. Get off my property now. How dare you . . ."

"I'm sorry," I said.

When we pulled away from the curb a minute or so later, I stopped at the corner to check my rearview mirror. Kristen was still there, standing perfectly still at the curb with the shovel in her hand and the uprooted hydrangea bush by her side. "Why did you have to do that?" I asked softly.

"Do what?" asked Monk.

"You know what. Her husband's in prison for life. His appeal isn't going anywhere. But she had a purpose. Why did you have to smash the one illusion that was keeping her going?"

"And let her stay happily married to a killer? Natalie, you don't mean that."

"I don't know what I mean," I said. And I slowly turned the corner.

CHAPTER FOURTEEN

Mr. Monk Makes a House Call

"I couldn't keep him home," said Trudy. She made it sound like an accusation.

Randy had put her on speaker. He leaned forward from the backseat as her voice filled the old Subaru. "Lieutenant Thurman came by and they went off to see his father. Arnold Senior is very sick, and Leland . . . Well, you know Leland."

"Captain Arny is sick?" asked Randy.

"Heart disease," Monk and I and the iPhone speaker said almost in unison. "It looks pretty bad," I added.

"I had no idea," said Randy. "We should go see him."

"We want to bring the captain up-to-date on the case," I said over my shoulder as I made an uphill light at Potrero Avenue.

"Well, he's at Captain Thurman's," said Trudy. "Do you want the address?"

"Sure," said Randy. "We can kill two birds with one stone. Oh . . ." He winced. "I didn't mean that. No one's dying, at least not Captain Stottlemeyer. I meant . . ."

"You don't have to explain, Randy. I know the expression." Trudy gave us the Thurman address and made us promise to get Leland home.

It was one of those old San Francisco houses, rambling, dark, and in disrepair from a hundred years of weather and fifty years of poor maintenance. You could just tell it had been in the same family for generations; no yuppie remodeling here. Rebecca, Arnold Thurman's daughter, met us at the door.

"He'll be so glad to see you," she said. "A.J.'s in his room, I think. But the captain's in the bedroom with Dad. It's in the back." And she led the three of us down a shadowy hallway. "You'll have to forgive the old place. It's falling apart."

"It's charming," I said.

"We had to take out a second and a third mortgage," Rebecca said, "for the medical payments. But we'll be okay. Something will turn up."

Until that moment, I'd never given a thought to A.J.'s living arrangements. Apparently, neither Arny Junior nor Rebecca had managed to fly out of the old wooden nest, which was probably for the best, given the current situation.

The room was set up like a hospital, with a regulation, adjustable bed, a heart monitor, a sideboard covered in medication, and an empty IV-drip stand over by the shaded window. The blips from the monitor grew slightly faster as soon as we walked in. "Monk and Natalie. And Randy Disher. My God, boy, I never thought I'd see you again."

I was shocked by Captain Thurman's appearance. He'd always been a hulking man, a larger, more substantial version of A.J. Now he seemed shrunken to half that size. "Clear off some chairs. It's like a damn visiting hour in here."

I did as I was told, taking a few glossy catalogs from a chair and setting them on the windowsill. "Sotheby's?" I said, looking at the covers. "Christie's. Pretty fancy."

"Yeah, my kids like to dream big. Don't know where they got that, not from my side. Becky, how's that herbal tea coming? Can you believe it? They won't let me have regular tea. And coffee's just a memory."

"Coming, Dad," said Rebecca in a tone of infinite patience, and exited the room.

"I guess this means you won't have any use for that whisky," joked Captain Stottlemeyer. "I should drink it now, right in front of you." He was sitting at Captain Thurman's bedside, in pretty much the same position as Trudy had been at his bedside.

"Gallows humor," growled the other captain. "I hope you choke on it."

"What's the joke?" I asked.

Captain Thurman smiled. "You may not know this, young lady, but Leland's pop was a renowned bartender."

"I do know that," I said. "I used to be a bartender myself."

"I doubt you were in Hamish's league."

"Well, I was pretty good. . . . Wait! Hamish Stottlemeyer? You're kidding."

Leland grinned. "A good old Scottish name, at least the front half."

"His pop had a gallows sense of humor, too," said Arnold. "There were six of us best buds in the old days. Fraternity brothers. I think we'd just turned twenty-one. Getting old and dying were the furthest things from our minds."

"As they should be," I agreed.

"Well, that's when his pop takes down from his top shelf an old bottle of whisky. He plops it smack down on the bar.

That was the night he'd gotten us all skunked. I'm surprised we remember anything."

Captain Stottlemeyer took over. "So us boys are already plastered and he plops down this bottle and he says, 'Boys, this is for the last survivor. Because all of you are going to get old and gray, God willing. And then you're going to die off one by one. In no time, there's only going to be one of you fine fellows left.'" The captain was imitating a decent Scottish brogue. "'So, boyos, I want you to promise me you'll leave this fine bottle untouched until only one of you is left. Then you'll go into a bar somewhere in the world, all by yourself. The last man. And you'll have the barkeep uncork it, and you'll drink a dram for every one of your fallen comrades, naming each by name as you slug it back and turn it upside down on the bar.'"

"Wow," said Randy. "Cool."

"The amazing thing is that we all loved the idea," said Arnold.

"It's a romantic notion," I said. "Kind of an old Scottish tradition."

"Ghoulish," Monk corrected me.

"We all solemnly raised our drunken hands and swore." Arnold sighed. "That's the kind of brotherhood you can't break up. Just the idea of it made us all stay in touch. Thirty-six years."

There was a respectful pause in the room. "Wow," said Randy again. "That's quite a story."

The captain nodded. "And the strangest part was my pop didn't have a Scottish accent."

"He didn't," Arnold confirmed. "Somehow over the years of telling, you gave him this mysterious brogue. But the rest is true, hand to God. The bottle's in some safety-deposit box."

"Five swigs of whisky will probably kill off the sixth then and there," said Stottlemeyer. Then his face turned serious. "You're going to outlive us all, Arny. You know that."

"Yeah." Arnold appreciated the sentiment. "Not if they make me drink herbal tea."

"Things will turn out. You'll get well enough for a transplant and we'll get you to the top of that wait list."

The two men clasped hands and locked eyes with real affection. When the moment ended, it was as if nothing had happened. "Well," said Stottlemeyer, turning to Randy, "tell me. What's happening with the wife killer's wife?"

Randy took the lead, filling in both captains. I didn't have the heart to talk about it. When it came time for the crowbar part, Monk jumped in with the color commentary—pink versus blue.

"Who knew you were such a gardener?" marveled Stottlemeyer.

"Only hydroponic, where there's no soil or insects. As for hydrangeas, they're unpredictable and disorderly. That's how they got on my watch list in the first place."

Through it all, I'm not sure how much Captain Thurman was listening. He'd been involved in enough murder cases of his own. Somewhere along the way, Rebecca arrived with her father's tea and left again, disappearing into the house. "Becky's an emergency room nurse. They gave her some sort of paid leave to deal with me."

"A nurse," I said. "It's nice to have a nurse in the family."

"Damn kids want me to live forever," he mumbled under his breath.

Stottlemeyer seemed pleased by our work that morning. "Well, it looks like we got one right, eh, Randy, even when Monk was off in Germany."

"Don't let my son hear you say that," said Captain T. "He thinks you can do every case without the magic of Monk."

"I think you know better than that," said Captain S.

"Hey, my son's a jackass, you don't have to tell me."

Adrian Monk smiled. But I felt mixed emotions. You never want a father saying something like that about his only son. On the other hand, it was true.

"So, where to now?" asked Captain S. "Mrs. Coleman doesn't look like a viable suspect."

"We're checking with the prison to see if Jasper has any other contacts on the outside," I said. "But it doesn't look promising."

"So who else wants to kill me?"

"There's still the robbery case," said Randy, holding up his dinosaur-covered journal. "A couple of rich college kids broke into their uncle's Nob Hill penthouse and stole a boatload of antique silver. Tens of thousands of dollars' worth. The responding officer's report said it was probably random. There had been several break-ins in the building. But the captain and I didn't think so. Well, the captain didn't think so."

"I remember those kids," said Leland. "Mean and entitled."

"Sounds like low-level stuff," said Captain T.

Randy shook his head. "Not if you're kids with your whole life in front of you and you get sent away for seven years."

Monk whistled. I didn't even know he could; maybe it was an accident. "Seven years. That's pretty harsh for a first offense."

Leland shook his head. "When we came to question them, they both pulled weapons, unregistered semiautomatics. That was worse than the burglaries, legal-wise."

"What did you do?" I asked.

"I sweet-talked them out of shooting me," said the captain. But I'm sure there was more to it than that.

"They served their time at Pleasant Valley," noted Randy. Pleasant Valley was a state prison in Fresno and even though it was minimum security, I'm sure it wasn't all that pleasant. "Both boys—men now, I guess—were released two months ago."

"It did seem harsh," Captain S. admitted. "The uncle, the one they robbed, he tried to get the charges dropped. By then it was out of his hands."

"I'd be mad, too," said Captain T. "At the judge who sentenced me and the cop who didn't fall for the random burglar theory."

"Two cops," Randy reminded everyone.

"Don't worry, Randy," said Captain S. "I'm sure they want you dead, too."

It wasn't more than a second later when Randy's iPhone pinged with a text. He jumped, as if expecting a death threat typed out on the display. "It's Trudy," he reported. My phone pinged and so did the captain's. Randy read the joint message aloud. " 'Enough fun, guys. Time for Leland's nap.' "

"The old ball and chain," chuckled Captain T.

"It's actually a pretty good ball and chain," said Leland. "And she's right."

We did our best to fade into the background as the two captains said their good-byes, perhaps their final good-byes, although neither one brought up the subject. "You take care of yourself," said Captain Thurman, and waved us out of his room.

Lieutenant A.J. Thurman stood waiting in the front hall. "Thanks for coming," he said to Captain S. "Seeing you really perked him up."

As we put on our jackets from the coatrack, I happened to glance out the window. "Where's Officer Nazio?" I asked. Now that I thought of it, I hadn't seen a patrol car when we'd pulled up.

"Gave him a few hours off," said Stottlemeyer. "I already had a police escort, right?"

"That's right," said A.J. "I'll call Nazio and tell him you're on your way. Meanwhile, if you guys don't mind escorting the captain home . . ."

"Hey, I'm not a five-year-old on a playdate."

"You're right. If this was a playdate, they wouldn't need sidearms." A.J. raised an eyebrow. Randy responded by patting the bulge under his jacket, while I patted the top of my PBS tote. I found myself carrying my Glock more and more these days.

A.J. was first out the door and onto the sidewalk. "Let me check," he said, motioning for us to stay back. He made a big show of looking up and down the street while the rest of us did a four-way eye roll, including Monk. Technically, of course, A.J. was right to check the perimeter.

"Suspicious vehicle at nine o'clock," he said, coming back to the doorway. Looking left past the stop sign on the next block, I could see it. I could also hear it, an oversized, dark SUV, idling loudly by the curb. The afternoon sun glared off its windshield. "It's not a neighbor," A.J. whispered. Why was he whispering? "The people in those houses are at work."

It seemed overly cautious to me. An SUV idling on the next block on a residential street is hardly a red flag. We couldn't even determine if anyone was inside. But this was A.J.'s territory. If anyone knew what would be out of place, it was him.

"What do you want to do?" asked Randy.

"I say we go out the back way," said A.J. "It's more controlled. You can pull the car around through the alley."

"I can't disagree with the lieutenant," said Monk, "although I really want to. A smaller, more controlled environment is safer."

"Oh, for Pete's sake." That was the extent of Stottlemeyer's protest. Police etiquette dictates you don't make a fuss when your safety is in someone else's hands. It's their business to keep you alive.

I crossed the street to my Subaru while the others retraced their steps back through the house. Before pulling out, I checked my mirrors. The SUV was still there.

After a few one-way streets, I found the narrow alley. It was also one-way, out of necessity, just wide enough for the household garbage cans and their weekly pickup. Halfway down the block I could see the captain, his lieutenant, and the Summit police chief stepping sheepishly out of the back gate. They began to walk my way as I drove slowly theirs. With any luck, they could get in without dinging my doors against a gate or a wall or a can. At some point I was going to have to bite the bullet and get all my current dings buffed out, just out of pride. Or I was going to have to sell the car, which might be easier and cheaper. These were the thoughts going through my head when I saw the stocky figure walk out into the lane behind them, in a black ski mask.

Before the figure even raised his gun, I honked my horn. Loud and long. I don't know if this was good or bad, if it wound up saving a life or making things worse. All three officers turned to face the intruder. Monk looked back and forth.

The first shot went wide, ricocheting off the aluminum siding of a house that had been built back to the property line. The second shot hit Captain Stottlemeyer in the left shoulder as he instinctively reached up for a shoulder holster that wasn't there. He reeled back and slammed to the ground. Randy and A.J. grabbed for their own sidearms. Meanwhile, I threw the stick into park and scrambled for my tote on the front passenger seat.

The assailant got off one more. The narrow alley made it seem like shooting fish in a barrel. But this one also went wide, pinging off a cement wall before lodging into A.J.'s upper right leg. Only a miracle or incredibly bad aim was preventing this from being a bloodbath.

It was Randy who got off the first response, dropping to one knee and firing into the sunlight. In his defense, it wasn't crucial that he hit his target. It was crucial that he respond quickly. The round from his Smith & Wesson spat into the ground at the shooter's feet, and that was enough. The man in the mask stepped back, took half a second, and retreated in a run to the end of the alley and around the corner.

CHAPTER FIFTEEN

Mr. Monk and Chicken Potpie Night

I didn't think about the oversized, dark SUV for a while.

Two-fifths of our team was on the ground, spurting blood. That left Randy and me to get on our phones to 911 and try to stabilize the scene. At some point, Rebecca Thurman came out of the house to join us, although I couldn't have blamed her if she'd stayed inside and bolted the doors. Her face went white as she saw the red stain seeping through my jacket, which I wasn't wearing at the time. I had folded it into quarters, pressed it to the hole in A.J.'s thigh, and kissed it good-bye. I needed an excuse to go jacket shopping anyway.

"He'll be fine," I assured her. "They'll both be fine."

The first time Monk and I looked for the SUV was after the ambulances had pulled away. It was where we'd last seen it—at the curb, past the stop sign, idling and empty and unlocked. It was, to be more precise, a Cadillac Escalade of a newish vintage. I took a Kleenex from my tote and opened the door.

Monk edged past me to bend inside and look. The speed of his deduction must have set a record. In less than ten seconds, he pulled his head out and straightened to his full height. "Stolen," he announced. "This morning on Bay

Street, a block or two west of Ghirardelli Square. Between
ten a.m. and noon. I could probably describe the victim if I
looked around, but that's not the point. The point is it was
stolen this morning by someone who knew what he was doing, for the purpose of attacking the captain. This person
willingly left the car behind, meaning we're not going to find
prints."

Every time he does this, I swear I'm not going to let it get
to me. How was he sure the SUV was stolen? And how, in ten
seconds, could he pinpoint the exact location and time?
"Okay, I give up."

"Give up what?" He looked genuinely perplexed. "Oh,
you mean . . . Natalie, please. The rightful owners are neat,
methodical people. There's no litter, no crumbs. The leather
is maintained regularly. I'd say once a week. Compared to
your car . . ."

"Yes, Adrian, I get that. Great car, great people. I'm a slob.
But . . ."

"That should tell you everything."

"Including it was stolen from Bay Street between ten and
noon this morning?"

Monk sighed and pointed to a single square of white paper with black printing, centered on the dashboard in plain
sight. I leaned over the hood, read it, and felt pretty foolish.
"A pay and display parking receipt."

"And since we accept that the owner would never leave a
piece of trash on the dashboard, we can conclude that the
car was stolen and this receipt was still in use at the time of
the theft."

Sure enough, it was there in black-and-white—the parking area, the time the ticket was printed, and the expected duration of their stay. Sometimes brilliance can be incredibly simple.

"So," I said, moving on to the next mystery, "what was the shooter's plan A? Hit-and-run? A drive-by shooting?"

"What do you think I am, a psychic?"

"Sorry."

"I'm leaning toward a shooting, since he brought a weapon. All we know is that he was a quick thinker and had cased the neighborhood beforehand. As soon as he saw us going back inside the house, he adjusted his plan. Afterward, he abandoned the car, just in case we'd left someone out front. Very admirable." Monk rolled his shoulders. "Except that he left the car running, which is environmentally wasteful. And he shot two police officers."

Reaching in with a fresh Kleenex, I switched off the ignition.

On this visit to San Francisco General, we found Captain Stottlemeyer sharing a room with the lieutenant. It made sense since their injuries were similar and it beat sharing with someone random. Both wounds—the one to the captain's left shoulder and to the lieutenant's right leg—were through-and-through, cop-speak for when a bullet passes through, leaving an entry and an exit wound. It sounds messy, but sometimes it can be good. In this case, the nine-millimeter rounds had passed through the fleshy parts and not caused any real damage, just a lot of blood and pain. Both men had undergone transfusions and were admitted for overnight observation. Any further attempt on the cap-

tain would have to go through the armed guard at the door
plus the guy in the next bed—plus Trudy Stottlemeyer, who
had camped out again at Leland's bedside.

"Are you going to take this seriously now?" she asked. She
was talking to all of us. "Whoever's out to get you is smart and
determined."

"What do you want me to do?" said the captain. "Hide in
a hole? I'm staying as safe as I can. Meanwhile, I have the
best detectives I know trying to find him—her—them."

"We're on the case," said A.J. from his bed. "Forensic
units are working overtime on the alley and the stolen car."

"I'm sorry, honey." She squeezed the hand connected to
her husband's good shoulder. "I'm not scolding. I just get
scared."

Today had been a full day, from the discovery of Jasper
Coleman's seven-year-old murder weapon to our time in the
emergency room. Rebecca Thurman had come by, looking
overwhelmed and feeling guilty about having to leave Arnold Senior.

"Go home," A.J. told his sister. "It's more important to
take care of Dad. How's he doing?"

"He has maybe a few days." It seemed a cold way of phras-
ing it, but of course, I'd never been through that nightmare.
Who was I to judge?

Officer Joe Nazio also dropped by. He felt even guiltier
than Rebecca. "I should have been there," he moaned. "But
the lieutenant said you had everything under control."

I tried to console him. "We had more than enough officers. One more wouldn't have changed anything."

On the way back to the Teeger residence, the three of us

made a pit stop at Whole Foods and picked up the makings for chicken potpie. It was Tuesday, chicken potpie night, as Adrian had reminded me more than once. This wasn't as sacred a ritual as it had been in the bad old days. But, all things being equal, why would we mess with chicken potpie night? We're not savages.

It was nice having Randy and Monk hovering over me in the kitchen and making suggestions. As usual, I neglected to slice my carrots to exactly equal widths and lengths, thus endangering the traditional family recipe, handed down for one generation by Adrian's mother. Randy was accused of miscounting the frozen peas and had to start over four times. Also, there was the familiar argument about pearl onions versus regular onions. A decade ago, on my very first chicken potpie night, I found the experience maddening and swore never to go through it again. By now it was therapeutic.

"So, what makes a hundred peas taste better than a hundred and one?" Randy was suppressing a sly smile.

"Are you kidding me?" said Monk. "A hundred and one is anarchy."

"Can you really taste the difference?"

"Taste. Smell. Feel the weight."

"He's exaggerating a little," I warned. "But please don't test him. I'm hungry and we still have thirty-five minutes of cooking time."

"This is kind of like 'The Princess and the Pea,'" said Randy. "You know, where there's a pea under a hundred mattresses and she feels it."

"That's not a fairy tale; that's a nightmare," said Monk.

"Who would do that to a princess? When my mother told me that story, I couldn't sleep for a week."

"Thirty-five minutes," I reminded them. "Let's get this assembly line rolling."

"I demand another recount of the peas!"

With the ingredients finally counted and measured, with the individual pies weighed on a scale and slipped into the preheated oven, we set the timer and settled into the living room with two glasses of Chardonnay and one bottle of Fiji Water.

"Like old times," said Monk, savoring the nonflavor of H_2O pumped from a pristine rain forest aquifer and then transported thousands of miles, probably on some filthy freighter. Fiji Water is the only thing Monk ever drinks. "I think everything should be like old times, don't you?"

"Don't get used to it," said Randy. "I only have two weeks of vacation saved up, and Sharona wants me to save some days for a trip to Bermuda."

"You know you don't have to go back. Natalie has a spare bedroom."

"I know. I'm using it."

"I think she's willing to rent it out long-term."

"He has to go back," I piped up. "Randy has a life—and people depending on him."

"He has a life here, too," said Monk. "And the captain needs him."

"I don't know if he needs me or not," said Randy. "Lieutenant A.J. took a bullet. I didn't take a bullet." He said it with real regret. "The guy didn't even aim at me. If I had any impact at all seven years ago, you'd think someone would want me dead."

"Life isn't fair," I pointed out.

"I know you're joking, Natalie. But people want to make an impact. When I arrested Mayor Cates, I made an impact. No one tried to kill me, but they threatened to."

"They did threaten him," Monk confirmed. "I was there in Summit and it wasn't pretty. Why would he want to stay?"

"To prove himself," I said.

"Randy doesn't need to prove himself. Remember the saying? You can run away from your problems."

"No," I said. "The saying is 'You can't run away from your problems.'"

"Can't? No, I don't think so."

"I think Natalie's right," said Randy.

"No, she's not," insisted Monk. "My dad used to say it all the time. You can run away from all your problems."

"Right," I said. "That advice came from the man who went out for Chinese food one night and never returned. Is that how you want Randy to wind up?"

"Hey, hey." Randy shook his head. "You guys can argue as much as you want. The captain has a lieutenant and I have a job. Matter settled."

"Exactly," I agreed. "So back to business." I took another sip of my Chardonnay, followed by a deep breath. "Tomorrow we get to work on the boy burglars."

"What if it's not them?" asked Randy.

"Then we'll have to develop new leads," I said.

"We just need to connect Judge Oberlin and the captain,"

said Monk. "The murders might not even be related to an old case."

"What about the note?" asked Randy. "The note said they stole seven years of someone's life. Why would the killer lie about that?"

"Why would he lie?" asked Monk. It was a rhetorical question but he answered it. "Because killers lie, Randy. They don't just kill, they lie. That's what makes them so treacherous."

"I suppose that's true."

"Monk's right," I said. "All we know for sure is someone murdered the judge and tried to kill Leland with the same umbrella method. And he, she, or they still want Leland dead."

"Everything else is a variable," said Monk. "The boy burglars are our best bet, but it's just a bet."

"Whoever it is, we'll get him," said Randy. His eyes focused on the timer sitting on the coffee table. "Twenty-four minutes until potpies. If you don't mind, I'm going to call Sharona. It's three hours' difference, so I don't want to be too late. I'll call from my room."

Monk waited until Randy walked out and Julie's bedroom door was closed. Monk grinned. "His room? Did you hear that? That's a good sign." I raised my hand and he flinched. "Ouch."

"I didn't touch you."

"You were going to punch me on the shoulder. I still felt the pain."

"Life is not going back the way it was, Adrian, so stop trying to manipulate things. You're not very good at it."

"I'm pretty good."

"And just because life used to be a certain way doesn't mean it was perfect. For instance, why do you like chicken potpie?"

"Chicken potpie? Are you disrespecting the potpie? What's not to like?"

"Well, let's see." I ticked them off one by one. "All the meat and vegetables are mixed together, which you hate. It's got milk, which you're phobic about. And it bubbles over the edge of the pan, which drives you crazy. And yet we make chicken potpie almost once a week."

"On a good week. We're getting a little lax. I've been meaning to talk to you."

"So why do you like it?"

"It's not that I like it." He set down his Fiji Water and thought seriously. "It's traditional."

"Like meat loaf—another recipe with milk and meat and vegetables squished together."

"My mother used to make them all the time."

"You know, just because the past was a certain way doesn't make it good."

"The past is comforting, Natalie. It's comforting because we survived it. The past also happened when we were younger and that's good, too. To be honest, Mother was a mediocre cook. She had to force us to eat that stuff. But Ambrose re-created the recipes. I have an extra copy in my safety-deposit box."

"Things change. And you can't try to force people back the way they were. Randy Disher has moved on."

"But you hate Lieutenant A.J. as much as I do. And the captain wants Randy back. You saw the way he jumped out of his bed."

I shook my head. Was he even listening? "I can see why Sharona left town without talking to you or leaving a note." I didn't want to be cruel, but it just came out. "She had to run. You would have done anything to keep her off that plane. And if you'd succeeded, then you never would have hired me. Think of that possibility. No Natalie. No Monk and Teeger. None of the past decade would have happened."

But Monk was in his own little world, not even pretending to listen. "Ooh, and the best part of Randy coming back is Sharona would come with him. Isn't that great?"

"Why is that great?"

"Because everything would be the way it was." He clapped his hands with excitement. "She can be our unpaid intern instead of Julie."

This time he didn't see it coming. "Ouch," he said, rubbing his shoulder. "That was totally uncalled for."

CHAPTER SIXTEEN

Mr. Monk and the Mini-Mall

After our evening of potpies and reminiscences, I took Monk back to his Pine Street apartment. When I came home, Randy's door was closed and I could hear him with Sharona, his voice warm and tender. Despite the time difference, they were still at it when I finally closed my door and went to bed. I missed that kind of long, loving phone chat, where you can talk about everything and nothing and never pay attention to the time or that your ear's growing moist from the receiver. When Mitch was away in Kosovo, we used to talk like that.

When I left the house the next morning, there was the gentle sound of snoring coming from Julie's room. I didn't have the heart to wake him.

Monk and Teeger, Consulting Detectives, opened to the public a little earlier than usual. I wanted to get a good start, harassing the records department at the DA's office and the warden at the Pleasant Valley prison. Neither of the Willmott cousins, Colin and Marshal, both barely eighteen at the time of their offense, had received a parole. This seemed odd. Young offenders waiting out nonviolent sentences almost always get a few years shaved off, especially on first convictions.

The DA records came through first, pinging into my in-box. I settled in with my second cup of coffee and read. From years of working through the dry legalese of the justice system, I'd developed pretty good skills at interpreting the data.

First off, both of their juvenile records were sealed. That's never a sign of good citizenship. There was no date associated with this, but there was a numbered code. Being a somewhat experienced detective, I compared this code with two other codes that I happened to know the dates of and came up with a ten-month window in which the record sealing had been filed for and granted.

My next step was using my SFPD passcodes to check the corresponding arrest records in specific neighborhoods, such as Pacific Heights, where the Willmott boys had grown up, and Nob Hill, where their uncle lived. None of this information gathering was foolproof. It was all chance. But my eye was drawn to the Pacific Heights arrest of two juveniles, names withheld, for breaking and entering and grand larceny. Very familiar charges. The unnamed youths in the case had been defended by one of the most expensive law firms in town.

A few more cross-checks showed that this same firm did the legal work for Willmott and Associates, a real estate development company that built high-end malls all over the state. The lawyers, who didn't have much of a record of defending petty criminals, were also the lawyers of record in five other cases involving a pair of juvenile male offenders.

I was a little surprised but not shocked to see that the defense for the last Colin and Marshal case, the one that had sent them away for seven years, was not performed by the high-end lawyers. The boys had been represented by a San

Francisco public defender. I'm no Adrian Monk, but it seemed to me that the Willmott family had finally grown tired of coming to the rescue of their wayward boys—with disastrous results for the boys.

I was still curious about the lack of paroles. But the Pleasant Valley warden had not yet returned my call. While I was waiting, I placed a call to Bethany Oberlin. Sometime during the funeral, between the time we walked into the Episcopalian chapel to view the body and the time Monk stood up and announced her father's murder, Bethany and I had exchanged business cards, just in case she wanted to talk. She'd never taken me up on it—surprise!—but I hoped she would at least not hang up on me.

"Natalie, I'd been hoping you'd call." The young woman's voice sounded strained and anxious.

"I didn't know if you were still in town."

"Of course. I have to stay for the funeral. They just released his body. It's hard to even think about going back to Thailand. I don't want to lose my job, but with Dad still . . . when his murder is still . . . You know what I mean. Not that there's anything I can do to help. Is there? Do you have any news?" Her voice grew excited. "Oh, my God, is that it? Did you catch his killer? Tell me."

I felt so guilty. For the past few days my focus, all of our focus, had been on trying to prevent the captain's death. We'd almost forgotten the first victim. Judge Oberlin still had a family that needed answers. "I'm sorry, Bethany. I should have stayed in better contact. No, we haven't caught the killer, not yet. But there might be something you can do."

I didn't check with my partner since I knew his schedule

as well as he did. Bethany and I set up a time—in one of the spaces between Monk's morning "ablutions," as he called them, and his cleaning schedule and his preparations for meat loaf night. It was Wednesday, after all. We're not savages.

There's never a lot of foot traffic coming by our door. That's both a good thing, in that it's not constantly distracting us, and a bad thing, in that, when it does happen, it's more distracting. When I glanced up to see a car pull into the parking space, I recognized Daniela Grace's silver Mercedes. Like her, the car always looked freshly waxed and detailed. Even though I knew she was on her way next door to Paisley Printing, I went out to greet her. "Daniela. How are you?"

"Not so well, dear." Daniela was the kind of person who took such questions seriously. "Not that it's your fault. Well, maybe your fault for asking."

"I hope it's not Peter and Wendy. I know they want to do a good job for you. If you just give them a chance . . ."

"No, Peter and Wendy are fine. They're rolling with the punches."

"What punches?" For a split second I thought Monk might be up to one of his tricks.

Daniela sighed and held up her leather Prada briefcase. "The IPO we're working on. We've had a security breach at the office. Two similar companies are going public next month and someone leaked information about our deal— things like the exact offering price, common versus preferred percentages. Profitability forecasts. Those little numbers mean millions. I say it's someone on the client side. The client says it has to be us. Meanwhile, we have to change the documents, just to prove the information false and pretend that the leak doesn't exist. Just a few more days." With her free hand, she crossed her fingers. "Wish me luck."

"If you want, Adrian and I could look into it," I suggested. "That's why you have us on retainer, right?"

"Right." Daniela cocked her head and laughed. "I'd completely forgotten about that." A few weeks ago, I had talked Daniela into paying us a tiny retainer so that we would stay available for emergencies like this. I hadn't even gotten around to telling Monk about it. "This is what I'm paying you for, isn't it?"

"You're paying us to be available, yes." I was already regretting my offer. "But we are a little busy right now." Why did I have to open my big mouth?

"Which is exactly why we signed that retainer. Rather clever of me, wasn't it?"

"Although we are busy with a murder right at the moment."

"Please. You're always busy with a murder. But it's good to know you can swoop in on the spur of the moment. Let me think it over and get back to you."

We were still standing there when the Gerbers happened to see us through their window. They came out, Wendy in a peasant skirt and blouse left over from the seventies and Peter in a tie-dyed shirt that blended into a pair of tie-dyed jeans, almost giving the impression of a jumpsuit. On second glance, I saw it was a jumpsuit. Tie-dyed. "Ms. Grace." Peter looked nervous and deferential. "Is there another problem? What can I do you for?"

"Natalie, I'll be in touch." And with a flourish, Daniela followed the Gerbers through the open doors of Paisley Printing, talking a mile a minute.

I stayed on the street. I was standing just a few feet, I realized, from where I'd first met Sue whatever-her-name-was.

Sue Puskedra non-O'Brien had been loitering at the curb, eyeing the Monk and Teeger storefront. Now she was gone without a trace, as if I'd simply imagined it. I couldn't get my friends on the force to help find her. This wasn't their fault. Nothing she'd done had been illegal, except not paying the bill I never gave her. Believe it or not, there's no statute against claiming to be married to a gay man.

I didn't even have a picture of her. That's literally what I was thinking when my eye wandered to the storefront at the north end of our strip mall. It was a charming establishment with barred windows and a steel gate, known as 24-Hour Holiday Pawn. My attention wasn't focused on the grimy windows, however, but on the two security cameras poised over the door.

A few months ago, when Monk and I opened up shop, we had a few run-ins with Al Wittingham, the owner. Monk had gotten into the habit of walking by the pawnshop on his way to work. His eye was naturally attracted to the filthy windows and the dusty displays—and, unfortunately for Mr. Wittingham, the items that were on display.

On three different occasions (it could have been four), Monk called the police. The first time it was a sterling silver punch bowl that he somehow knew was stolen property. The second time it was a Mickey Mantle baseball card. The third time was a forgery, a dozen Morgan silver dollars mounted in a felt display case. Of course it wasn't Adrian's fault that Wittingham occasionally turned a blind eye to customers with stolen goods. But it got to the point where the man had taped pictures of Monk and me on the wall beside the cash register, barring us from ever stepping inside.

"What did I tell you? Hey, don't come in here. You're banned for life."

"Sorry," I said to the man behind the counter. "I was hoping you could help me."

"Help you? Don't make me laugh." Al laughed anyway. He bore a striking resemblance to a small, dirty owl, with round-framed glasses and permanent stains on his collection of vintage T-shirts from the 1980s. He wobbled out to try to block the door.

"I noticed your cameras," I said, getting right to the point. "You've got one of them pointed at the street, if I'm not mistaken."

"One on the door, one out to the street to catch license plates, and three of them inside, all angles, so don't try anything funny."

"For how long do you keep the footage?"

"What's it to you, Miss Nosy? Now get out."

"Mr. Wittingham, please. I did nothing wrong. My partner did call the police, yes—"

"Not to mention the EPA. That was the worst. I had an antique tablecloth from Germany, sold to me legitimately by an old widow. How was I supposed to know—"

"It was made from asbestos." (Four occasions. How could I forget the asbestos tablecloth!)

Asbestos, I learned, had been used for all sorts of things in the bad old days, even clothing. The emperor Charlemagne was said to have had the first tablecloth made of it. At the end of a banquet, he would throw it into a roaring fire and watch as the dirt got burned up but the tablecloth remained unharmed. Like a magic trick.

Wittingham scowled. "Thanks to your friend, they closed me down for a week and made me pay for the whole cleanup. I lost a ton of customers."

"Well, it was asbestos. You should be grateful you're not sick."

"I could have sold it," he snapped. "People were looking at it all the time."

"Really, people were handling the asbestos tablecloth?"

"No, they weren't," he shouted. "I misspoke. It's your word against mine."

I held out my hands in peace. "Mr. Wittingham, I'm not here about the asbestos. I'm here about a woman who was standing in front of your place less than a week ago. I'm hoping your camera caught a glimpse of her. If we check the tapes . . ."

Wittingham smiled a toothy yellow smile. "So you need something from me, huh? You guys nearly ruin my business and now you want something. You don't know how happy that makes me. NO! Not on your life, missy."

"I completely understand." It was the answer I'd been expecting. "I just want you to know that, after much effort, I finally got my partner to come into work from the south side of the parking lot, by the Laundromat."

"Lucky for them."

"Yes, lucky for them. But that's another story. My point is that it took some effort, but I did it for you. I could just as easily talk Adrian Monk into taking his old route again—if you don't appreciate all the effort I went through."

It was an odd sort of blackmail. I'm not sure it's ever been used before, threatening to get someone to change his walking pattern. And I didn't feel guilty about it. If Wittingham didn't keep illegal items in his shop, if he managed to clean his windows so they didn't attract Monk's irritated stare, none of this would be a problem. "He can't really help himself, you know. Once he has you in his line of vision, it's over."

Wittingham folded his pudgy arms across his pudgy middle. "I can take everything out of the window. How about that? Or I can black it over. Give him nothing to see."

"That would really help your walk-in traffic." I took a step back and tried to look all sweet and innocent. "Wouldn't it just be easier to check your security video? It won't take long. We can look at it together."

"I'm not letting a detective look at my video. What kind of idiot do you think I am?" I didn't answer, just kept up my sweet expression. "How much trouble is this going to be? Do you have a date and a time when this woman was here?"

"I do."

CHAPTER SEVENTEEN

Mr. Monk Refocuses

The usual suspects, plus a few extra, were crowded into the semiprivate room at SF General. Trudy Stottlemeyer gathered her husband's bag of dried, bloody clothes, ready to make their exit, while I adjusted the captain's shoulder sling and tried to get him into a wheelchair. The captain wasn't cooperating.

"I'm perfectly capable of getting around under my own power."

"Everyone leaves the hospital in a wheelchair," said Trudy. "It's a rule."

"A dumb rule," said Stottlemeyer. "If I'm fit enough to go back to work . . ."

"You are not going to work," Trudy informed him. "Banish that thought."

"Why not? I dare you to find anyone more capable of tracking down my killer."

"Leland, that's not funny."

"Trudy's right." Randy tried to guide his former partner into the wheelchair. "You can't be part of the investigation. We need you safe at home with a guard at the door."

The captain found it hard to argue, not after what had

happened the previous day in the alley. "Okay. But I need you to keep me constantly updated."

"Will do," said Lieutenant A.J. He was lifting himself out of the next bed, with his sister helping him into the other wheelchair. Since he could put only limited weight on his right leg, the process was more difficult. "I'll keep you in the loop, Captain."

"Not you," said the captain. "If I'm getting bed rest, you're getting bed rest."

"Sir, that's not fair. I'm perfectly capable of returning to the field."

"Not with that leg. Chief Disher is on loan from the Summit PD. Between him and our consultants, they can handle it."

"You're trusting your life to them?" A.J. stubbed his foot onto one of the wheels and let out a little scream.

"Sorry, Arny," said Rebecca, as if she were somehow to blame. "So sorry."

Her brother brushed her hands aside. "Captain, you can't be serious. Some doofus with a dinosaur diary? A pair of strip-mall detectives? Look at Monk. He can't walk down a street without stepping over every crack. They're not even with the department."

"Well, I'm authorizing them. You're going home and they're in charge."

"You can't do that. I'll file a complaint."

"You do that, A.J. Meanwhile, will someone please get me out of this damn place?"

"It is not a dinosaur diary," muttered Randy as he straightened the captain's wheelchair and started pushing. "It's a journal."

"I wouldn't trust this bunch of misfits to make me a sandwich," shouted A.J. into our backs.

By the time the old Subaru made it through the crosstown traffic and was being flawlessly edged into a tight parallel parking spot on Hyde Street, the three of us had all calmed down. Pretty much. "How can you work with him every day?" Randy asked from the backseat.

"That's my point," said Adrian. "That's why we need you to come home."

"Monk, it's not going to happen."

"Then I'll figure out some other way. Maybe Luther can help."

"Luther?" said Randy, looking puzzled. "You mean your driver friend?"

Monk grinned. "Luther and I have our own ways of solving problems."

I heard this and nearly scraped the bumper in front of me. "No. You and Luther are not going to pull one of your pranks. I absolutely forbid it."

"We'll see," said Monk. "We'll see."

As we walked up to the porch of Judge Oberlin's house, I noted the sturdy stone umbrella stand, the spot where the captain had sat down and chatted with me one day prior to his own poisoning. The answer had been right under him and we never suspected. Monk also saw the stand and gave it a wide berth.

Bethany Oberlin must have been waiting because the door flew open almost before I touched the bell. "Come in, come in. Please." We wiped our feet on the mat and followed her instructions. The front door opened directly onto a wide, homey living room with a stone fireplace centered on the rear wall. Before sitting down, Randy introduced himself.

"A police chief from New Jersey?" Bethany stiffened. "Are murders like this happening in New Jersey?"

"No, no," Randy assured her. "I worked with Captain Stottlemeyer seven years ago. And your father, too. On those trials where someone wanted to kill us."

"Seven years ago? What happened seven years ago?"

I tried to explain in as few words as possible. Someone had dropped a note on the captain's desk, claiming that the attacks were revenge for stealing "seven years of my life."

"We think it may be a trial the judge and the captain were involved with," said Monk. "But it could be anything. Were you living with your father back then?"

She thought for a moment. "I was in high school. Sixteen. Mom had just died in a car accident."

"I'm so sorry." That's what I say when someone mentions death, no matter how long ago.

"Thank you. It was a rough patch for Dad. He was just going through the motions. Some of his old friends tried to reconnect, but I couldn't tell you who. I spent a lot of time with my high school friends. Captain Stottlemeyer . . . I know he and Dad used to be close. But that was before I was born. I think the first time I met the captain was at Dad's first funeral." She shuddered at the memory. "His second funeral is tomorrow, by the way."

"Tomorrow?" Monk turned to his appointment secretary. "Is that on our schedule, Natalie? You didn't mention it."

"It's a small event," said Bethany Oberlin, biting her lower lip. "I didn't think to invite you. But if you really want to come . . ."

"Thanks, but we'll let you grieve privately." The last thing the poor girl needed was Monk bending over her father's casket again.

"Do you think Dad did something bad?" she asked. "To make someone hold a grudge strong enough for murder? For seven years? He was in mourning at the time and not always rational."

"Whatever he did, it involved the captain," I pointed out. "We're checking the trials, but there might be something else. Do you have any idea?"

"Dad wasn't the type to make enemies. But he was known for his strict sentencing. Several of his decisions went in front of review boards. I don't think any of them was overturned."

"Was he a strict father, too?" I had to ask.

"Dad was . . ." She thought hard before going on. "I'm not sure he liked children, even his own. Growing up, I got treated like a little adult. Mom was different. I could always go to her for sympathy and a hug. I work with kids myself now. Kids aren't always perfect. They like to experiment, try on different personas and behaviors."

"Make mistakes," I said, thinking of my own relationship with Julie.

"Yes, but that doesn't make them bad. They're discovering who they are, what works for them. Dad didn't get it. 'As the twig is bent, so grows the tree.' He used to say that a lot. His mission, I think, was to straighten the twigs, which wasn't always easy on the twigs. Maybe that's why I got into teaching, to try a gentler way of bending the twigs. Who knows?"

"If you heard that your dad sentenced a couple of teenage boys to seven years each for stealing antique silver, would that surprise you?" I was interested to see her reaction.

"Stealing silver and threatening two officers with semiautomatics," Randy reminded me.

"He really gave them seven years? Those poor boys."

"They used to be poor boys," said Chief Disher. "Now they're grown men, ex-cons who probably have chips on their shoulders."

"Well . . ." She sighed, the weight of the world on her thin shoulders. "To answer your question, I can see Dad doing that. He'd say it was grand larceny. He'd look at their priors and how they dressed and comported themselves. These boys who stole the silver, you think they killed Dad?"

Randy shrugged. "They could be our best lead."

"Do you think whatever Dad did back when he was grieving, right or wrong, is putting your captain in danger?"

"You can't think of it that way," I told her. "Nothing can excuse murder. If those men did it, they're responsible. No one else."

"They're not trying to kill me, if that makes you feel any better," said Randy.

Bethany looked puzzled. "Why would that make me feel better?"

Sometime in the middle of our visit with Bethany Oberlin, Harlan Brown phoned me from the Pleasant Valley facility near Fresno. I let it go into voice mail and returned his call as soon as the three of us got outside.

"Warden Brown, thanks for getting back to me," I said, even though I was the one getting back to him.

"No problem, Miss Teeger." The man had a warm Southern accent. Is it a cliché, or do most of the nation's wardens come from the South? Maybe they just like the accent. "The Frisco police commissioner says I should answer whatever questions you and your partner might have."

"That was very nice of him." I sometimes forget the power Adrian Monk's name carries in the world of law enforcement.

"Your message said something about the Willmott cousins. I gotta tell you, ma'am, I had mixed feelings about their release. On the one hand, I'm glad those boys are gone. On the other, I feel sorry for the general public."

I let out an inappropriate chuckle. "I guess that answers my question about why they didn't get paroles."

"It's a shame, really. They come in as a couple of entitled yuppie kids and wind up covered in neo-Nazi prison tats, spouting all kinds of hateful stuff and getting into knife fights. We tried everything on them."

"Neo-Nazis? Oh, dear."

"You heard me, Ms. Teeger. In a maximum- or even medium-security prison this behavior wouldn't be a big deal. But Pleasant Valley is minimum security. Half our population is white-collar offenders in on bank fraud and insider trading. Some of them are Jewish. Then, out of the blue, these clean-cut kids start watching that TV show *Lockup* on MSNBC. You know the prison show about life behind bars?"

"I've seen bits and pieces." *Lockup* was one of those reality shows that makes you question everything you thought you knew about humanity and want to hide under the covers.

"Well, these two kids started their own branch of the Aryan Brotherhood. From scratch."

"I didn't realize the Aryan Brotherhood had branches."

"I think they got all their information from *Lockup*. That basic cable. I tell you, it's more trouble than it's worth."

"Why didn't you have them transferred to another facility?"

"Ma'am, we tried. But the parents pulled some strings with the state. Funny how they couldn't use their juice to keep the boys out of prison, but when it came time to mess with my facility . . ."

"They probably thought it would just make them worse, putting them in a tougher prison."

"I'm sure that's what they thought."

"I know I'm going to regret asking you this." I stepped away from the car and out of earshot. "Do your records show a current address for the Willmott boys? Are they in the Bay Area by any chance?"

"They're living together, if I'm not mistaken." I could hear the warden tapping away on his keyboard. "Yep. Right in San Francisco. You thinking of visiting them? You're not African-American, are you?"

"No."

"Good. How about Jewish? If you're Jewish, I can't give you the address. For your own protection."

"I'm not Jewish."

"Good." And he gave me the address.

When I got back to my perfectly parked car, Monk and Randy were looking quizzical. "Well," said Monk. "Who was that? And why is there a drop of perspiration above your right eyebrow? It can't be over sixty degrees."

"Adrian, how do you feel about neo-Nazis?" I didn't think Monk had any Nazi-related phobias, although I couldn't blame him if he did.

"Neo-Nazis?" He rolled a single shoulder. "They're not as bad as the old-fashioned original Nazis, from what people say—although the original Nazis were a lot neater and they dressed better. Is there a reason why you're asking me this question?"

CHAPTER EIGHTEEN

Mr. Monk and the Urban Château

The address I'd written down wasn't far away, about twenty blocks north toward the bay and another twenty blocks west. It wasn't until I was getting close and the neighborhood kept getting nicer that I realized. Our two young neo-Nazis, fresh out of prison, had set up house in Pacific Heights, otherwise known as the land of you-can't-afford-to-live-here. And then it hit me. Of course.

"They're residing in their parents' basement, aren't they?" said Monk. Great minds think alike. "I hate basements."

"It doesn't have to be the basement," I said. "But you're probably right."

"What if they're not home?" said Randy from the backseat. "We should have called ahead."

"I didn't want to give them advance warning." I turned on Broadway Street and started looking for a parking space.

Monk agreed. "It's an historical fact. You don't give Nazis advance warning."

Colin Willmott's parents certainly had enough room to accommodate their son and nephew in the spare bedrooms on the second or third floor of their faux-French urban château, situated on a spacious corner lot. But I guessed it was some sort of mutual agreement that kept all the Oriental rugs and hunting paintings above ground level and all the swastikas and survival gear and military-style cots in the basement, with its own bathroom and separate entrance from the street.

It was late afternoon on a Thursday, but Ben and Olivia Willmott were both working from home. We identified ourselves and held up our IDs to a camera above the doorbell. An alarm system beeped on and off, followed by the sound of more than one dead bolt being unbolted.

The weary, middle-aged couple were at first reluctant to sit down with two private detectives and a police chief from New Jersey. But this, we told them, involved their Colin, and as painful and intrusive as it might be, they knew they had to make one more effort, and probably a dozen more after this.

Ben Willmott did something or other in banking. Olivia Bowersox-Willmott, as she introduced herself, did something in the advertising world. Both were perpetually confused and exhausted with their only son, who, despite having love and every other advantage showered on him, had turned into a Hitler-loving ex-con.

They walked us back to the kitchen—through the front room, a second living room, and the dining room. Along the way I noted a framed photo on the fireplace mantel, the younger-looking Willmotts, all scrubbed and happy-looking. An earnest but smiling Colin, blond and perhaps ten years old, stood between them, the Eiffel Tower in the background.

We sat on leather-topped stools around a marble island big enough to have its own zip code. Olivia offered us something to drink and Adrian was impressed to find that their imported water of choice was from Fiji. Good start.

Ben took a sip from his own bottle. "I used to look at people in our situation, on the news, and think they must have been bad somehow or overindulgent. But we didn't do it any differently from the way dozens of our friends raised their kids. There was just something about the way Colin and his cousin interacted. They were the same age, only a month or so apart. From the time they were toddlers, the boys brought out the worst in each other."

"When was their first arrest?" asked Monk.

The Willmotts exchanged wary glances. "Those records are sealed," said Ben. Then he sighed. "They were fourteen or fifteen."

"Fourteen," his wife clarified. "It was small stuff at first. Taking a car for a joyride, shoplifting. There was at least one convenience store. And of course, there were the drugs."

"Two convenience stores and a gas station," Ben added. They almost sounded like a pair of proud parents reciting their child's long string of accomplishments—but exactly the opposite.

"The nice thing about prison was that it got them off drugs. They say. We hope."

The Willmotts, Olivia and Ben and his brother's family, had done everything they could—counseling, drug rehab, trying to keep the boys apart, a lot of patience—probably what I would have done if Julie had gone down that path and I'd had the Willmotts' money and clout.

When the cousins finally turned eighteen and Captain Stottlemeyer arrested them for stealing their uncle's silver collection, pieces that had been in the family since the Revolutionary War, the Willmotts decided on a little tough love. Suddenly gone were the slick lawyers and the legal favors that had worked during the previous four years. The boys were on their own with a court-appointed attorney just out of law school. Having pulled semiautomatics on the arresting officers didn't help their chances.

"The judge completely went out of bounds," said Olivia. "It wasn't fair."

"You mentioned them doing a joyride," said Monk. "At fourteen? Did they take the keys or hot-wire it?"

"It was a car off the street. Colin is very mechanically minded," said Colin's father. Another one of the child's accomplishments.

"We'll assume he still knows how to hot-wire cars," said Monk.

Ben Willmott's sad smile faded. "Are you saying they're in trouble again? Please don't say that."

"It could be very big trouble," said Randy. "Mr. Willmott, do you own a handgun?"

"Handgun?" Olivia looked to her husband. "We don't have to answer that."

Monk cricked his neck and rolled his left shoulder. *Here it comes,* I thought. I felt sorry for the poor couple.

"The answer's yes," Monk announced. "No one says, 'We don't have to answer that' if the answer's no. Under normal circumstances, you would keep it in the bedroom, the usual spot for a law-abiding household needing a gun for protection. But Mr. Willmott's eyes just flitted out toward the front of the house."

Monk got off his stool and crossed to the doorway. "The second living room. When we walked through, I noticed two antique end tables with locks on the drawers. The one on the left side of the sofa had scratch marks around the lock mechanism. Fresh ones, not yet polished over by the maid. My guess—and it's not really a guess—is you tried to hide the weapon from your son in the past, before prison. The end table was your new hiding spot and the boys found it."

Ben sputtered. Should he be outraged or impressed? "What the hell are you doing? This is an invasion of privacy."

"Just observing the obvious," said Monk.

"Colin and Marshal aren't allowed in the main house," said Olivia. "We had the inside stairs removed. They don't have keys and we always lock up and set the alarm. It's impossible for them to break in."

"Hardly impossible," said the master of the impossible. "What's your alarm code? Your birthdays, your anniversary, your son's birthday? Something easy for Colin to figure out?"

Ben's embarrassed expression said it all. "We've done everything to protect ourselves. We're not responsible anymore. He's a grown man."

"A grown man living in your basement," Randy pointed out. "What kind of handgun is it? I'm going to guess, like Mr. Monk. A nine-millimeter?"

"We don't have a gun," said Ben defiantly. "If you check state registration records, yes, you may find a nine-millimeter Beretta under my name. But that gun went missing. Years ago. I never reported it. That's not a crime."

"I'll tell you what's a crime," said Randy. "For a convicted felon to possess a firearm. That's at least eighteen months plus a ten-thousand-dollar fine. If you know they took your gun and didn't report it, that makes you an accessory."

"And if we report it?" Ben asked.

"Then we can get a search warrant for your basement."

"Well, that's not going to happen," said Ben.

"What did the boys do?" Olivia asked softly. It seemed she couldn't help herself.

"That's no longer our responsibility."

"Benjamin! That's what you said when they turned eighteen." She raised her voice, as close to shouting as she would get. "You said it was time the boys learned the hard way. Tough love. Well, this is what your tough love did. Are you happy?"

Ben turned to me, as if sensing I was the one other parent in the group and that I'd understand. "Before the trial got under way, we knew it was a mistake. We tried to fire the public defender and get a top-notch lawyer, but the boys . . . They were so enraged at the whole family."

"Can you blame them for being mad?" said Olivia.

"They were adults and we could no longer make their choices. They reacted out of spite."

I found this hard to fathom. "They rolled the dice with an inexperienced public defender rather than let you tell them what to do? Weren't they scared? They were just boys."

Ben nodded. "That's what we're dealing with. They're filled with so much hate. Getting even is what they live for."

"We lost our son and our nephew forever," said Olivia, her voice cracking with emotion. "Their other cousin, from my side of the family, is getting married this weekend."

"A very nice Italian girl," added Ben, with a what-can-you-do shrug. "We were a little surprised, to be honest. One generation off the boat. But very nice people. Very lively."

Off the boat? I thought. *Lively? And they wonder where their son got his prejudices from.* I just nodded and kept smiling.

"A wedding is supposed to be a joyous occasion," said Olivia. "Instead, the boys aren't even invited. Their own cousin they grew up with. Everyone has cut them off. Everyone's too afraid."

"And yet they're living in your home," Randy said.

Olivia bristled. "What do you want us to do, make them live on the street or worse, with a gang?"

"Have you and your husband lived here a long time? In this house?" asked Monk. The question seemed to come out of the blue, but I knew better. "The name Willmott is etched on the mailbox and the mailbox looks at least thirty years old."

"Who said you could examine our mailbox?" said Ben. "I'm feeling violated here."

All four of us did some form of eye rolling, including Ben's wife. "Yes," said Olivia. "Almost thirty years. The house was a wedding present from my parents." Wedding present? Really? I think my parents gave Mitch and me a Cuisinart. "Why do you ask, Mr. Monk?"

"I was thinking about your mice problem," said Monk. "Well, not your mice in particular. In general. In a lot of garden sheds and basements, there's leftover rat poison, just sitting on the shelves. Not used for years. A lot of those old rat poisons used thallium as an ingredient."

"Thallium?" said Randy, his interest in the Willmotts growing.

Monk went on. "It's been outlawed in the U.S. for quite a while. Highly lethal, even to touch or breathe. But if you've had the house for thirty years, it's more than likely . . ."

"Rat poison?" said Ben Willmott. "You ask us about guns and stealing cars? Now rat poison?"

"Yes," said Monk. "It's a regular smorgasbord of crime. And it probably isn't over."

"Oh, my God," said Ben.

"We don't have a garden shed," said Olivia. "All the garden supplies . . . they're in the basement."

"In the basement with the boys," I pointed out.

We left the Willmotts in a state of stunned wonder. I thanked them for their time, Monk thanked them for the Fiji Water, and Randy advised them to change their alarm code immediately. Also the passwords on their computers and bank accounts and whatever else they wanted to keep safe.

After the front door closed behind us, I listened for the dead bolts being locked into place and the pings of the alarm system being reset. "You have to feel sorry for them," I said softly.

"Because they raised a boy who's trying to kill the captain?" asked Randy.

"We don't know that," I said, then turned to Monk for his expert opinion.

"Earplugs," said Monk.

"Earplugs?"

Monk held a finger in the air, as if testing the direction of the wind. "Rock-and-roll music. It's even worse than the hippies."

"What hippies?" Randy asked.

"Don't ask," I said.

"Earplugs," repeated my partner. As I scrounged through my tote, Monk led the way around the left side of the urban château, down a slate gravel path toward a door near the rear of the house. "Augh. The noise!"

"I don't hear a thing," said Randy, shaking his head in wonder. "Monk, you must have ears like a blind person. You know? How they say when you lose one sense, then all the other senses become better."

"Really, Randy? And what sense has Adrian lost?"

"I don't know. The sense of normal? No offense, Monk."

"I can barely hear you over the din," shouted Monk, more for effect than anything. He took my pack of earplugs, broke the plastic wrap, and stuffed the buds firmly in his ears. "That's better. What were you saying?"

"I can hear it now," said Randy as we got closer. There was indeed a thumping bass beat coming through the basement door. "It's Nirvana."

"No, it's like the opposite of Nirvana."

"Adrian." I had a question. "If the earplugs block the music, don't they also block Randy's voice?"

"I'm sorry, Natalie, I can't hear you." And he began pounding his fist on the door.

All three of us tried pounding on the thick wooden door, one after the other.

The music was indeed Nirvana, "Heart-Shaped Box" to be specific. Not my favorite. The denizens of the basement apartment did their best to ignore us, but at some point they realized we were interfering with their music and we weren't going away. They cranked it down to half volume, probably just in time to hear Randy shouting, "Police—open up" in his deepest voice. He continued to shout "police" but added "Summit, New Jersey" under his breath each time, just to keep it legal.

CHAPTER NINETEEN

Mr. Monk and the Basement Nazis

"**A**nd I swear that I don't have a gun. No, I don't have a gun. No, I don't have a gun."

Monk tried not to listen, but the words came through. Even with the distraction of earplugs and the pounding guitars, it was the lyrics he found most disturbing. "Did you write this song for me?" he asked, staring at the tall stereo speakers. "Just now? How did you do that?" His voice held a note of paranoia.

"I wish." Marshal Willmott smirked. "It's, like, Nirvana, dude."

"Why does everyone compare bad music to Nirvana? Are we in opposite world?"

I tried to explain, almost shouting. "This is a famous song. 'Come as You Are' by a group called Nirvana."

"Okay . . ." He thought about it. "And the words just happen to answer my question?"

"That's right," said Colin. "We don't have a gun. And you don't have a search warrant."

"Are those some more of the lyrics? Because that would really freak me out."

We were in the main room of a wood-paneled basement.

High in a side wall, just under the ceiling, was a cemented-over door, barring what had been an entrance up to the rest of the family's world. The cement door simply hung there without a staircase.

The center of the space was defined by a moth-eaten Oriental rug and two reclining easy chairs facing a TV against the wall, a real, old-fashioned TV, as deep was it was wide. The remainder of the four walls were decorated with Nazi flags and Nazi eagles and framed, smiling photos of the original Nazis. You could squint and imagine yourself in the Hitler bunker during the final days of the war.

On either side of the "living room" were the sleeping areas, each with a garment rack for hanging clothes and cinder-block shelves crowded with personal items. The beds were army-style cots, each perfectly made, with tight hospital corners. This was actually Monk's doing, the first thing he took care of after we came down the steps from the garden. Monk didn't explain and the Willmott boys didn't ask, as though grown-ups were always coming down to make their beds.

Being the only real officer, Randy took control, telling them that we would like to ask a few questions. Colin and Marshal were cocky enough to agree. They pointed to a stack of folding chairs, probably stored for family events, back when the Willmotts held family events. They were now stored under a portrait of Eva Braun. We unfolded them in a semicircle in front of the leather recliners and Randy started in with his first question about the gun, a moment that happened to coincide with the current song on the playlist.

Monk was still fidgeting when Randy crossed the concrete

floor to the stereo receiver. A second later the room fell into a merciful silence. Colin and Marshal looked like they were about to object but didn't. "So," said the ex-lieutenant, coming back to the semicircle. "We've established your claim not to be in possession of a gun."

"What?" said Monk, then remembered he was wearing earplugs. He removed them with a disposable wipe and handed the whole mess to me.

Colin looked quite different from his Eiffel Tower photo, even taking into account the fifteen years. His head was shaved, although his thin eyebrows proved he was still blond. He was prison thin and prison pale, with just the first signs of age starting to crease around his hard blue eyes. His outfit, identical to his cousin's, was black jeans and an orange T-shirt. A lot of ex-cons I've met refuse to wear orange. Too many memories. But the Willmotts seemed to embrace it.

I would describe Marshal next, but his look was almost identical. They could have been mistaken for twins, which might have been part of their affinity in the first place, two handsome, golden-haired sons of privilege growing up a mile or so from each other. I might have had trouble telling them apart if it weren't for the tattoos. Colin's crawled up the left side of his neck and incorporated a swastika in a red circle. Marshal's was on the right and featured the jagged lightning bolts of the Nazi storm troopers edging up toward his ear.

Monk seemed mesmerized, his gaze jumping from one pulsing swatch of neck skin to the other. I was just thankful that there was no ink on their prominent, bobbing Adam's apples. That might have sent him over the edge.

"Now tell us what you know about rat poison," said Randy, making the most of his tough-cop persona.

"Rat poison?" The light was beginning to dawn in Colin's eyes. "You mean like the stuff that killed Judge Oberlin? That kind of poison for rats?"

"I'm telling you, that was a good day," said Marshal. "Talk about karma."

"How did you know that?" asked Randy. "The type of poison."

"It was on the news," said Marshal. "Channel Four. Oberlin was the prick who gave us seven years. I Googled this thallium junk. We had some of it here in the basement, but Col and me threw it out after seeing the news. Seemed too dangerous to keep around, you know?"

I couldn't believe my ears. "You threw it out?"

"Yeah," said Colin. "We put the containers into some old Tupperware, sealed it up tight, and tossed it. Couple days ago. So, you know, if anyone was to get a search warrant and happen to go through our quarters and find some microscopic trace of it, that's why. Easily explained." He didn't seem to care if we believed him or not.

"We're good citizens," added Marshal. "Some people I know wouldn't have used Tupperware."

"Is that what they teach you in prison?" asked Monk. "How to get rid of toxic evidence?"

"Yeah." Colin grinned and for the first time I saw the perfectly orthodontured teeth his family must have spent a small fortune on. "We learned a lot in prison."

Monk nodded. "Did you learn it from your white-collar, minimum-security prison mates? Or from TV?"

"You shut up." Colin's grin faded. "What kind of name is that? Adrian Monk."

"It's my name." Monk couldn't stop looking at their necks.

"Is that Jewish?" asked Colin.

"Monk is English," I interjected. I'd actually looked it up some time ago. "It was the name given to someone working for a monk or a monastery."

"So I guess not Jewish," said Colin, although he didn't seem convinced. His hand went up to scratch his tattoo. When Monk winced, he saw it.

"You say it was a good day when you heard about Judge Oberlin," said Randy. "How about Captain Leland Stottle-meyer?"

"Stottlemeyer?" said Marshal. The cousins exchanged glances. "The captain who arrested us. What about that scum-bag? Is he dead?"

"Yeah, is he dead?" echoed Colin. "Serves the bastard right."

"Sorry, he's not." The Summit police chief leaned forward in his folding chair. "And neither is Randall Disher, the lieu-tenant who put the cuffs on you. Remember me?"

"Who?"

Randy looked deflated. "Guys, come on. Me. You don't remember?"

The shaved-headed Nazis leaned forward in their reclin-ers for a better look. "Sorry, dude," said Colin. "That was you?"

"Did you put on some weight?" asked Marshal.

"No, I didn't put on weight. Maybe five pounds. But that was me with the cuffs. Don't say you wouldn't like a little re-venge."

"You were just doing your job," said Marshal. "No hard feelings."

"No hard feelings?"

"It's not like the captain," said Marshal, his eyes narrowing with the memory. "The rest of you were happy with 'person or persons unknown.' But he kept at it. Like he didn't have any bigger crimes in town."

Marshal had also raised a hand to scratch his tattoo. This time both cousins noted Monk's wince of distress. Their eyes met and their crooked, smug grins returned. What happened next was fascinating, like some nature film showing predators in the wild, communicating without sound, silently stalking their prey.

Colin went first, making sure Adrian was watching. He began to scratch at his tattoo. For the first time, I saw that the nail on his pinkie was longer than the others, and was sharpened to a point. He pulled the nail slowly down his neck, through the red circle and the black swastika, leaving a mark all the way. Monk winced again, this time with sound, an audible shudder. "Augh, what are you doing?"

Marshal's turn was next. His nail looked identically sharp. It came down through the lightning bolts to his collarbone, then across the pale skin of his throat, straight across the Adam's apple to his other collarbone.

"What are you . . . That can get infected," groaned Monk. "Stop that."

Adrian Monk is perfectly fine with blood and guts and dismemberment, as long as the subject has stopped breathing. Then the person becomes a thing, a part of a puzzle. His mind divorces itself from its need for order and perfection.

But if the subject is still breathing . . . If the damage is self-inflicted with a fingernail, done perhaps with four manic eyes and a pair of menacing grins . . . Even for me, the sight was unsettling.

Colin was next. He mimicked his cousin's movement across his throat. Then he went to work on his left arm, drawing upward along the skin from his wrist to his elbow. Marshal giggled like a kid of five and did the same.

"Stop that," Monk shouted. But he couldn't tear his eyes away.

Both of them were giggling, goading each other on as they'd done for most of their lives. Keeping Monk in their gaze, the Willmotts went simultaneously for the other arm, starting from the wrist, this time digging deeper. I couldn't believe they were hurting themselves like this, just to momentarily torture a man they didn't even know. Their giggles had grown into full-blown, Charles Manson–type laughs.

Monk threw a hand across his eyes and stumbled to his feet, skidding his folding chair back across the concrete floor and heading blindly for the basement stairs.

CHAPTER TWENTY

Mr. Monk Takes a Nap

We all have our ways of coping with traumatic events. And in our business, there are a lot of them. Adrian likes to stay cloistered in his apartment; Randy likes to hang out with his cop buddies; and me, I like to switch gears—to keep busy, but on something else, something to distract me, in this case, from the image of our primary suspects grinning like skinhead banshees as they drew bloody designs on their necks and arms.

That night, all three of us coped according to expectations. Monk was at home, his phone unplugged; Randy was exchanging macho tales at the cop bar over on Turk Street where they have the best hot wings in town; and I spent a lovely evening with Al from 24-Hour Holiday Pawn, fending off his friendly advances and trying to isolate a few frames from his security camera footage.

Not so bright and not so early the next morning, I filled my travel mug with Peet's House Blend, grabbed my keys and tote, and tiptoed by the guest room door. I could tell Randy was up by the sound of sneezing and sniffling. I knocked. "Morning, sunshine. Everything all right?"

"Morning," he moaned back. "I think I caught a cold last night. Or some allergy or something."

"It's more like Sharona's revenge for deserting her."

"You think I caught her cold?"

"Probably."

"Wouldn't it be funny if I went back and gave it to her all over again? Okay, maybe not funny." He took several inhalations and exploded in one big sneeze. "Can you do without me today?"

"Absolutely. I'm just meeting with a computer geek." I didn't say who the geek was because then he might come along and the last thing I needed was him giving me his cold. "Take care of yourself."

My daughter isn't really a geek. But she is a college-educated twenty-one-year-old living in the Bay Area, which makes her pretty much a geek in my world.

Julie had taken the BART over from Berkeley and was waiting for me at the strip mall. Al and I had managed to isolate a few blurry images of Sue Not-O'Brien pacing out in front. I remembered the moment well, her thoughtful, confused expression. And the relief she'd shown when I'd walked up and offered my services.

The five best images were clumped together in my Photoshop file. Julie was in my chair and I was behind her in Monk's—although if you tell him I was using his chair, I will deny it, and he'll probably believe me rather than some stranger like you.

"It's just like some old-time movie," said Julie. I'd finally broken down and told her about Sue. "Some mysterious woman comes to a private eye begging for help and then she disappears and it's all mysterious. Like *Chinatown*."

"*Chinatown* is an old-time movie?"

"You gotta admit, it's pretty cool. I texted my friends and they have a lot of theories."

"Julie, this isn't a game or a brainteaser. I may have gotten myself into some weird situation I don't even know about."

"That's why I'm here to help." She enlarged the image one more time.

"Why is it still so blurry?"

"Mom, this isn't *Mission Impossible.*"

"I know. But I was hoping for maybe *Law & Order: SVU.* Some picture I can show around, maybe put up on a billboard. 'Do You Know This Woman?'"

"You're kidding, right?"

"Right. Look, is there any way you can combine some of the images—a clear nose from this one, un-fuzzy hair from that one?"

"You're still kidding, right?"

"Right."

"Stop staring over my shoulder and talking like a Tom Cruise character. I'll do what I can."

I arranged Monk's chair back under his desk in exactly the same position and same height, making sure there were no skid marks. It was the best I could do.

I stepped outside and away from the windows, so as not to be accused of hovering, and used this break to check in with Monk. He had replugged his phone. "Those guys are crazy. I can't get them out of my mind." It was his way of saying hello.

"Good morning, Adrian," I replied. "Did you get any sleep?"

"Forty-eight minutes. But if I don't get in my solid two

hours, I'm a mess. Every time I closed my eyes, I saw their dirty fingernails scraping across their skin."

"Try thinking of them as corpses."

"I wish."

"Do you think they killed the judge?"

There was a pause. "They're up to something, and it's not over. That performance was meant to scare me. Colin-the-swastika knew my name was Adrian, even though Randy introduced me as Mr. Monk. We've put away more than one resident of Pleasant Valley, so someone must have mentioned my name and my OCD."

"Any other leads—besides they wanted to scare you?"

"The two of them share a kind of unspoken communication. Very dangerous. I didn't get much else. I was distracted."

"Anything at all?"

"Well, they're fixated on revenge. That's clear. They still talk to Colin's mother, not his father or to Marshal's family, whom they hate even more than Colin's. The boys applied for passports, expedited ones, so the documents may have already arrived. They're planning something secret for Saturday, after which they're fleeing the country." He paused for effect. "Other than that, I know nothing."

I both love it and hate it when he does that. "Adrian, don't make me beg. The passports?"

He sighed dramatically, but moments like that are what he lives for. "There was a white sheet taped up against the wall in a corner. That and the glossy paper in their computer printer scream, 'homemade passport photos.' In their wastebasket near the bottom were two FedEx strips for sealing overnight envelopes, so they were in a hurry to go somewhere."

"You're right. I should have seen that."

"You're forgiven. Do you want to take a crack at the Saturday thing? It's not that hard."

"It'll be faster if you do it."

"Agreed. There was a calendar on the wall above Marshal's cot."

"I saw it," I said, a little proud of myself. "You think it's odd that ex-cons without a job or a lot of appointments would have a calendar on the wall?"

"No. I think it's odd that the calendar page was for August, next month. The July page was torn off."

"Huh." Okay, this was puzzling, at least to me. "It's still early. Why would they tear off July?"

"Because they didn't want a cop and two private detectives to walk in and see it. While I was making up Marshal's cot, I caught a glimpse of the torn-off page. It was on the floor."

"And . . . ?"

"I couldn't see much, not without them noticing. But this coming Saturday was circled in red with a little skull and crossbones drawing."

"A skull and crossbones? In red?"

"Something bad is happening Saturday."

"You think?"

"Yes, I do." Monk was getting better at detecting sarcasm, but there were occasional lapses.

"You think it'll be another attempt on the captain?"

"I can't say. Maybe if I went back in . . . But I'm not going. No way."

"Then how do we find out what they're up to?"

"You go back. You're a detective. Meanwhile, I'm heading

to bed and trying for another forty-eight minutes. I'm hanging up now. Don't call until after I'm done."

I had just hung up myself and was heading back into our storefront when Julie signaled me from the doorway. "I have a class in an hour," she said, then noticed my expression. "What's wrong? Something's wrong."

"It's just Adrian. He's being pigheaded."

"You know I can handle him pretty well." Her smile was instant, warm and manipulative. "If I was in the office every day, I could get closer to him. . . ."

"We are not hiring you as an intern," I told her, cutting to the chase. "It's a dangerous, dead-end job that won't look good on your law school résumé."

"I'm not going to law school."

"Julie, please. I have too much on my mind to get into this discussion."

Her smile flicked off like a switch. "Fine. It's on your screen. And next time, get someone else. This work's too dangerous and dead-end for me." And she walked off in the direction of the BART station.

I hate arguing with my little girl, but it's part of my job. At least she hadn't stolen the family silver and wound up with prison tats. I should count my blessings.

The image on the screen was not as good as I'd hoped, but not as bad as I'd feared. It was definitely Sue, cropped to the size of a blurry, off-kilter mug shot. Perhaps if I showed it around, someone might be able to put a real name to the face. But where to show it? I had joked about renting a billboard. But how about a flyer taped to a telephone pole?

"Have you seen my fuzzy client? Answers to the name Sue. Reward."

I printed out a copy and taped it on my wall, right beside the piece of notepaper with the mysterious numbering that Monk had retrieved from my wastebasket—the eighteen rows of crossed-out numbers and letters "0-0," "1-2," "A-B." Monk hates when I tape things up. But I find it helps me focus, a reminder of the puzzles yet to be solved.

A minute or so later when the phone rang, I picked up without looking. "Natalie? Don't hang up." There was no way I was going to hang up.

"Where are you?" I said as soon as my head stopped spinning. "Who are you?"

For lack of a better name, it was Sue. "I'm sorry, Natalie. I know I put you through a lot. But I can explain."

I focused on the fuzzy picture. "I'd love to hear you explain."

"That day . . ." She lowered her voice. "I was scared. I wound up not checking into the hotel and I ditched my phone. I thought they might be tracking me."

"They? Who's they?"

"Can I trust you, Natalie? I have to know I can trust you."

"Of course you can. The point is, can I trust you?"

"I'm sorry for lying and using you like that. It was terrible. But I didn't know what else to do."

"Is your name even Sue?"

"Yes. Suzanne."

"Puskedra? Because I did some Internet searches and there's no Sue Puskedra in the entire world."

"You were right. It's a made-up name. If I told you my real last name, you'd know what this is about."

"I would?" That was oddly reassuring. There actually might be some explanation. "So tell me. Why did you say you were married to Timothy O'Brien?"

"I needed to find out something. And you helped, even if you didn't know it."

"How did I help? Was it legal?"

She didn't answer my questions. "I know you went to see Timothy. What did he say about me?"

"Say about you? He has no idea who you are. No one does."

"He's lying, the scumbag. How about Gayle Greenwald? What did she say?"

"No one knows who you are, Suzanne." I was almost shouting.

"Oh, they wish they didn't know me. It would make everything easier. But they're lying, Natalie."

"Why would they lie? Sue. Suzanne, you have to tell me what's going on. You owe me that."

There were several seconds of dead air and I'd thought she'd hung up. "Not over the phone."

"You're sounding paranoid now. Come to the office."

"No, they could be watching. You come to me. You remember that place I said had a fitting name? Don't say the name out loud, just yes or no."

"Yes." She was talking about Jezebel's, the trendy bar around the corner from her nonhusband's office. "You think someone's listening to us?"

"Better to be safe. Meet me there as soon as you can."

"Is this your new number?" I said, and looked at my screen.

"I'm calling from a pay phone. It's safer."

"I can meet you now if you want."

"Good. Don't let yourself be followed."

"Then give me a half hour. Be safe."

"You, too."

We hung up and I went into warp speed. I grabbed my key ring, locked up the office, turned on the alarm, and checked my surroundings on the street. It's times like these that my years of unofficial PI training come into play. One of the hippies next door, Peter, was in his hand-painted VW van, just pulling out of the parking lot. We waved hello or good-bye and I waited another two minutes. When nothing passed by except the usual midmorning street traffic, I got into my Subaru.

Between the usual traffic and my diversionary tactics, it took almost thirty minutes before I turned onto Market Street and scooted up the ramp to the first parking structure on the right. It was a textbook move, guaranteed to lose anyone who wasn't directly behind you. I traveled the last two blocks on foot.

By the time I walked into Jezebel's and checked my phone, thirty-five minutes had passed. The place had just opened and seemed deserted, except for a bartender who was emptying a steaming rack of glasses from the dishwasher. I gravitated to the booth I'd used last week to eavesdrop on the nonhusband, sat down, and waited.

I didn't start to worry until after I'd nursed my way through two club sodas. I checked my phone—just over an hour at the table. What the hell could have happened? I'd been a few minutes late, but that shouldn't have made a difference. Could I have been followed? Had she been followed? Was she in danger? Or had she just changed her mind?

As long as my phone was out and staring at me, I pressed "call last." After four rings, a recorded voice came on, informing me that the phone was not receiving calls. A lot of pay phones do that.

"Another one on the house?" asked the bartender gently. A few early lunchers were straggling through the door and soon he would be busy.

"No, thanks," I said. "Just the check."

He crossed to the register and touched the screen a few times. "Waiting for someone?"

"I was."

"Bummer. Be right with you."

As he slipped the printout into a check holder, I rummaged through my tote, reaching past my wallet and my Glock and my keys to the folded piece of paper I'd taken off my wall. He pushed the check holder my way. I unfolded the paper and pushed it his. "Have you ever seen this woman?"

"What are you, a private detective?" he joked.

"I am." Usually I love saying that, but this time it didn't cheer me up.

"Surveillance?" he guessed, examining the grainy black-and-white shot, enlarged and photoshopped to within an inch of its life. "Sorry."

"Sorry about what?" I needed specifics.

"I see a hundred women in here like that. Do you have a name? Or a better shot?"

"I've got nothing," I said. "Just that."

When he left to process my card, I used the time to make another call. "Adrian?" I'd promised to keep Monk in the loop on the Sue case from now on, and I was keeping that promise.

He was still upset. "You should have called me right after she called you."

"You told me not to interrupt your nap."

"Honestly, Natalie, there's no winning with you."

"That's what I was going to say."

"This Sue woman is bad news. She lies, manipulates, disappears. . . ."

"Maybe she's just in trouble. Who do you think she is?"

"Someone not named Sue or Suzanne."

"She said if she told me her real name, I would automatically know what this is about. She said it was some crime or scandal involving Timothy O'Brien."

"She said that to gain your sympathy."

"Why would she do that?"

"Your guess is as good as mine. No, that's not true. My guess is better, and I don't even have a guess."

"Or maybe she was telling the truth. What do you think happened?"

"If we're lucky, we'll never find out. If we're lucky, it's all over and done with." His sigh lasted a good five seconds. "Of course we're never that lucky, are we?"

CHAPTER TWENTY-ONE

Mr. Monk Waits for the Weekend

"**R**andy, buddy, I hear you're a bit under the weather." Captain Stottlemeyer had wandered to the front window of his living room where the cell reception was better.

"Sir?" Lieutenant A.J. motioned his boss to move away from the window. The captain motioned back, rejecting the request, then switched the phone to speaker mode.

"It's just a cold," said Randy, his voice a lot raspier than when I'd last heard it. "Unless you don't think it's a cold. What does Monk think?"

"What do I think?" Monk spoke in the general direction of the cell phone.

"You think it could be poison? Those neo-Nazi skinheads were pretty angry."

"Not at you," Monk pointed out.

"I know they didn't attack me with an umbrella," said Randy. "But maybe when I unfolded my folding chair. I think I saw some dust."

"But you have the symptoms of a cold," I said. "My money's on Sharona, not heavy-metal poisons."

"Randy, you should drive yourself to the hospital and get tested," said the captain. "Just to be sure."

"Thanks, Captain. Good idea." Randy's mood was brightening. "I'm going now."

"And after they tell you it's a cold, get back to bed and drink plenty of liquids. Monk, Natalie, and Lieutenant Thurman will hold down the fort. Don't worry about us."

Monk had enough self-control to wait until the captain hung up. "What do you mean Lieutenant Thurman? We're not working with him."

"Yes, you are, Monk. The three of you need to learn to get along. This will be good training."

"We can do it on our own," insisted my partner.

"No, you can't," said A.J. He was hobbling across the room, his right leg heavily bandaged beneath his khaki slacks. My guess was that a lot of painkillers were involved.

"The lieutenant's in no condition," I said.

"Nattie, I'm fine. I'm running an investigation, not a track-and-field event."

"He's been cleared for duty," the captain agreed.

"What about your father?" I asked the lieutenant. "If he only has a few days, don't you want to be there?" It wasn't my best moment, bringing up his dying father, but I was desperate.

"You leave my dad out of this," said A.J. There were times when he would just hover by his father's bedside, so concerned about Arnold Senior's health, and other moments, like this one. . . .

A.J. sat down on the edge of a sofa. "The captain stretched the rules when he let you guys investigate with a visiting officer. You're consultants. Imagine if this ever goes to trial and you're asked to testify about a chain of evidence. The defense will have a field day with your habit of wiping down everything with sanitized wipes. All a lawyer has to do is shake hands with you and there goes our credibility."

"I have never wiped down evidence," Monk sputtered, which wasn't quite true. Luckily, in that particular instance, the suspect had already confessed and it didn't matter. "Never," he repeated for emphasis. "I was a detective first grade when you were still in diapers."

"Yeah," said the thuggish detective. "You must have been something back in the day. But the only Monk I know is a basket case who waves his hands around and makes lucky guesses half the time."

"Monk's the best detective I know," said the captain sternly. "Keep that in mind."

"Yes, sir."

The captain was fully dressed. His arm was still in a shoulder sling, held tight with a Velcro strap. He looked healthy enough. But I knew he was under orders from his doctor and from his security detail and, most important, from his wife to stay away for a few more days. "On the other hand, Lieutenant Thurman is my second-in-command. I trust him the way I always trust my partners."

"Thank you, sir," said A.J. "I will consider any input from any private investigators the department wants to hire."

"It's not just input," growled Stottlemeyer. "We have a dead judge and two attempts on my life. You guys work it out." There was no arguing with that tone of voice. Monk and A.J. nodded reluctantly.

"Do you think it was the Willmotts? Monk?" It was A.J.'s first attempt at trying to be cooperative.

"They're guilty of something," said Monk. "Their release

corresponded with the attack on Judge Oberlin. They're angry. They had access to poison, possession of a nine-millimeter handgun . . . and they're planning something secret for Saturday."

"How do you . . ." A.J. rephrased it. "How do we know that?"

Monk explained about the Willmott visit, about the missing gun and the calendar and the skull and crossbones for Saturday. "I'm eighty-two percent sure about the gun and ninety-five percent about Saturday. The expedited-passports theory is only seventy-one percent."

"You see?" A.J. interrupted. "This is what I'm talking about. These crazy percentages. What the hell do they even mean?"

"Well, the captain always asks how sure I am about things. This is my way of quantifying. You may have noticed that seventy-one percent is lower than ninety-five."

A.J. came nose to nose, way too close for comfort. "Are you ridiculing me, Monk?"

"No, no. But you're not making it easy."

Lieutenant Thurman shook his head and started to pace, wincing violently with each step. "You know what, Monk? You know what? I'm ninety-eight percent sure you're crazy. And one hundred percent sure I don't give a damn."

"That's enough," said the captain. "Lieutenant, you listen to Monk. If things get heated or you have real concerns— real concerns—then you call me and I'll take over."

"You can't do fieldwork," I said.

"Wanna bet?" The captain sighed and winced and pressed a hand to his throbbing, injured arm. "This is going to be one long investigation."

*   *   *

The next day was Friday, otherwise known as the day before skull-and-crossbones Saturday. Since we weren't expecting any real developments, Monk didn't argue with A.J. being in charge of surveillance. The lieutenant kept in close contact with the two units, one parked in front of and one on the side street of the urban château in Pacific Heights. At a little before eleven a.m. he called in a report, keeping his tone relatively civil.

"There was a FedEx delivery at ten forty-one," he told me. "The mother sent the driver around to the basement door. The one with the lightning bolts took the delivery."

"Two envelope-sized packages?" I asked.

"Yeah. The driver let me check his tablet. They were both from the passport center on Hawthorne Street, just like Monk said."

"Good," I said, resisting the temptation to rub it in. Monk said something from his desk across the office and I relayed the message. "Today is garbage day in Pacific Heights."

"How does Monk know that?"

"He just does."

Monk kept talking and I kept relaying. "If the cans are on the street and haven't been emptied, they're fair game, legally. Adrian wants you to go through them. Let us know what you find."

"I'm not going through their garbage."

"Then have a patrolman do it."

"I can't spare a patrolman right now."

"Is the big lieutenant too squeamish?" Monk taunted

loudly from the other side of the room. "Afraid to get his hands a little dirty?"

"Adrian, stop it. Lieutenant, get a pair of gloves and make a list of what you find. We're not interested in food. Anything else. And try not to be seen."

"I need to call the captain."

"You don't need to call the captain."

"Does the big lieutenant need the captain to sort his garbage?"

"What did Monk say?"

"Nothing. Look, if their garbage can help us get a handle on what they're doing tomorrow . . ."

"I got it," said A.J. "That doesn't mean I like it." And he hung up.

"Adrian, please. Don't antagonize him any more than you have to."

"My antagonism is just the right amount, thank you."

"Fine." I checked the time on my phone, then gathered my keys and my tote. "I'm off to see Daniela Grace. Can I trust you not to insult the hippies or fight with the pawnshop or start a fire?"

"Why are you seeing Daniela? She's not going through a divorce, is she?"

"No. No divorces, I promised you."

"How about murder? She's not planning another murder?"

"No murder." Monk and I had first met Daniela at a low point in her life when she, a successful trial attorney, was actually trying to kill someone. I won't go into the details, but Monk talked her out of it. I make a point of checking the obituaries, and the object of her murder plot is still alive and well. But Adrian's been a little wary of her ever since.

"Then why are you seeing Daniela? What are you keeping from me?"

"Nothing. You can come with me if you want."

"Okay, I will."

"Good. Come along." This was exactly what I'd wanted and I was relieved that my plan had worked so well.

"What about lunch?"

"What about lunch?" I echoed.

"I brought Spam sandwiches on white bread." He held up a brown paper bag that he'd bleached white. "As a treat for you."

"We'll bring them along. Put them in my tote."

We made it to the offices of Grace, Winters, and Weingart in plenty of time for our eleven forty-five appointment. Monk found the one chair in the waiting room that fit his needs, and luckily for everyone, it was unoccupied. I took the chair next to him and we waited.

"You know we can't take on a case," Monk whispered. "Maybe after skull-and-bones Saturday. But not now."

"I know," I whispered back. "But we'll make a little time. Daniela is paying us a retainer."

"Wait. What?" He was reacting like he'd never heard this before, which was technically true. "We're on a retainer?"

"Yes. It seemed like a good idea, getting paid to be available."

"Well, we're not available."

"Adrian, please, as long as we're here . . ."

"We?" He scowled. "You tricked me. I didn't come prepared to work."

"Well, prepare yourself."

"Mr. Monk, thank you." It was Daniela, of course, at exactly eleven forty-five. "Natalie said she'd try to drag you along. Welcome to our little digs." She proceeded to lead us back through the warren of wood-paneled spaces to a corner office, decorated in British colonial furnishings with a stunning view of the Transamerica Pyramid. *Why can't I have an office like this?* I wondered. *It probably has a bathroom. Just add a microwave and a wine rack and I could live here.*

Daniela closed the door, offered us the chairs in front of her blank expanse of a desk, and quickly brought Monk up to speed.

The intricacies of the initial public offering were complex. Even what her client did was a little fuzzy in my mind—some social media company that had a best-selling phone app that let you spy on your friends, presumably with their consent.

This app was now worth hundreds of millions. In three months it might be worth billions or next to nothing. That's why the app company wanted to do an IPO as soon as possible. They also needed to keep the details hidden until just the right moment, from both a legal and a profitability standpoint. That's where the law firm of Grace, Winters, and Weingart came in, to comply with all the filing requirements and produce the thousands of pages necessary—government forms, offering documents, glossy brochures—all for the big day.

Out of all of this detail, the only part Monk and I needed to understand was that the company's name was JAS, Joyful App Services, and that they had a leak. "To be absolutely accurate, GWW has a leak." Even with her mahogany door closed, Daniela said it under her breath. "One of our other contacts in the software business heard the rumor and gave us a heads-up. We denied the leak came from us, of course. We're professionals. We deal with clients' secrets all the time. So we all worked overtime, the JAS people and us, to change some details of the offering, just enough to mitigate any damage or possible lawsuits."

"And it happened again," said Monk.

"Right," said Daniela, looking embarrassed. "Only this time, we accidentally got a few numbers wrong. We corrected them here at the office, not at the JAS office. These corrected numbers were the ones that got leaked the second time, just yesterday."

"So it's clear," said Monk. "Your firm has a leaky employee."

"It appears that way," said Daniela. "We've narrowed our working group to just a few, which makes the work all the harder. But we can't afford another leak. Even with our liability insurance, it could put us out of business."

Daniela had seen Adrian Monk pull off instant miracles and she needed him to do it again. Monk understood her predicament. And he didn't care. "We can't do this right now."

"Yes, you can. That's why I'm paying you."

"No. We have a murder and two attempted murders. We don't need something with four squares or some disgruntled birds on a phone."

"We can devote today to your problem," I said guardedly, my eyes focused on Monk in my patented don't-contradict-me stare. "Tomorrow is the weekend. But we can come back on Monday, if we need to."

"But not tomorrow," said Monk. "Tomorrow is skull-and-crossbones day."

Daniela had no idea what that meant, but she was fine. "I suppose I can't force you to work weekends. But if you can wrap this up in the next few hours, that would be perfect."

"We'll do our best," I said.

"Then it's settled." Daniela stood up and straightened her lightweight pink tweed jacket.

Before I knew what was happening, she had escorted us to the cubicle just outside her door. "This is Booker, my paralegal and right hand. Booker knows everything. He'll give you a rundown on the others you need to speak to."

"Mr. Monk. Ms. Teeger. Daniela has told me so much. I'm a big fan."

"Don't gush or they'll raise their fee," said Daniela, only half-joking. Just before she closed her mahogany door, when Booker wasn't looking, she tilted her head in his direction and raised a plucked eyebrow. Message received: Even her right hand was not above suspicion.

Booker Sessums was a short, thin, neatly put-together black man in rolled-up shirtsleeves and a tie. Mid-twenties was my guess. As I get older I'm finding it harder to estimate age. It's easier to just separate adults into four groups: my daughter's age, younger than me, my age, and older than me. He was my daughter's age, plus.

Booker's work space was large and fairly private for a cubicle. He removed a folder full of files from a chair. Monk didn't look like he wanted to sit, so I did. "I'll help as much as I can," said the paralegal. "We're pretty slammed, but I know it's important."

"We'll try to make this quick," I promised. "How many people are on the JAS team?"

"Before the last leak there were seven. Now there are four, including Daniela and me."

"Only four," I said for Adrian's benefit. "That shouldn't be too hard."

Booker sat down and reached over to his keyboard. A machine out in the corridor began to whir. "I'm printing out their vitals from the personnel files. If there's anything else . . ."

"We'll need to meet with each one."

"I can take you by their offices," said Booker. "Whenever you want."

I lowered my voice and leaned in. "What can you tell us about Daniela? Is she a good boss?"

Normally I wouldn't consider Daniela a suspect. She was the one who had hired us, and the one with the most to lose. On the other hand, she did once try to murder someone, so nothing was off the table.

"She's great," Booker said without hesitation. "Honest, straightforward, funny at times. A good boss."

"Then why are you quitting?" Monk had wandered his way around the cubicle and was now on Booker's other side, flanking him.

"Quitting?" Booker looked stunned, but he didn't deny it.

"The other men came to work in a sport coat or blazer. You came in a suit, a new one." Monk pointed to a jacket on a hook. "The breast pocket is still sewn up. Your shoes are freshly shined. Obviously, you're going somewhere important. During lunch, because you keep checking your watch."

"That doesn't mean . . ."

"I'm not through," said Monk.

"Booker." I smiled sympathetically. "It's less painful if you don't interrupt him."

Monk pointed to the man's trash can and continued. "There's a crumpled-up invitation to a baby shower. It's obviously work-related, since it was sent to the office. You threw away the RSVP notice along with the invitation, so it seems like you're ready to burn some bridges. I don't blame you. Baby showers!"

"That doesn't mean . . ."

"I'm not through."

"Less painful," I repeated.

"You used to have things on your wall, but the empty picture hooks show you've been removing them. Also, you're an organized worker with a file cabinet, but there was a folder on Natalie's chair. When you moved it, you placed it facedown on the other side of your space. Personal files to take home, I hope? Not business ones?"

"Yes. Personal," said Booker. He looked defeated.

"I'm not through."

"Mr. Monk, please," Booker Sessums whispered. "I am leaving the firm. I'm having lunch with my new boss today and leaving as soon as this leak situation is solved."

"No two-week notice?" I asked.

"With Daniela Grace, there's no grace period. You quit and you're out."

"And why are you leaving?" I asked.

"He's going to law school at night."

"Adrian, let him tell his story."

"It's faster my way."

"Just try to be polite."

"He's right," Booker admitted. His voice was so low I almost had to read his lips. "I'm in law school. My new place promised to accommodate my schedule. Daniela is a lot of great things, but accommodating isn't one of them."

"This place you're going," Monk said. "Do they represent any of the competing IPOs?"

"They do not. It's family law. Less pressure and more meaningful. I'll give you their contact information, but you have to promise to be discreet."

I made the promise, even though I was sure Monk could have figured out the firm's name, given another minute of glancing around. Booker had just handed me his future boss' card when my tote began to vibrate. I excused myself, went out to the hallway, and answered.

"Nat, girl?"

"The name is Natalie. What is it, A.J.?"

"The name's Lieutenant. We did your garbage search. Two unhappy patrolmen scouring through six bags. I tell you, everybody's got a Monk story."

I should have known he'd get someone else to do the dirty work. "You separated the family garbage from the boys?"

"It was pretty obvious. Whole Foods versus Domino's Pizza."

"And?"

"Here's the highlights reel. Empty box of nine-millimeter rounds. Empty box of forty-five caliber rounds. Each one a hundred-round value pack."

"So they have two guns?"

"Two illegals, at least. But the boxes aren't enough for a

search warrant. I checked. Neither are the tags and receipts of two cartridge belts. We also have tags and receipts for four duffel bags. Camouflage colored from the looks of it."

"No ski masks?" I was remembering the attack in the alley behind the Thurman house.

"If they bought ski masks, it was probably at some earlier date."

"Right," I said. "Looks like skull-and-crossbones Saturday will be eventful."

"I wish we could go in and arrest them now. It seems like probable cause. But there's no law against buying ammo or cartridge belts or circling dates on your calendar."

"I know." For once, A.J. and I were in agreement. "Let me put Adrian on."

While Adrian was on with the lieutenant, getting whatever other details he could out of the garbage team, Booker retrieved the personnel records from the printer and pointed me in the direction of the last two leakster suspects. Compared with what the blond Nazis were planning in the basement, this seemed like such small potatoes.

CHAPTER TWENTY-TWO

Mr. Monk and the Stakeout

The day didn't end with a breakthrough. Our defecting paralegal answered a few more questions, then donned his suit jacket and sneaked out for lunch with his new boss. We commandeered his cubicle for our own lunch of Spam sandwiches, washed down with mini bottles of Fiji Water and topped off with individually wrapped oatmeal cookies.

Adrian and I stayed for another two hours, interviewing the head of the firm's finance department and a fourth-year associate who had yet to be named a partner, even though she'd been promised it. They seemed like reasonable suspects to me, both of them nervous and overworked and seemingly frustrated by the unstoppable leak.

"I don't see how it could be anyone at GWW," said the fourth-year associate. "It damages the firm. And even if I did it and had another job lined up, it would be doomed. No one likes a spy."

"And yet there is a spy," I pointed out. I looked to Monk to say something clever or point out that the associate raised carrier pigeons that could sneak secrets out of the high-rise window. But he seemed to be losing interest. We wound up sneaking out of the wood-paneled confines of Grace, Winters, and Weingart without checking in with Daniela or saying good-bye.

"What do I say when she calls?" I asked.

"Tell her sometimes the magic works. Sometimes it doesn't."

"I can't tell her . . . Wait. Are you quoting something? From a movie or a book? It's not like you to quote things."

"I'm quoting Captain Leland Stottlemeyer, who might have been quoting a movie or a book. I don't know which one. If it's important, you can call him up."

"It's not important. I was just surprised."

"Well, you can tell Ms. Grace that I can't create evidence like magic. Sorry to disappoint."

Daniela Grace called twice that evening. Both times I let her go to voice mail and didn't listen to the messages. I went to bed early and tried to put skull-and-crossbones Saturday out of my mind. But even when I managed this feat, there were other thoughts right behind it: Daniela's unanswered call, disappearing Sue, and the hacking cough coming from the guest room all night. Several times that night I woke up to hear Randy shuffling through to the kitchen. The light scent of chamomile tea should have been soothing to me, but it wasn't.

The next morning, before leaving the house, I knocked on his door and poked my head in. "Are you surviving? Is there anything I can get you?"

The Summit police chief looked like a little boy, dressed in blue pajamas, with the covers almost pulled up to his neck. The bed was littered with used tissues, but he reached out and made an effort—a noble, painful effort—to clear a spot for me. I chose the chair by Julie's old homework desk and wheeled it over to within five feet. No closer.

"I feel so horrible," Randy rasped.

"I have some NyQuil," I offered. "It may be a few years old."

"Not about the cold. Not just about the cold. I feel horrible about coming all this way and taking over your house like a hospital ward."

"It's not your fault. It was so generous of you to drop everything and try to help."

"Some help I turned out to be." Throughout a lifetime of treating colds and flu attacks, I've learned that one of the most common symptoms is a bout or two of self-pity. I don't mean to belittle it. This is a real symptom and needs to be treated like any other.

"You're a big help," I replied. "Your journal brought up some details no one remembered. And the captain. Did you see the way he lit up when you walked in? Oh, and then there was the gunfight in the alley. You were the only one on our team who got off a shot."

Randy thought this over and sniffled. "Maybe. But it just reminded me of the old days, when you and Monk and the captain did the important stuff and I was just along for the ride."

"Randy, you were never along for the ride." That didn't come out right. "You know."

"I do. It was always Randy and his stupid theories."

"That's not what I meant."

"Remember when I suggested that Dale the Whale committed murder by using liposuction to get rid of six hundred pounds of fat, then had reverse liposuction to put all the weight back on and fool us? The whole department was laughing."

"That was before my time," I said. "But I heard the story."

"Exactly. Everyone heard the story. If I ever came back, it would be the same thing."

"Randy, that was a long time ago. You're smarter now. You're a police chief."

"I still make mistakes."

"So what's the answer?" I asked. "I say go back to New Jersey and make mistakes on your own."

He considered my advice. "I guess the grass is always greener, huh? When I was here, I always wanted to be the guy in charge. Then I got to be the guy in charge and I felt lost. I missed being part of a team. Then I showed up here and I'm suddenly a third wheel."

"I think you mean fifth wheel."

"Fifth wheel?" Randy coughed phlegm into another tissue. I rolled back my chair another two feet. "Isn't this a bicycle comparison? Two wheels versus a useless third wheel?"

"No, I think it's a car analogy," I said. "Four wheels versus a useless fifth wheel."

"Hm." He gave it some thought. "What if you're referring to a couple? That's only two. You'd be the third wheel, right?"

"You're right," I had to agree. "When you're talking about a couple, then it's a third wheel. I think I've heard it used both ways."

"Of course, in reality there are three of you guys and I'm the useless fourth. So maybe we should make it a tricycle analogy. I'm the fourth wheel—of a tricycle." He sighed. "All I know is I should go home."

"Not until the captain's safe and you're over your cold. Now, how about that NyQuil?"

I spoon-fed the police chief a full dose of the green liquid, tucked him in bed, and still kept to my schedule.

A stakeout team had been on-site at the urban château through Friday night into Saturday morning. At ten a.m., the "A" team would take over.

When Monk and I arrived, A.J. was already there, his Honda Accord having just replaced an unmarked patrol car. A.J. saw us driving up, held up his phone for us to see, and pressed a speed dial button. I don't know why but I was flattered to realize I was on his speed dial.

"Morning, sunshine," he quipped. "You guys park on the next block. We already have a two-vehicle presence." I could see him point around the corner of the big corner lot.

"Then we'll relieve the second vehicle," I said.

"Already done. The new second vehicle just got here." There was a certain lightness to A.J.'s voice that made me nervous. I shifted into park and turned my head to spy a familiar brown Buick sedan.

"No. What the hell is he doing here?"

I didn't wait for an answer. I hung up, drove right past the dusty Honda, and made the next three left turns. I double-parked beside the brown Buick and rolled down my passenger window. The captain's window was already down.

I leaned over to speak, but Monk said it for me. "If Natalie were an assassin, you'd be dead by now."

"From the look of her, I'd say she wants me dead anyway." Stottlemeyer's arm was still Velcroed to his body, but he was grinning like a schoolboy.

"Captain," I shouted. "We're doing this to protect you. And you purposely put yourself in danger?"

"We're doing this to catch Judge Oberlin's killer," Stottlemeyer countered. "Every officer puts himself on the line every day. The average bad guy would shoot through any of us to get away. From the way I see it, this is no different."

"What about your shoulder?"

"My doctor came by and cleared me last night. It's like A.J. told me. . . ."

"A.J. talked you into this?" I asked, shaking my head. "I should have known."

"Hey. No one has to talk me into doing my job. Besides, as A.J. pointed out, if these boys are after me today, it's a lot safer to be behind them than in their sights."

"What about your wife?" I asked. "Where is she?"

"Trudy's staying with her sister in Santa Cruz. She left last night."

Our debate was interrupted by the communicator on the captain's uninjured shoulder. It buzzed and Lieutenant Thurman's voice crackled. "We've got the elder Willmotts leaving the house. Does the wizard of odd want to give them a glance?"

"Does he mean me?" Monk asked.

"He means you," I said.

Monk and I had to scramble out of the Subaru to get a better view. From a spot behind a hundred-year-old maple, we could see the trunk of a black Lexus pop open. Ben and Olivia worked together to clear a space for a large shopping bag. Ben was in a black suit, Olivia in a dress of flowery, tasteful pastels, knee-length, with a small white hat perched on her head. They reminded me of my parents heading out for a weekend brunch at the country club.

No one even suggested following them. In fact we felt relieved that they were out of the picture. We settled into our three vehicles—the Honda across the street, the Buick around the corner, the old Subaru farther down the block—and wasted the next few hours getting on one another's nerves.

"Wizard of odd," Monk mumbled under his breath. He was in the passenger seat, belted in. I was kneeling down on the sidewalk by his window, eating a Fig Newton. Monk doesn't allow eating in my car.

"Let it go, Adrian," I mumbled between bites. "Sure, he's obnoxious and mean. But I think everyone realizes that. In some ways, A.J. is his own worst enemy."

"Not as long as I'm alive."

"Well, get used to him. Arny Senior and Leland have this bond. When Arny dies, it's only going to get stronger. You know how loyal the captain is."

"What if something unexpected happens to A.J.? You know, like a bomb. Or he gets pushed off a cliff. Accidentally."

"Really? You?" I had to laugh. "You could never kill anyone. First off, you're not the type. Second, I know you. You'd confess within five minutes. Even if you didn't confess, you could never get away with murder."

"What do you mean? I'm an expert in killing. I have lists of every possible way to die. I have a hundred locked-room murder methods that look like suicide."

"So you're constantly thinking how to kill people?"

"I'm a dangerous man, Natalie. I review and update the lists once a month."

"Update? Why do they need updating?"

Monk sighed. "It's the bane of technology. I had a perfect

murder method using a Western Union telegram, another using Morse code. Both of those had to be eliminated. I have six that involve pay phones, which are dangerously close to extinction. On the plus side, I do have two new ones that didn't exist before Candy Crush. That's a mobile game people play on their phones."

"I know what Candy Crush is. I'm just surprised you do."

"A possibly lethal application like that? I'd be remiss in my duty to humanity."

"Okay, I'll bite. How do you kill someone using Candy Crush?"

There was just the hint of a crinkle around his eyes. "If I told you, I'd have to kill you—with Candy Crush, just to make sure it worked."

"You're all talk, Adrian."

"I know." And the smiling hint disappeared. "Meanwhile, our careers are ruined."

"Not ruined, just changed. Change is good."

"How is it good? Give me one example."

"Okay, change is not always good. But it's inevitable. We'll do fewer cases with the police and more civilian cases, like the one for Daniela."

Monk scowled with disapproval. "Trying to patch a leak. That's not why I became a detective."

"It may not be as exciting as murder. But there's millions of dollars at stake and her company's reputation." My phone rang and in one fluid motion, I stashed the remaining Fig Newtons in my tote and pulled out the phone. "Finally, some action!"

I checked the display, sighed, and pressed "ignore." "Was that Exciting Daniela?" Monk guessed.

"Yes," I admitted. "Her fourth call and, unless you've solved her case, I don't want to talk about it."

The phone rang again and I almost pressed "ignore" again. But this time it was Lieutenant Thurman. "They're on the move," he said. "Dressed in black. One backpack. Four duffel bags that look empty. Don't seem to be in a rush. You got the plate number?"

"The old Volvo? Sure." The boys were in the habit of driving a forest green Volvo SUV, decorated in dings and rust, at least a dozen years old, undoubtedly lent by one of their begrudging families. A fresh bumper sticker sported a skull with tiny swastikas in the eye sockets. Colin was behind the wheel.

Tailing the Willmott cousins wound up being like a weird, secret parade. They were in the lead, of course, followed by the Honda a block behind, the Buick in point position two blocks back, and my Subaru on a parallel street. Things became more organized once we hit the 101 heading south. The neo-Nazi cousins engaged in no evasive action. They didn't even break the speed limit.

"They're not anywhere near the captain's house," Monk observed.

"Is that good or bad?" I asked, but he didn't answer.

CHAPTER TWENTY-THREE

Mr. Monk and the Ballrooms

Fifteen minutes later, the parade led us off the 101, around the bend of an off-ramp, down an access road, and into the oversized parking lot of the Tuscany Pines. Not one of us had ever been here before.

Our three tail vehicles idled on the access road as Colin backed the Volvo into a handicapped space by a side door. The cousins took the duffel bags out of the back, hefted them on their shoulders, and disappeared into the building.

"A restaurant?" asked A.J. Everybody had everybody else on speaker.

According to its bright signage, the Tuscany Pines was several things: restaurant, catering service, banquet facility. The section of the parking lot in front of the main doors with the faux-Roman columns was crowded with a hundred or more cars, from shiny and expensive to more than a few pickups.

On instructions from the captain, we all parked in different spots, facing out, giving ourselves quick access to various exit routes. It was reassuring to see Stottlemeyer once again in command of the situation.

We met by the captain's Buick. He had already grabbed

his duty handgun from his glove box and slipped it under the Velcro strap of his sling. "Monk, Natalie and I will go in the front. Natalie, I'm going to need you to keep your weapon locked and within reach."

"Got it," I said. I was going to keep my Glock .22 in my PBS tote on top of my packets of disposable wipes. Instead, I left the tote on Stottlemeyer's front seat and stuffed the Glock into the oversized pocket of my thigh-length, truffle-colored Calvin Klein belted trench coat. It looks much nicer than it sounds.

The four of us made our way to the Roman columns. "Should we call for backup?" I asked.

"We don't have a crime," said A.J.

"But I have a bad feeling," Monk said. "I estimated a sixty-eight percent chance—"

"Shut up, Monk."

"Lieutenant . . ." Stottlemeyer's gaze fell to A.J.'s right leg. "You keep a position out here. We don't know what they're up to, but the Volvo is their transportation."

"Let Monk do it," said A.J. "He's useless in the field."

"He's not useless in the field. Besides, he doesn't have a driver's license."

"I do have a driver's license," said Monk. "I just choose not to use it."

"Why can't Natalie stay back?"

"Because Natalie has two good legs. End of discussion."

The lobby of the Tuscany Pines gave the veneer-thin appearance of an Italian villa, with marble tiles and crystal chandeliers. In front of us were the oak doors of a closed restaurant. To the left and the right and up the polished stairs were doors and hallways leading to the event rooms. Around the staircase, on a trio of freestanding signs, were listed the afternoon events. Pointing right: BOWERSOX-CASTELLO WEDDING. BALLROOM A. Pointing up the stairs: RODRIGUES QUINCEAÑERA. BALLROOM B. Pointing left: ANDREW AND ADAM GREENBERG BAR MITZVAH. BALLROOM C.

Adrian, Leland, and I stood in the empty lobby, staring at the signs and listening to the distant sounds of music and celebration. Where the hell were the Willmott boys in this monstrosity? And why?

"A bar mitzvah?" whispered the captain, focusing on the third sign. "You think they'd actually shoot up a bar mitzvah? With kids?"

It was a frightening thought. "We know they're here with guns," I answered. "They hate Jews and they drew a skull and crossbones on their save-the-date calendar."

"Maybe," said Monk.

"What do you mean, maybe?" I asked.

"According to the parents, these boys are motivated by revenge and spite. Do they even know the Greenbergs?"

"It's a Jewish name," I said.

"I know. But this was carefully planned, whatever it is, not some random hate crime."

"So, what now, Monk?" said the captain. "We just stand here until you figure it out?"

"Yes, that's pretty much what I do."

"Well, we can't afford to wait." The captain obeyed the arrow on the sign, hurrying down the hall on the left toward Ballroom C. Monk and I were right behind him. The weight of the Glock and its full clip rubbed against my hip.

As we came closer, we could hear the commotion. It was the good kind of commotion, made up of singing and music and shouts of laughter. What a relief. And then, just as we arrived at the double wood-paneled doors, the good commotion was overshadowed by the sound of a crash. Something breaking, like glass and wood. A few screams. A few more shouts and screams. Then the music stopped.

"Captain, I'm still not sure—"

The captain used his good arm to take out his cell phone and toss it at Monk. "Call for backup and nine-one-one. Both." He used the same good arm to take out his Beretta.

"Captain . . ."

"Now, Monk. You ready, Teeger?"

"Yes, sir." The gun was out of my trench coat in a second and I was following the captain through the unlocked doors. So far we'd heard no shots. That was good, I thought.

The banquet room was crowded and in total confusion, with a well-dressed crowd shouting and pointing and trying to get a better view amid the chaos. We only succeeded in adding to the confusion—two strangers in civilian garb, one with an arm sling, one in a stylish trench coat, their weapons pointed down and held tight to the body, textbook-style.

I don't know how we got to the center of the action so quickly. The guns might have had something to do with it. Small shards of mirror crunched under our feet as we came closer. Someone, a woman, raised her voice, calling for a doctor. A half dozen doctors, at least, raised their hands and began to crowd forward. They stopped when they saw us and the guns. A few screamed.

In the middle of the huge room, under the broken remains of a half-hanging mirror ball, were two teenage boys sprawled on the parquet floor. They wore matching white dress shirts and ties and could have been twins. They probably were.

"Police," shouted the captain. "Is everyone all right?"

"We don't need the police. We need a doctor," shouted the same woman. Again, a half dozen people, maybe more, surged their way forward. This time, they weren't deterred by the man in the sling and the woman in the trench coat. The boys on the floor were moving now. One of them even managed a weak laugh. Two banquet hall chairs, one with a broken leg, were sprawled beside them. For the first time since entering, I realized something was terribly wrong—or rather wasn't terribly wrong.

"Will someone please tell me what happened?" the captain barked.

The information came from several sources all at once, but it wasn't hard to piece together. The coming-of-age ceremony had ended and the celebration begun. The bar mitzvah boys, Adam and Andrew Greenberg, had been participating in the hora, a dance involving chairs held aloft by a throng of friends and family. The boys had been in the chairs at the time, waving with the music and laughing, and—here's where the stories differed, but only slightly—somehow in all the excitement, they and the chairs and the mirror ball, which should never have been hanging so dangerously low, had all managed to collide. It had been traumatic, of course, but nothing compared to the nightmare of a couple of neo-Nazis with handguns.

Two internists and a cardiologist were checking for blood

and broken bones, while a representative from Tuscany Pines finally arrived to deal with the damage and the interrupted party. Several lawyers in the crowd were in the process of canceling their day off and starting to take statements. We managed to escape questioning by the uncle of the twins who was demanding to see identification and get a written statement on what we'd witnessed.

"Where's Monk?" asked the captain. We had put away our weapons and were letting ourselves be pushed toward the door.

"The last thing I saw, you were telling him to call nine-one-one."

"Shoot." Stottlemeyer and I stumbled out into the hallway. "Something else to deal with. Monk!"

"He wasn't enthusiastic about this lead," I said, looking around. "Adrian!"

We quickly made our way back to the lobby and there he was, glancing between the closed restaurant and the other two signs. He didn't ask any questions about our adventure, just handed the captain his phone. "I didn't call."

"Monk!" The captain's voice held a strange combination of anger and relief. "When I tell you to call for backup, do it. It's the chain of command. What if there'd been a mass shooting? Every second counts."

"But there wasn't."

"There wasn't." The captain sighed. "Thank you. You were right. I should have listened."

"What was it?" Monk asked.

"It was a hora accident," I told him.

"Horror?"

"No. Hora, the Jewish dance. Never mind. Where are the Willmott boys?"

"I checked with Lieutenant Thurman," said Monk. "As far as he knows, they're still in the building."

"But where?" asked the captain. "They're obviously not after me, not unless they're three steps ahead of us and led us here on purpose."

"Those two?" Monk scoffed. "They're not three steps ahead of anybody. My guess is they're here for their cousin's wedding."

"What cousin?" I asked.

Monk pointed to the freestanding sign and reminded us. "Olivia Bowersox-Willmott. That's how she introduced herself. The family's other nephew, she said, was getting married this weekend to an Italian girl whose Italian last name I'll wager is Castello."

There it had been, right in front of us. Bowersox-Castello Wedding. Ballroom A. "I should have seen it when we walked in," said Monk. "I don't know how I missed it."

"You were distracted," said Stottlemeyer. "Sorry, buddy."

The captain took a second to check in with A.J., still working backup in the parking lot. "Stay put, that's an order," he argued as we started down the Tuscany Pines' other wing. "We're fine. Just had a little delay."

As we approached Ballroom A, we could hear the live music coming from behind the double doors. "Don't Stop Believin'" by Journey, which I suspect is a fairly popular wedding song, although, for pure energy, I think I'd go with the hora.

The captain stopped, undecided about pulling his weapon this time. I was skittish, too. "What do you think, Monk?"

"You should ask them about the wedding gifts. Where are they?"

"Wedding gifts?" The captain laughed. "You think our skinheads are here to steal the happy couple's blenders?"

"As far as we know, the skinheads only have two hand-guns. If they were preparing to shoot up a ballroom, they would have brought more power. Plus, in my personal opinion, they're not killers. They're spiteful and sick. Seven years ago they had a chance to shoot you. They didn't."

Stottlemeyer thought it over. Behind the doors, we could hear the band switch over to "The Wind Beneath My Wings." "Okay, Monk. We'll do it your way."

Our entrance into Ballroom A was much more subdued. There was no dancing with chairs, no broken mirror ball, no guns. And, more important, not a neo-Nazi in sight. There were just a hundred or so guests dawdling over drinks and wedding cake. The bride and groom were on the floor, slow-dancing photogenically while an exhausted photographer balanced on one knee, still doing his job.

I found the Bowersox-Castello crowd to be an interesting mix of old San Francisco and old-school Italian. Pacific Heights meets North Beach. Each side kept pretty much to itself. The team colors made it fairly evident, beige and taste-ful pastels on one side and bolder, more vibrant hues on the other.

"No gift table," said Monk. "Do you see a gift table?"

"They often keep them separate," I said. "Let's try not to cause a panic."

Since I'd previously met Ben and Olivia Willmott and had a few more people skills than my partner, I was the one enlisted to get the information. I spotted Olivia. She had crossed the border to join a pair of her new in-laws, women approximately her own age and just as concerned, in their own way, with the subtleties of makeup and hair.

"Ms. Teeger." She remembered me almost instantly and her face went ashen. "What's wrong?" She excused herself and we stepped a few feet away.

"Nothing's wrong. We just need to speak to Colin and Marshal. You had mentioned the wedding today and I was wondering if they were here."

"Here? God forbid. If they're not in the basement . . . It's not our responsibility."

"It's not important," I said, and wracked my brain for a new approach. Why don't I ever think these things through? "Mr. Monk and I brought a little present for the happy couple."

"Oh." She was taken aback. "That wasn't necessary."

"It's our pleasure."

"But you don't even know them. I'm sure they'd love to meet you. Why don't I introduce you?"

"No, we don't have time. Is there a space for wedding gifts? We'll just add it to the pile."

"Uh, yes." She pointed toward the double doors. "I believe if you go out, there's a room across the hall. Be sure to leave a card mentioning the gift and your names. We'll try our best to get Monica to write real thank-you notes. But you know kids."

"I do. When my daughter gets married, knock wood, I'll be lucky if she doesn't send out a mass e-mail. 'Dear everyone, thanks a bunch.' Or worse, set up a Twitter feed where everyone can comment on the other people's gifts."

Olivia chuckled, and I wondered whether it had crossed her mind that she might not ever have this moment, seeing her only child get married with a hundred loved ones toasting the young couple's future. "Are you sure you don't want me to introduce you?" she asked. "They're really a lovely couple."

"No, we have to go. We'll just drop off the gift."

"I think the room is locked. Why don't I get my husband to get a guard or an usher—"

"No need to disturb him," I said quickly. "We'll ask a guard ourselves."

As I walked away, I could feel Olivia's eyes following me. Monk and the captain were waiting impatiently by the door, but I refused to look hurried. "Across the hall," I whispered. I was going to warn Adrian not to wave to Olivia or draw attention to himself. But he'd never do that in the first place.

The room across the hallway had probably been built for this purpose, to discreetly hold the wedding booty. In a way, it was comforting to see that the old traditions had not been completely replaced by gift registries and e-commerce and UPS delivery.

There was no sound, not a peep, coming through the thick single door. The captain pulled his ear away and inspected the sturdiness. It was a traditional lock and key system, in keeping with the old-world pretense of the Tuscany Pines. "I could probably take my shoulder to it," he whispered, shrugging his sling. "Under normal circumstances."

"Why don't I get a guard with a key?" I whispered.

"It's not locked," Monk whispered. He motioned us all

down to the lock level and he pointed out the signs. "Someone used a set of picks. Amateur job. You can see the scratches."

"That doesn't mean it's unlocked now," I whispered back.

"Dead bolt." Monk mouthed the word. And sure enough, no dead bolt was visible in the crack between the door and the doorjamb. From inside the room came a muffled sound, like something falling over. "The idiots didn't even relock it."

The captain and I drew our weapons. "Odds are it's just a robbery," he reminded us. "Nobody be a hero." And we stood to the side—the captain to the left, me to the right—as Adrian turned the knob and threw open the door.

CHAPTER TWENTY-FOUR

Mr. Monk and the Money Tree

Our first sight was of the young neo-Nazis, all in black, rolling on the parquet floor. They were snatching bills off a fallen tree made out of wire—twenty-dollar bills, one-hundred-dollar bills—and laughing under their breath like kids. I won't say it was the strangest sight ever, but it's not something you see every day.

Much later, when I had time to think and Google a few things, I would realize that this was a money tree, an old Sicilian tradition in which wedding guests pin money to a tree symbolizing good fortune. It might seem tacky, but I suppose it's no different from slipping the groom a check in a plain white envelope, or buying the couple a house in Pacific Heights.

The rest of the room reminded me of Christmas morning, a Christmas morning where two home invaders got there first, tore open most of the smaller, easier-to-carry presents, and stuffed them into four camouflage duffel bags.

As soon as Colin and Marshal saw us, they froze. Then they dropped the bills and rolled sideways toward the open backpack on the floor. "Police," barked the captain. "Hands up. Stand up. Now."

"You heard him," I added in my toughest voice. My Glock was trained on Marshal; Stottlemeyer's Beretta on Colin. I only knew which was which because of the tattoos.

The young men stopped rolling five feet away from the backpack and the handguns inside it. "Stand up," the captain reminded them. "Hands behind your heads."

They did as they were told, not saying a word, just glaring. With their arms up and their fingers laced, the scars, the fresh red lacerations on their necks and arms, almost glowed. Monk closed the door behind us and refused to look their way.

Colin was the first to speak, his eyes boring into the captain's. "You're the scumbag who arrested us. What is this, a damn vendetta? Following us around? What are you, the only cop in town?"

"Sometimes it feels that way," said Stottlemeyer.

"All because of a couple pieces of silver," snarled Marshal. "Like a friggin' Judas."

"Just doing my job." The captain kept his voice calm and even, but I could see that he was thrown. The last time he'd seen them, they'd been a pair of demented, clean-cut high schoolers with their whole lives in front of them.

"Doing your job, hell," said Colin. "The other cops were fine. But you had to keep nosing around. And now look. The second we get out of the joint. Unbelievable."

"It's persecution," chimed in Marshal.

"You're profiling us because of our political beliefs."

"Typical Jew-run system."

"Colin? Son . . . ?"

While we'd all been occupied, the door had opened. Olivia Willmott stood there in her flowery dress and little white hat.

"What are you boys doing?" It was more of a gasp than a question. Olivia closed the door behind her and glanced around, taking in the torn-open boxes and the strewn gift wrapping and the half-naked money tree.

"Mom, get out of here."

"You're stealing from George's wedding? Your own cousin?"

"Yeah," said Marshal. "And by the way, thanks for the invite."

"Who in the world steals wedding gifts?" Olivia went on. "Is that what you learned in prison? What are we going to say to the guests? Did you stop to think of that?" The woman had a lot of questions.

"We're not going to say anything. We'll be in Mexico."

"It serves them right," said Colin.

"Really, Colin? What did George ever do to you? What did any of us do? Your father and I devoted our entire lives—"

"Mrs. Willmott. My name is Captain Stottlemeyer, SFPD." The captain was trying to regain some control of the situation.

"Stottlemeyer?" Olivia seemed to see him for the first time. "Oh, I know who you are. You're the son of a bitch who sent my boy to prison."

"Mrs. Willmott, I'm going to have to ask you to step back."

"And Natalie." Suddenly I felt self-conscious about keeping my weapon out and pointed. "You were a guest in our house. Then you come here and crash a wedding and lie about bringing a wedding gift?"

Monk looked confused. "We brought a wedding gift? We don't even know them."

"No, Adrian."

"Did you put my name on the card?"

"Monk!" Stottlemeyer tried again. "Mrs. Willmott, I'm asking you to step to one side. Monk, I've got a couple sets of zip-tie handcuffs in my right jacket pocket. Take them out for me."

"Can't Natalie do it?"

"Natalie's busy. C'mon, buddy. There's nothing else in the pocket. Not even lint bunnies, I swear. You can do it." As he was saying this, I actually was busy, moving to the right, positioning myself between the cousins and the open backpack.

"Are they going back to jail?" asked Olivia. Her hand went to her throat. "No, please. They just got out. It's not fair."

"That's not my call," said the captain. "Monk? If I had two good arms, I'd do it myself."

"Was the jacket recently dry-cleaned?" Monk reached a hand toward the captain's right pocket, then drew it back. "It's important that I know."

"The jacket's clean. We need to get these guys in cuffs." The captain shifted his footing, still keeping Colin in his sights. "Mrs. Willmott, please. Step back."

"Colin's not a bad boy." She was pleading now, inching closer toward her son. "It's all Marshal. He's the one."

"Aunt Olivia," protested the nephew skinhead. "That's cold."

"It's true. Colin's your puppet."

Colin bristled. "I'm no one's puppet, bitch."

"Do not talk that way to your mother." Olivia was within arm's reach now. "You know better."

"I'm no one's puppet."

"You tell her." Marshal's eyes wavered. He was eyeing

something on the floor, but in the confusion of gift boxes and wrapping paper, I couldn't see.

"Step away, ma'am." The captain moved sideways, trying to keep his shot clear. "Monk, the zip ties. Do it now."

"Okay." Monk was gearing himself up. "Let me count to three. One, two . . ."

The rest happened in an instant. Stottlemeyer shifted his hands; Monk went for the jacket pocket, squinting and twitching, as if about to stick his hand into a jar of scorpions; I tried to keep my gun trained on Marshal, who was edging away. And Colin took advantage of the moment, grabbing his mother by the arm, pulling her straight into him.

Olivia Willmott screamed, not a loud scream. But it was distraction enough to let Marshal dive for something on the floor, something with a black handle, and toss it up to his cousin. Colin had both arms around his mother, but he managed to catch the black handle in his right hand. He saw what it was and he almost giggled at the sight. In one motion he removed the plastic sheath, tossed it aside, and spun his mother around. She put up next to no resistance.

They were in the typical hostage pose, facing us, the son behind the mother, his one arm draped across her shoulder and his other holding a knife—a good-quality kitchen knife with a long, narrow blade—across her throat. It had happened so quickly, neither the captain nor I could have risked a shot.

"Put down the knife," said the captain. "This doesn't have to end in jail."

"That's what you said last time," said Colin. "How about you put down your guns?"

"Not gonna happen." Stottlemeyer shot me a quick glance and I knew. Keeping guns away from them would be a high priority. He'd been through this same scenario seven years ago. It had worked that time. He'd managed to talk them down, promising them who-knows-what. Leniency from an understanding judge? But this time . . .

Before Marshal could think of it, I walked over to the backpack and, with my free hand, grabbed it by a strap and slid it across the floor. "No guns for you," I said, and went back to my two-handed stance, feet spread, knees flexed.

"Sorry, bro," said Marshal. He retreated behind his cousin, making his aunt the biggest part of the trembling target.

"We're still good," said Colin, and he adjusted his arm and pressed the knife against his mother's neck. Olivia Willmott took in a quick, sharp breath. "Put down the guns or I kill her. Plain and simple."

Marshal laughed. "You'd kill your own mother? Bro!"

"Believe me, it would be a pleasure."

Olivia had the good sense to remain stiff and stoically silent.

"And then what?" asked the captain. "Kill her and you'll be back inside for life. Both of you."

"He's right," said Marshal from his place at the back of the pack. "If it was your dad instead, I'd say, 'Go for it.' If it was my dad, I'd say, 'Go for it twice.' If it was my mom—"

"Put down your weapons," Colin said. The captain shook his head. "I'll kill her—I'm serious." I couldn't imagine what was going through Olivia's mind. "You don't think I'm serious?"

"Colin, I know you're serious," said the captain. It was Hostage Negotiation 101. Don't provoke the hostage taker. "But it's not going to get you out of here."

"We'll just see." There was an emergency exit door behind them and Colin began dragging his mother slowly back. "Don't make me cut her." For a second he stumbled, then recovered. "Marshal, move your damn feet."

Marshal was the first at the door. He backed up against the push bar, but there was no alarm, just the door opening and the three Willmotts backing themselves out. The captain followed, with Adrian and me right behind.

Why wasn't Olivia struggling more? Was she in some way a willing hostage, willing to risk serious injury, maybe death in order to help her son escape? And if this was the case, what was our responsibility? Should we rush Colin and Marshal and risk it all? If we were pursuing them on a murder charge, maybe yes. But before they had grabbed Olivia, their only offense had been felony theft of wedding presents. All of this was going through my mind. I'm sure it was going through the captain's.

"Get the car," Colin ordered his cousin as they backed into the side parking lot of the Tuscany Pines.

"Damn," muttered Marshal. "Damn it to hell."

"What?"

"Keys. They're in the backpack."

"Why'd you leave them in the backpack?"

"You left them in the backpack, bro."

"Okay, okay, okay," mumbled Colin, thinking hard. The backpack was still in the room, out of play, behind the emergency exit door.

Every few seconds I would get a clear shot. But there were two of them. And the knife, still at Olivia's throat. And they were just mixed-up kids. And where the hell was Lieutenant A.J.? I looked around. Nowhere in sight. We had left him out here specifically for something unpredictable like this. The moron.

"Okay, Mr. Adrian Monk," said Colin. "We need your car."

Monk winced. "Why does everyone have to have a car? I do have a driver's license, but that's because I use it as ID and I don't have to take a test to renew it. If I had to take an actual driver's test . . ."

"Shut up," shouted Colin. "Okay, you. Captain. Your car keys. And don't tell me you don't drive."

"You can stop now," said Stottlemeyer calmly. "You don't have to make things worse."

"Car keys!" And the young skinhead readjusted the blade. Olivia cried out, a frightened little bleep of pain.

"Okay." The captain didn't lower his Beretta. "Monk. Left jacket pocket."

Every now and then, I catch a glimpse of the old Monk, the way he must have been before Trudy's death sent him down the rabbit hole of OCD dysfunction. This was one of those glimpses.

In a stream of deft, self-assured moves, Adrian reached into the captain's jacket, making sure not to endanger the delicate standoff. He pulled out the Buick key chain, held it high so the Willmott cousins could see, then pressed the unlock button. Just fifty yards across the parking lot was the captain's car, pointed out toward the exit, blinking its lights, ready to go. Adrian pressed again, just so Marshal could pinpoint the vehicle. Then he tossed the key chain in a perfect arc. Marshal stepped out from behind his human shields, catching it without having to stretch his arm.

"C'mon, Mom, let's go," said Colin. He took a quick glance behind him to his left and let the kitchen knife slack just a few inches off his mother's throat. He stepped back, putting a little air between mother and son. And that was the exact moment A.J. rounded the corner.

I don't know how much of it was dumb luck. My guess is a lot. A.J. had obviously been circling the perimeter of the sprawling facility, checking the exits, dealing with our periodic updates, and wondering why those periodic updates had stopped. He must have heard or seen something from just around the bend, because his attack was quick and a little chaotic.

On the run, the husky lieutenant assessed the situation, made a course correction, and barreled into Colin from the side. Colin's knees buckled and he collapsed. The kitchen knife went skittering across the asphalt. His mother fell to one side.

It took Monk and me several seconds to adjust. But Captain Stottlemeyer was right on it. With Colin safely under the weight of the homicide lieutenant, the captain re-aimed his Beretta on Marshal, still upright and suddenly exposed. The skinhead instantly raised his hands.

"What took you so long?" That was the captain's code phrase for thanks.

"Sorry," said A.J. "It's a big building." He was the first one to his feet, grabbing Colin by both arms and yanking him up. For the first time since we'd barged into the money tree room, I relaxed my grip on my Glock, handing it off to Monk and crossing over to where Olivia was still sprawled in an empty parking space.

"Mrs. Willmott? Are you all right?" She didn't answer.

Instead, she attacked.

I was within ten feet of her when this middle-aged mom with a red welt across her throat found the strength to push herself into a half crouch and ram right into me. The attack was wordless, with just an angry grunt of effort from her and a startled cry of pain as I lost balance and tumbled back on my keister, a straight, unbroken fall.

Before anyone could react, Olivia had turned and was focused on her next target. By now Lieutenant A.J. had brought Colin into a secure armlock and was just reaching for the handcuffs snapped into the leather loop on the back of his belt. A second later, Olivia was on him, all desperate determination.

"Run," she screamed. "Colin, run."

For probably the first time in a decade, Colin Willmott listened to his mother. So did Marshal. Both boys turned and began to run, swerving through the rows of parked cars. The rest of us picked ourselves up and gave chase. The captain's Buick beeped twice as Marshal, car keys in hand, followed the sound and flash, like a beacon to freedom. Every half second we could see a shaved head bob up above a car roof, Colin or Marshal. Impossible to tell. My worst fear was that a departing civilian—a wedding guest, a kid from the bar mitzvah—might get caught in the cross fire.

The lieutenant, his own sidearm now drawn, rounded the last bend. It was a straight shot to the Buick and an even straighter shot to Colin's back. For the first time in I don't know how long, the young officer raised his weapon and used it in the line of duty.

A single gunshot echoed across the field of cars and the nine-millimeter slug shattered an Audi taillight just inches from Colin's leg. The young man stopped, scared and undecided. The car was still twenty yards away. "The next one's in your back," shouted A.J.

There are departmental regulations against shooting an unarmed suspect in the back. I knew that. A.J. knew that. But, lucky for everyone, Colin didn't. He hesitated just enough to let Lieutenant Thurman catch up.

"It's over, kid," he said breathlessly.

Meanwhile the captain, one arm in his sling, one arm with his Beretta, was one row over, grunting with every stride as he gained ground on Marshal, who was almost into the car.

"Let my son go," screamed Olivia. She was on top of the lieutenant now, hitting him in the back and giving Colin the chance he needed to run again toward his cousin and the getaway car. From my spot one row farther away, I could hear the Buick's door slam shut. The engine turned over.

And then the explosion, deafening and percussive.

A yellow-and-red fireball engulfed the captain's car and threw everyone else back and to the ground.

CHAPTER TWENTY-FIVE

Mr. Monk Can't Listen

We were lucky, all things considered. Everyone except Marshal.

Monk and I did not have to be hospitalized. We were examined in one of the emergency response vehicles that came whizzing down the 101 and were released with nothing worse than hearing loss—temporary, they assured us—and a persistent ringing in the ears. It seemed illogical to have both hearing loss and ringing in the ears, but that's how it was, believe me. I was prescribed a Xanax to help with the anxiety and the ringing, but Monk refused. He thought it might turn him into a pill-popping drug addict, reduced to selling himself on street corners for another fix. He might have actually said those words, but luckily I couldn't hear.

My only permanent loss was the PBS tote, which I'd left on the captain's front seat.

Next on the lucky spectrum was A.J. Thurman. He'd been one row and a few vehicles closer. He had our hearing loss plus a laceration on the upper left leg, his good leg, from a piece of flying Buick. It might leave a scar, the doctor advised, which A.J. would probably be bragging about for the next twenty years sitting on a stool in his favorite cop bar.

Olivia Willmott had a similar shrapnel wound to her left arm. The main damage she suffered would be the wounds that no one could see and that might never heal.

Colin Willmott was in the lockdown ward 7D/7L at San Francisco General. He had received two broken ribs and a punctured lung. Recovery time was estimated at eight weeks, but he would be indicted well before then, as soon as the DA could figure out the precise charges. This time a full regiment of Willmott family lawyers would probably be playing defense.

Leland Stottlemeyer had been approximately forty feet from the explosion, and had been running toward it before he was blown back by the force. He wound up on his regular floor of SF General just down the hall from his previous two rooms, this time with a fracture to his tailbone, or coccyx, a word I had only previously known from playing Scrabble. It would keep him off his feet for some time, but the doctors were predicting a full recovery. Despite this, the captain was probably the luckiest of us all, since he'd managed to avoid being in his car when the bomb meant for him was detonated.

At the far end of the lucky spectrum was Marshal Willmott—who was dead.

My plans for that evening were low-key, as you might imagine. Monk and I stayed with the captain until Trudy Stottlemeyer made her way back from her sister's place in Santa Cruz. We filled her in on the situation, trying to make it sound like no big deal.

"Who could possibly hate my husband this much?" she shouted over the deaf ringing in my ears.

"WE HAVE NO IDEA," I shouted back. "I'M SORRY."

"Someone tried to kill him three times. You'd think he'd at least have an idea."

"WE DID HAVE AN IDEA. WE WERE WRONG."

It's hard to carry on a serious, sympathetic conversation when you're shouting back and forth. I stayed a few more minutes, helping Trudy set up camp in yet another armchair beside yet another hospital bed. Then I called my daughter and yelled at her.

I'm not sure she understood much of it, other than I LOVE YOU, I LOVE YOU, I LOVE YOU. I certainly didn't hear much from her end, even with the phone's volume turned up. Being a budding detective, she sensed something might be wrong and shouted that she would meet me back at my cozy house in my cozy neighborhood of Noe Valley.

Monk's part-time babysitter, Luther Washington, met us by the emergency room doors and took Adrian off my hands. The last thing I saw before I crossed away to my old Subaru was Adrian using his skills in American Sign Language to communicate with Luther about his plans for the evening. Adrian had memorized the manual alphabet and a few hundred signs, just in case of an emergency like this. Unfortunately, Luther hadn't.

As soon as I pulled into my driveway, Julie came running out. "MOM, ARE YOU OKAY?" she shouted, then took me by the arm and began to gently guide me toward the porch. "THIS WAY."

"I CAN SEE FINE. IT'S MY HEARING."

"WELL, I DIDN'T KNOW. WHAT HAPPENED?"

"WHAT?"

"WHAT HAPPENED?"

I know it doesn't make sense that I was shouting. But it's hard not to shout when you can barely hear your own voice, only the insanely loud ringing in your ears.

Randy must have heard the commotion, because he also came running and said a few things I couldn't hear. He looked better than he had that morning, well on his way to recovery, although Julie and I still gave him and his germs a wide berth.

I don't know about you, but witnessing a murder and narrowly escaping death gives me an appetite. Julie had anticipated this by picking up pizzas—a large with pepperoni and mushrooms, a small meat-lovers for Randy, and three side salads, which was our way of trying to eat healthier.

Dinner was quick and comparatively wordless. I could tell they were dying to hear the story. So, after we dumped the dishes in the sink, I brought my laptop out to the living room, they brought out their smartphones, and all of us sat around with glasses of Chardonnay and e-mailed back and forth in glowing, electronic silence.

I started by outlining the afternoon's events, letting my fingers fly and ignoring anything like sentence structure. I also ignored the red squiggles that popped up under my endless misspellings. It took a few minutes, but I sent off my first e-mail and watched their expressions as they read it. Both of them looked suitably horrified and concerned.

"RU sure UR OK?" e-mailed Julie. "How about Adrian? OK?"

"I'm fine," I mouthed from across the room. I still couldn't speak without shouting and my voice had become hoarse from the effort. "Adrian's fine."

"Was it A.J.'s fault?" typed Randy.

While waiting in the ER, I had given this idea some thought. "I'd love to say yes, but I don't think so. The captain left A.J. outside with no instructions except to stay in touch and watch for the cousins. The parking lot goes around the building with a dozen exits. He couldn't be expected to keep an eye on everyone's car."

"What do U think?" wrote Julie on her phone. "Killer followed captain from home? Had bomb? Planted bomb?"

Yes. I nodded half apologetically from across the room. Then I typed. "Big mistake for the captain to leave his house. At least we know it wasn't the Willmott skinheads."

Randy frowned. "RU sure it's not them?"

"Sure I'm sure. You think the boys knew we were tailing them and rigged the car and proceeded to blow themselves up?"

Randy shrugged. "Suicide by exploding cop car. I've heard of that."

"You have not heard of that, Randy. No one's heard of that." I actually said those words aloud. Without shouting. I must have been getting better. Perhaps it was the combination of the pepperoni and the Chardonnay and the leftover Xanax in my system.

"Can you hear me now?" asked Julie at a normal-ish volume.

"It's better," I said, again not shouting.

We all turned away from our screens and gathered around the coffee table, with Randy still keeping a germ's throw away. Julie hugged me tightly and I hugged back. "Much better," I said.

"When you called and started shouting, I got so worried." If I looked at her mouth when she spoke, it was easier.

"I know, honey. I'm sorry. But now you know how I feel. If you came to work with Monk and me, I don't think I could take it."

"No, it's just the opposite. If I was working with you, knowing what's going on and having your back, it would be so much better."

"For you, maybe."

"Yes, for me. Is that wrong?"

I didn't have a good answer for that. And I respected my daughter enough not to give her a bad one. "We'll talk about this later."

"Fine."

An awkward silence fell over the room. It was finally broken by a fake, exaggerated yawn. "Awwwh!" Randy Disher vocalized, stretching his arms wide for emphasis. "Time for me to get back to bed." He pushed himself to his feet. "Don't worry about me. You gals can talk as long and as loud as you want. It won't bother me. Not that I'm going to be listening. I'm going to be sleeping, that's what I meant."

"Good night, Randy," I said. And I blew him a kiss.

Julie and I sat up for another hour, until the aches and exhaustion of the day caught up with me. Julie asked if she could spend the night. I said yes and resisted offering her the other half of my queen-sized bed, just to keep her close. Instead, I helped her pull out the couch and grab the sheets from the linen closet.

I thought sleep would come instantly that night, but it didn't. I couldn't stop thinking about Olivia. As much as she'd wanted to abandon her once-golden son to his own choices, she couldn't. What mother could? And yet the result of her meddling had been so much worse. From the moment she'd walked in and allowed herself to be taken hostage, things escalated. Now she had the memory of her son holding the point of a knife to her throat. Plus the sight of her nephew being blown up in a fireball. And the nightmare for her wasn't over. Lawyers and publicity and family grief all lurked on the horizon.

I broke down and took another Xanax. When finally I drifted off, I think I dreamed about Julie, about trying so hard to protect her from something. A monster? And what made it harder was that she was trying to protect me from the same monster. I woke up the next morning with no clear memory. Only a feeling of frustration that was impossible to shake.

CHAPTER TWENTY-SIX

Mr. Monk Finally Listens

One nice thing about nearly being blown to bits on a Saturday afternoon is that you can take all day Sunday to recover.

Just getting out of bed helped me shake off the dream. I washed my face, made sure I had a nightgown on, and followed my nose out to the kitchen. Julie and Randy were putting the final touches on my favorite pancakes, with perfectly curled strips of bacon for the smiles and slices of strawberries for the eyes. From the crusty mouth to the bloodred eyes, it seemed a remarkable portrait of my current state.

"HOW ARE YOU?" asked Randy.

"Hungry," I whispered back.

"CAN YOU HEAR ME? NOD IF YOU CAN HEAR ME."

"Yes, I can hear you. It's much better."

"YOU'RE NOT NODDING."

"Sorry." I nodded, thanked them for the breakfast, and poured myself some coffee. A half hour and three grinning pancakes later, I was almost ready to face the day.

"You going to be okay by yourself?" asked Julie. Just hearing her say that made me feel a hundred percent better. I assured her I was fine and that I would be staying close to home, a promise made easy since my car was still in the parking lot at Tuscany Pines.

Randy had plans to visit the captain in the hospital, then spend time with the old garage band he'd played with on and off for the past twenty years.

"I miss jamming and being one of the guys," he said, wiping away the last vestiges of his runny nose. "That's one thing you don't get when you're chief of police. Hanging with your buds. Making jokes. Not being ridiculed month after month for arresting the mayor just once."

"Randy!"

"I know, I know. I have to stick it out."

Neither one volunteered to clean up the breakfast mess before leaving, but I didn't mind. It was nice spending a day at home, with just the ringing in my ears for company. I read the paper, focusing on the comics and the horoscope and avoiding the front-page news about the car bomb. I watched two episodes of *Game of Thrones*. I Googled tinnitus, the medical name for ringing of the ears, and grew anxious over the possibility of it never going away. For some people it doesn't.

After my afternoon nap, an old Subaru just like mine pulled up at the curb followed by a patrol car. Officer Joe Nazio came to the door and handed me the keys. I invited him in, but he couldn't stay. "I'm assigned to the forensics bomb squad. We're just cleaning up. Hope to get some of Sunday off."

"Sure," I said. "Do you have any leads? Size and placement of the bomb? Triggering mechanism?" I could see him eyeing his watch. "Joe, please. I was there."

"You're right," he said.

Joe didn't stay long, maybe five minutes, not that there was much to tell. The device had been magnetically attached under the chassis, not far from the gas tank. It had been equipped with a tilt fuse, which was activated by the vibration of the car starting up. "It depends on your luck," said Joe. "Sometimes a tilt fuse will detonate when you slam the door, sometimes when you go over your first bump."

"It doesn't sound very sophisticated," I said.

"It's not. You can build one by going online. You just have to be careful not to set the fuse before the bomb's in place."

"So it was set in the parking lot."

"Absolutely. Just bad luck he didn't get seen."

Joe promised to keep us in the loop. But, being consultants, we were already part of the loop. "Go home, Joe," I said. "It's Sunday. Hug your family."

By the end of my afternoon, I had watched two more episodes of *Game of Thrones* and come to the conclusion that the show needed less female nudity and more dragons. The only other interruption was a call from Daniela Grace. It was around six p.m., right as I was scouring the back of the freezer, trying to decide between two containers of frozen brown leftovers. I sighed. But I knew there would be no better time to take the call.

"Daniela, hi. Sorry to be calling so late on a Sunday."

"You're not calling me. I'm calling . . . Oh, I get it. Humor."

"I should have tracked you down before leaving your office. My fault. No excuse. We interviewed everyone who had access to the IPO information and we came up blank, I'm afraid. But we're still working. We haven't given up."

"Natalie, I'm not an idiot. I watch the news. It seems you two had plenty of time to attend a wedding reception."

"Wedding? That was a murder case. We were almost blown up."

"You don't have to shout, dear."

"I'm sorry. I'm just getting over temporary deafness—you know, from almost getting blown up."

"Still shouting."

"That was for emphasis. Daniela, I'll talk with Adrian first thing tomorrow and give you a call. I promise. I know you're on a deadline and there's still a leak. We'll do our best." Somehow I managed to say good-bye and hang up.

That night I got to bed right after the news—not the eleven o'clock news, the six-thirty news. The next morning, I was almost back to normal, just a steady little tone in my ears that I could ignore if I hummed the opening notes to "Somewhere Over the Rainbow," just the first four words, over and over. It seemed to be in the same key as my hum.

It was early, only a little after nine, when I pulled into the strip mall. I was surprised to see the lights on and a black Lincoln Town Car in my space. Adrian and Luther were there. As I parked beside the Lincoln, I realized that one of them was shouting. "YOU HAVE TO CLEAN BETWEEN THE CRACKS. OTHERWISE DUST WILL BUILD UP AND SPLIT THE WOOD. THAT'S JUST SCIENCE."

"Huh. I bet that takes like a thousand years," said a more normally regulated voice.

"STOP YOUR MUMBLING."

"Adrian?" I walked in to find Monk vigorously polishing

the wood surface of his desk. Luther stood beside him in his black chauffeur-style suit. "What's the matter?" I asked.

My partner looked at me. "I'M SHOUTING SO I CAN HEAR MYSELF."

"ADRIAN, DON'T TALK. WRITE THINGS DOWN." I went to my desk and got a pencil and a pad.

"ALL NIGHT AND DAY! WHEN IS IT GOING TO STOP?"

"Whatever medication they gave him to calm down, he didn't take," explained Luther. "He's getting worse."

"NO PILLS!" Monk informed the surrounding two-block radius.

"OKAY, NO PILLS." I knew from experience that anxiety can build in situations like this and really affect you. "YOU NEED TO CALM DOWN." I handed him the pencil and pad. "WE'LL START WITH THE SHOUTING."

"Excuse me!" It was Peter Gerber, standing in our doorway, backed up by Wendy Gerber. They were both in baggy, tie-dyed T-shirts, and it was hard tell where one ended and the other began, like a herd of hippie zebras on the Serengeti.

"Mr. Monk, I know you complain about our noise, but this is just mean." Gone was Wendy's sweet, forgiving, live-and-let-live demeanor. "Peter plays very softly. You don't have to re-taliate by screaming like Godzilla." Then she caught sight of Luther. "Oh, you. Clyde or Luther or whatever."

"Hey there," said Luther, with the wave of a hand and the hint of a grin. "The poster worked out great. Did exactly what we wanted."

"We know," said Wendy.

"Hey, hardly anyone saw it."

"We saw it," said Wendy. "It affected Peter's aura for days. It was nearly black."

Peter bit his lip and shook his head. "Is this shouting another one of your pranks? Does it make you feel good, huh? Bullying a couple of pacifists."

"I ought to punch you in the nose," said Wendy, looking like she meant it.

"WHAT DID THEY SAY?"

"ADRIAN, WRITE THINGS DOWN." I pointed to the pad. "PLEASE."

"What's wrong with him?" asked Peter.

"It's not on purpose," I assured them. "Adrian's been through a concussion."

"Oh." Wendy blinked, a little embarrassed. "So this isn't some kind of getting even?"

"I don't believe them," said Peter.

"It's true," said Luther. "He was right near that car bomb. You must have heard about it."

"We did hear." Peter seemed unconvinced, especially since the information was coming from the man who commissioned the hip replacement poster.

"He needs to take his medication," I added.

"WHAT? MEDITATION?" Monk shouted.

"Meditation?" said Wendy, her face brightening a bit. "We can help with his meditation. We meditate all the time."

"No," I said. "No meditation." I couldn't imagine anything making Monk more nervous than engaging in gratuitous meditation with his hippie neighbors.

"It will relax him," promised Wendy. "Calming him will go a long way. Look at the poor man's aura. It's reddish purple."

"They're just going to make fun of us," said Peter, motioning toward the door. "We should get back to work."

Wendy smiled sweetly. "There's always time to do a session with someone in need. Natalie, what do you think his weakest chakra is?"

"My guess is they're all equally weak."

"It doesn't matter. I'll get the mats. Do you guys have incense, or should I bring some back?" She was almost bubbly again.

Wendy was just heading out the door when she happened to glance over to my desk, more exactly the wall above my desk. It was one of those chance things, a glance out of the corner of her eye. But it was enough to stop her in her tracks. "Who is that?" She was pointing to the bleary security photo of Sue Puskedra O'Brien that I'd re-taped behind my monitor.

"I don't know who it is," I said. "Do you?"

"You don't know? You put up her picture." It sounded almost like an accusation. Peter joined her, both of them tiptoeing up to the image, as if it were about to bite them— or disappear.

"This just beats all," said Peter. "You guys have no shame."

"Do you know her?" I asked. "She told me her name was Sue or Suzanne."

"Go ask your prankster friends," said Peter, pointing an accusing finger at Monk and Luther. "They'll tell you all about Sue—or Marjorie—or whatever else she calls herself."

"Adrian?" The Gerbers looked so offended, it was hard to doubt them. "Is this true? Do you know her?"

"WHAT?" Monk replied.

"Know who?" Luther asked. He joined the tie-dyed couple at my desk. "Crappy picture. But I've never seen her."

"She wasn't part of your prank?" asked Wendy.

"What prank? Mr. Monk and I only did one, which was pretty funny and awesome if you ask me."

"Did you ever meet this woman?" I asked. "Wendy, this is important."

Wendy rolled her eyes but gave me the benefit of the doubt. "Okay. She came in last Thursday. Marjorie Mapplethorpe. I should have known by the fake name. Made us drop everything with some sad story about her little consignment shop and how desperate she was for business. We wasted an hour with her on a four-color newspaper ad. She never paid and she never picked up the file."

"A sweet prank," said Peter. "Just like your others. We tried tracking down Marjorie Mapplethorpe, but her e-mail was fake. Her phone number was fake."

"No such person exists," I guessed.

"Oh, she exists," said Peter. "You have her picture on your wall."

"No, honestly," I pleaded. "I got that from Al's security camera at the pawnshop. This woman did the same with me—walked in with a phony job and didn't pay."

Peter huffed, unconvinced. "Why would she do that?"

"We don't know. I grant you, she did exactly what Luther and Adrian did. But they have no connection to this woman, I promise."

"You'll forgive us if we don't believe you," said Peter, and he led his wife out the door.

I waited until they were safely in their own space, out of earshot. "Luther, please tell me you don't know her."

"I said I didn't. Man, this is some world when you don't trust your friends." Before I could apologize—not that I was going to, but before I could—Luther was checking his watch and walking out the door. "I got real customers and a real business to run. You guys have fun." Monk and I watched him drive off.

"YOU KNOW I DIDN'T HEAR ANYTHING, RIGHT?"

"ADRIAN, SHUT UP AND SIT DOWN."

"Yeah, shut up," came Peter's voice through the thin wall. He pounded it twice for emphasis.

Without another word, I managed to get Monk into his chair and wheeled it over to my desk. I adjusted the monitor so we both could see, created a Word document, and set the font size to fourteen, nice and large. Just for emphasis, I pressed a finger to my lips—shh—sat down, and started typing.

I could feel Monk wincing at every little typo, but that didn't stop me, or make me go back and self-correct. I just went with the flow and wrote down everything that had happened in the past five minutes, along with my own little opinions.

"WHERE WERE YOU ON THURSDAY?" he shouted right in my ear.

I yelped, jumped about a foot, then settled back and typed. "I was sitting at a bar waiting for Sue. DON'T SHOUT. I know. She lured me away so she could come here and pull her prank on the hippies. DON'T SHOUT. What a jerk. You were right about her. DON'T SHOUT."

Monk didn't shout any more. He just sat there behind my

shoulder, his brows furrowed, thinking. It was what he did best, the thing he felt most comfortable doing in the world. I could almost feel his nervous energy draining away.

I was just sitting there, deep in my own thoughts, when the office phone rang. I picked it up, just on reflex. "You said you'd call this morning, although I don't know why I expected you to."

"Daniela, hello. Adrian and I were just talking about your case." I put the phone on speaker, in case I needed to type something for Monk.

"Well, that's an unfortunate waste of time because you're fired."

"Fired?" I don't know why people repeat words that they've obviously heard. It may have something to do with shock or to give us time to process. "Did you say fired?"

"That's right, dear. We have that little retainer agreement we're going to let expire. It was a bad fit."

"No, it wasn't. Daniela, please." I won't say I've never been fired before (one bartending job, a waitress job, and a gig as the California Lottery Girl). But this was something I cared about.

"Your firm is young and small," Daniela went on. "Your first loyalty is to the police, I get that. Old ties. Life and death—blah, blah, blah. But it makes it hard for you to give me the dedication I need. I'm wondering how we ever got involved in the first place." Her laugh was light and cheery, as if she'd just told a joke.

I'll tell you how we got involved, I wanted to say. *Because Adrian caught you trying to kill someone and I talked him into giving you a pass.*

It was a painful conversation. Grace, Winters, and Weingart had been our first corporate client, our only one. We'd done good work for them and I was hoping they'd turn out to be a gateway to more clients and a higher profile. Instead it would be the opposite. Getting fired doesn't make for a good reference.

I did my best to argue my case, but of course it was too late. "How are you going to handle the leak in your office?"

"I made several calls this morning, the top notch, all with vast experience in corporate espionage, which is not your strong suit, I'm afraid. All except one said they could take us on immediately. Devote their top people today and guarantee results. I went with Elliot Brown. I'm having lunch with Elliot himself at the Fairmont at noon."

"Who turned you down?"

"Mr. Monk, is that you?"

It was indeed Mr. Monk. He was speaking at a normal volume and seemed to be able to hear just fine. "It's me," he confirmed into the speaker. "Adrian Monk."

"I'm sorry about the news, dearest one. But I had no choice. You should talk to Natalie about handling clients and returning calls."

"Don't blame Natalie. She's the very best"—he cleared his throat and I felt great for a second—"I can do, given the circumstances. You said all the firms except one were able to take your case. Which one wasn't?"

"I'm not sure what concern that is. But I'll check my notes." She paused, then came back on. "It's West Bay Investigators. They're supposed to be the best. Unfortunately, they were busy."

"Yes, they have a good reputation. So does Elliot Brown. You'll be in good hands. Sorry it didn't work out. I apologize for Natalie." Without another word, he started pressing buttons on the phone until he managed to disconnect the call.

"You apologize for Natalie?" I asked. "What was that about?"

"Those were just words. I wanted to hang up without her being mad." Monk opened his mouth wide and wiggled his jaw. "I'm feeling better, thanks for asking. There's still the ringing, but if I think about other things . . ."

I didn't care. I was so angry and hurt. "I can't believe Daniela fired us. Do you know how hard that makes it? No one's going to hire us but the police. And A.J. is cutting back our fees. He's also a Neanderthal jerk you can't work with. What are we going to do?"

"I can fix this."

"You? And how can you fix it?" I might have been close to tears. "How?"

"Natalie . . ." Monk looked me in the eyes, about to say something serious and heartfelt. Then he popped his jaw again and wiggled it. "I can't believe how much better I feel."

"You were going to say something. What?"

He closed his jaw. "I was going to say I haven't been the best partner. I know that. I make you responsible for everything and maybe I complain more than I should."

I was taken aback by what, for him, amounted to a full-throated apology. "Well, it's nice to hear you admit it."

"I'll make it up to you. I can fix this thing with Daniela."

"You? What are you going to do?"

"I'll take care of it. I know how. All I need you to do is be ready to have lunch today at noon. Can you do that? We'll be eating at the Fairmont Hotel."

"Where at the Fairmont? You mean the restaurant where Daniela's having lunch? Please don't say we're going there to blackmail her about her murder attempt. That would be cruel."

"I didn't even think of that. But no. Just leave it to me."

I wasn't so sure. "Does this involve Luther again? No more pranks with Luther. Promise?"

Monk promised.

CHAPTER TWENTY-SEVEN

Mr. Monk Takes Control

I left everything in Monk's hands.

Those might be the scariest six words I've ever written.

But scary doesn't always mean bad. Sure, there was the possibility of disaster, or of being led into a moment of embarrassment that would haunt my dreams. His OCD and/or his limited knowledge of human behavior might ruin our business in a dozen different ways. On the other hand, Adrian is the world's best at what he does, pulling sense out of a world of chaos. I could only hope this was one of those times. And, let's be honest, I had nowhere else to turn. That's what I meant by scary.

I did my part, going home, puttering around, changing into something presentable—a navy shirtdress, belted, with a turned-up collar—then picking up Monk and getting to the Fairmont. At a few minutes past noon, we walked through the lobby to the Laurel Court Restaurant, an immense circular room that's actually made up of several intersecting circles, with faux-marble pillars and domes and chandeliers and landscape murals on the curved walls.

Monk avoided the hostess station. "Do we have a reservation?" I whispered.

"Nope," he said, and began to look around, all the while humming the opening bars to "Somewhere Over the Rainbow."

"Why are you humming that?" I asked.

"Because you're humming it," he said.

"Oh." I had to pay attention and stop myself. "Sorry. Still some problem with the ringing ears."

"Mine's much better. You need to focus on something, Natalie. It's mind over matter."

The restaurant's multiple circles gave the illusion of openness while preserving a surprising amount of privacy. I followed Monk as he wandered from space to space and finally headed in one direction. I'd known Daniela was going to be there, but I didn't expect to see her alone at a table for two, nursing an iced tea and looking impatient.

"Natalie. Mr. Monk." She wasn't pleased. "I'm not about to change my mind. Elliot Brown is going to be here any moment and—"

"Elliot won't be here until twelve thirty," said Monk. "I had my assistant call and postpone your lunch."

"What assistant?" I blurted out. "It wasn't me. Daniela, I'm so sorry. I have no idea what he's doing."

"And yet you're here, enabling whatever nonsense he's up to."

"True. I suppose I trust him," I said. That was my excuse. "He's trusted me dozens of times—well, more than once. And I probably should trust him more often."

Monk smiled. "Have a seat, Natalie. We don't want Daniela uncomfortable." I lowered myself into the wingback chair opposite the steely-eyed lawyer. Monk remained standing between us, his eyes flitting out to the circles of the Laurel Court. "How is Booker Sessums, your paralegal?"

"Booker is fine. He's a hard worker and very loyal."

"He's quitting as soon as I solve this case. Going to another firm."

"Adrian," I hissed. "We promised to keep it secret."

"You know I can't keep a secret. Anyway, I'm solving the case right now, so he can leave."

"Booker?" Daniela looked stunned. "Are you saying the leak was Booker?"

"No," said Monk, eyes still flitting over my shoulder. Had he seen something? "It wasn't Booker or the guy in your finance department or the fourth-year associate who wants to be partner. I'll give you a hint. It's someone in this room. And I don't mean Natalie."

"What?" A ridge of lines popped up between Daniela's brows. Time for more Botox. "Are you accusing me, Mr. Monk? Are you saying I purposely sabotaged an IPO worth over a million to our firm? Unbelievable."

"Adrian? That's kind of far-fetched. Not that I don't trust you."

"Did I say Daniela? No, I think I said someone in this room." The fact that Monk was so bold and sure of himself was a good sign. He gets this way only when he's vacuuming or solving a case. "Under normal circumstances I'd just tell you. But my partner has a business to run."

I shrugged, trying to look helpless. "It's true, Daniela. We do have a business to run."

Daniela didn't know Monk the way I did. But she'd been

part of two cases. She knew something was up. Instinctively, she stood and glanced behind her, just in case the perpetrator might be obvious—like a Wall Street investor wearing a little burglar mask. Instead it looked just like the Laurel Court with a Monday lunch crowd.

"All right," she said, settling back down. "Our conversation this morning didn't happen. And Elliot Brown. He's not hired. And we'll renew your retainer, if this all pans out."

"And how about an apology to Natalie? For doubting her. She always makes me apologize."

"Let's not press our luck," I said, and held out my hand to Daniela. "Deal?"

"Deal," said Daniela, shaking the offered hand. "And if it makes him get to the point any faster, I do apologize."

"Deal," echoed Monk. "Let's go."

Just like that, we were all on our feet, crossing through the curves of the dining room, with Monk in the lead and at least two of us softly humming "Somewhere Over the Rainbow." Monk slowed as we rounded another bend and a table for two came into view. He stopped and we stopped. So did the humming.

A very attractive young woman in a business suit sat in a wingback chair facing us. My first reaction was that she was in her late twenties with too much makeup and an unflattering hairdo. My second reaction was that she was my daughter in disguise. "Julie?" I whispered.

"Julie, your daughter?" said Daniela. Her eyes went wide. "Your daughter is our spy? I take back the apology."

"Adrian?" I looked at him pleadingly. "What the hell does this mean? What is Julie doing here?"

"Do you trust me?" he asked.

"Yes, I trust you," I said. "But . . ."

"No buts."

Julie looked up from her iced tea, saw us, and allowed herself a smile. It was just a hint, but enough to make the person sitting opposite her stand up and turn.

It was Sue Suzanne Puskedra O'Brien, minus the open, warm smile and the infectious laugh. She did not look happy to see us.

"Sue?"

At first it seemed like she wanted to run. I could almost see the options going through her mind. How much danger was she actually in? What would be the consequences? And how fast could she go, given the maze of the restaurant and her four-inch heels?

"Her name is Claudia Collins," Monk informed us. "She's an investigator at West Bay. You know, the PI firm experienced in corporate espionage, the one too busy to consider your case? This is why they were too busy. They were working the other side."

"You can prosecute if you like," said Claudia/Sue/Suzanne, her voice even and cold. "But I'm not sure you want to, given the circumstances."

"That's not my call," said Monk. "My job was to track you down. You're down."

"I've never seen her before in my life," said Daniela. "How could she . . ."

"She was hired by the competition," said Monk. "I have no idea what these telephone applications do. But someone cared enough to try to disrupt your stock going on sale."

"My client's identity is confidential," said Claudia/Sue/Suzanne. Heck, I'll just call her Claudia.

"Every secret has a weak link," Monk explained. "And when Ms. Collins heard you were going to a commercial printer for your documents . . ."

"You mean . . . That's why you were hanging out in front of the mini-mall," I realized out loud. "It was Paisley Printing you were staring at, not Monk and Teeger."

"You came outside and invited me in." Claudia smiled, all teeth. "What was I going to say? I have a dozen business cards with aliases. I used the Sue O'Brien card and was lucky enough to remember Timothy from a divorce case we did for his firm six months ago. The fact that Timothy is gay and single didn't seem to be a problem."

"So you made it up? On the spur of the moment?" asked Julie. "All the stuff about the high-powered husband and the mistress?" My little girl sounded impressed.

"It wasn't hard," said Claudia, "especially when your target is sympathetic. Natalie practically did it for me. On my first visit, I checked for a Wi-Fi signal from the printing shop next door."

"I warned you about those thin-walled hippies," said Monk. "But no, you wouldn't listen."

"On my second visit, I got Natalie to leave me alone for half an hour. Altogether too trusting for someone who's supposed to be a trained investigator."

"You leave my mom out of this," said Julie. "She's twice the investigator you are."

"She's your mom?" Claudia looked back and forth between us and finally laughed. "Touché. I should have known by the fake name. Yamilla Applethorne, coming to me for a divorce. It beats the hell out of Sue Puskedra O'Brien."

"I used to know a girl named Yamilla Applethorne," Monk confided. "She looked quite a bit like Julie, just not as tall or thin or as attractive. She was also half-Hispanic."

Julie couldn't wait to tell her part of the story. "Adrian got in touch this morning and asked me to help. When I walked into West Bay about divorcing my husband, Trevor, I insisted they assign a woman to my case. I knew from the second I saw Claudia, she was the one. From your photo."

"Photo?" asked Claudia.

"Security camera," I explained to her. "From the pawn-shop."

"Of course." Claudia shook her head. "I should have been more careful."

A waiter tried to pass by with a tray full of salads and we all had to rearrange ourselves. Claudia settled back into her chair while the three of us spaced ourselves around the small circular table. On his way past us again, the waiter avoided us and wisely refrained from asking, "How is everything?"

Monk pulled a piece of scrap paper out of his jacket pocket. It was the page of cryptic codes he had rescued from my trash, the one I'd taped up beside Sue's photo: 0-0, 1-2, A-B, etc. "You were trying out passwords to get into their system. Being shiftless, drugged-out hippies, they probably used something simple."

Claudia smirked. "Their Wi-Fi signal was unprotected, and the password to their files was the most common in the world: "password." It took me thirty seconds, even with a weak signal."

"And a few days later," said Monk, "when you found out

they'd changed the documents, you couldn't go back to Natalie. So you sent her on a wild-goose chase and walked right into the hippies' lair."

"While they were mocking up my newspaper ad, I was ten feet away, downloading the new version of the IPO."

"Excuse me." Julie raised a timid hand, like a student in a criminal law class. "Did you just admit to a crime?"

"Don't get too excited. No one's going to prosecute," said Claudia.

"She's right," said Daniela. "Unfortunately."

Claudia smiled. "Grace, Winters, and Weingart would be admitting their negligence. So would Joyful App. And my God, Monk and Teeger? For them to admit corporate spying under their own roof? If this hits the news, it would hurt them much more than it would hurt me or my client."

"But that isn't fair," said Julie.

"Welcome to the world," said Claudia, still smiling.

"No, Julie, this is good. We can mitigate the damage," said Daniela. "As long as the leak is plugged, I can advise my client to proceed. The IPO isn't until Wednesday."

"No harm, no foul," agreed Claudia, turning up her palms in surrender. "I tried my best."

Julie couldn't understand any of this. And I couldn't have been prouder of her. "Wait. You're the one who did something wrong. Adrian and my mother . . ."

"Adrian and your mother don't have the first clue about running a business. No offense, Natalie. You're a lovely person. But it's not about being a sympathetic listener or working cheap on a police case. It's about knowing how hard you can push things and getting results."

"Well, that's not how I want to do business," I protested. "Even if we aren't successful. Look, I broke our rule about divorce cases because I liked you. I cared."

"We all gain people's trust. Usually it's a bad guy; sometimes a good guy. It's the business we're in, nothing personal. You can't be ruled by emotion." Claudia checked her watch, then wiped the corners of her mouth with her linen napkin. "Well, Ms. Yamilla Applethorne, since you don't have a divorce, I should probably skip lunch and get back to work. You're a good little actress. It's been a pleasure."

One thing about Claudia/Sue/Suzanne, she didn't lack confidence. Or nerve. She took her time, pulling herself together and making her exit. She even pushed in her chair before adjusting her scarf and heading for the door.

"She didn't leave money for the iced tea," said Monk. "One criminal act after another."

"I'll pay the bill," said Daniela. "And I'll pay your bill, Mr. Monk. Gladly." The coral red corners of her mouth turned up in a grin. "How did you know?"

"I wasn't trying to solve your problem," Monk admitted. "I was solving Natalie's. A woman plays a prank on our office and the office next door. What do these places have in common? A paper-thin wall, that's it. What do they have of value? Nothing at Monk and Teeger. But over at the hippies' . . ."

"I get it," said Daniela. "Once again I underestimated you. I won't do it again. Now, if you'll excuse me . . ." She was looking out over my left shoulder when she groaned. "Elliot Brown has just walked in, kiddies. Looks like my fun is never done."

CHAPTER TWENTY-EIGHT

Mr. Monk and the Very Last Man

So let this be a lesson to me. Adrian Monk is no man-child. He is not some idiot savant with just one special skill. He is a brilliant detective who was once a seminormal human being and could still be that man. The fact that he could solve this case and orchestrate a perfectly timed redemption in front of Daniela Grace proved it. There had been no great embarrassment, no OCD faltering. Even Monk's use of Julie. Had I known what he was up to, I would have totally objected. But it worked.

Given Julie's little adventure with playacting, I'd thought she'd be ecstatic, like the times when I'd accidentally given her too much sugar before bedtime. Giddy and bouncing off the walls. But she was relatively subdued. I took it as a sign she was growing up.

After Claudia Collins walked out and Daniela left us in order to deal with Elliot Brown, we had the table to ourselves. I dragged over a wingback chair. Monk arranged it evenly with the other two, and we all sat down to celebrate with an expensive lunch. Two iced teas, two Cobb salads, and, since they refused to allow Monk to go back and inspect the food preparation area, no matter how nicely we asked, one bottle of Fiji Water, opened at the table.

I don't recall everything we said. But Julie re-created her meeting at West Bay and how she talked Claudia into going out to lunch. Monk talked about our landlord and how he should be criminally prosecuted for the thin walls. And I reveled quietly in my great good luck. And by saying "quietly," I include the ringing in my ears. Almost gone. I had to focus to notice it at all.

"How is the captain?" Julie asked at one point.

My sense of well-being faded. "Physically, he's fine," I said. "He should be released anytime, although he'll have trouble sitting until his tailbone heals."

"Why did you say 'physically'?"

"Someone's tried to kill him three times. Other people were injured, one was killed. All collateral damage. I have no idea how this is all affecting him."

"Plus, it's escalating," said Monk between sips of his Fiji. "The last attack was just hours after he left home. Whatever the note said about already having waited seven years, someone's in an awful hurry to kill him."

Nothing puts a pall over a celebration like a death threat to one of your best friends. Even after Daniela dropped by our table to thank us again and pick up the tab, we were all sobered by the reality of the situation. This wasn't over.

"Is there anything I can do to help?" asked Julie.

"No, absolutely not." I'm glad Monk said it before I had to.

"Good. I mean . . ." My daughter blushed. "To be honest, I'm not so sure I want to be a private eye after all. No offense."

"Oh." This was a surprise. After so many months of hounding me . . . "What changed your mind, honey? Was it seeing how Claudia worked?"

"No, it's nothing."

"It's not nothing. Look, I can't pretend I'm upset by your change of heart. It's a tough business. And not everyone in it is moral or ethical, at least not all the time."

"Don't worry, Mom. I still respect what you do. I just think it may not be right for me."

"I'm glad to hear it." Actually, I was a tad disappointed. I don't know why.

"You can still be an unpaid intern," Monk suggested.

"No, she can't," I said. "How about an internship at a law office? That will help prepare you for law school. Daniela Grace was very impressed by your ability today, I must say."

"She was?"

"Absolutely. The way you went in there. Your confidence and initiative. I'm proud of you."

"She thought I was convincing?"

"Of course you were convincing. I barely recognized you myself."

"So, you're saying I could be a good actress."

"An actress? Heavens no. That's not what I'm saying at all."

"You don't want me to be an actress?"

"It's even worse than being a PI."

"Well . . ." Julie squinted and pursed her lips. "I'll just have to give it more thought."

A few minutes later, Adrian and I were on the street, watching as my daughter, in her grown-up disguise, walked south on Powell toward the nearest BART station. "She takes after you," Monk said as Julie faded into the crowd.

"Was that meant as an insult or a compliment?"

"An observation," said Monk. "But I'll say compliment if that makes you feel better."

"Good," I said. "Now let's go see the captain."

Monk was silent, all the way from the Fairmont parking garage to the hospital parking garage. He emitted no loud warnings for me to yield at every intersection, no constant reminders about my speed, like a speedometer with audio. This should have been a nice change, but it wasn't. I knew what he was thinking. How could we be so clueless for so long on this case? We didn't have any suspects left. And we certainly didn't have a motive, which was probably the most puzzling part.

As always, there was an armed officer in a chair outside the door. As usual, A.J. Thurman was at the captain's bedside. The three main differences, on this particular visit, were the absence of Trudy Stottlemeyer, the absence of a heart monitor, and the position of the man in the bed. Leland was facedown, his upper chest resting on a pillow, his head resting on his folded hands.

"That's a very unnatural position," said Monk.

"Good afternoon, Monk," said Leland without looking up. "It's actually quite comfortable. I can also rest on my side. And with my inflatable doughnut, I can manage lying on my back. Want to help me with my doughnut?" Monk shivered audibly and the captain chuckled. "Ow, don't make me laugh. Natalie, are you there?"

"I'm here," I said. "How is Trudy holding up?"

Stottlemeyer lifted his hands, a helpless gesture. "Even with the poison and the bullet and the fractured tailbone, I think this damn assassin's doing more harm to my marriage than to me. Anyway, Trudy will be sorry she missed you. The lieutenant persuaded her to go home a few minutes ago."

"You don't need more than two or three babysitters," said A.J. He was in Trudy's usual chair, with a pair of crutches leaned up against the wall, one for each injured leg.

"How's your dad?" I asked. Between the captain and the retired captain, A.J. must have been spending half his life looking down at sickbeds.

"Not good." A.J. bit his lower lip. "It might be as soon as tonight. That's what the doctor says."

"Shouldn't you be with him?" I asked. It seemed like a reasonable question.

"I love my dad, okay? I just needed to take a break."

"Not much of a break," said Stottlemeyer.

"At least you're going to live," said the lieutenant. "That beats a deathbed vigil."

"Don't make me feel more guilty, okay?" Captain Stottlemeyer grunted and managed to turn over on his side. "People have paid the price for me being alive. A twenty-five-year-old boy paid the price."

"Sorry, Captain." A.J. lowered his eyes and rubbed his outstretched legs. "I'm just trying to deal with it."

"I'll get out of here today," promised the captain. "Then we'll all go over and see your dad."

"Thanks. Dad would like that." A second later, his phone rang and he picked up instantly. "What's up?" He paused.

"Good, good." A hand over the receiver. "It's Rebecca. He's still with us." Back on the phone. "No, I'm not alone. Monk, Natalie. The captain, of course."

"Hello, Rebecca," I said in the phone's direction.

"I'll get there when I get there," A.J. told his sister. "Damn it, Becky, I'm doing my best."

"Why do I always feel so awkward around him?" I asked. It was less than five minutes later. After the call from A.J.'s sister, Monk and I had cut our visit short, promising to visit the captain at home, as soon as he was released. We were in the hospital stairwell, getting our exercise and avoiding the horrors of the elevator.

"You feel awkward?" said Monk. "Good. I thought it was just me."

"Well, it is you. You feel awkward around everyone. But A.J.'s a special case."

We emerged from the stairwell into the lobby just in time to see Randy Disher and Bethany Oberlin come in through the automatic doors. We all saw one another at the same moment and joined up by the elevator bank. Three out of four of us hugged.

"I came by your house to say good-bye," said Bethany. "Randy was there. I'm so glad I ran into you like this."

"I had my phone off," I explained. "You're leaving?"

"Back to Thailand, through Tokyo. It's about a twenty-four-hour flight."

"I don't envy you that. How was the second funeral?"

"Uneventful," said Bethany with a sad smile. "Thanks for asking. It might have been a blessing for the first one to be such a mess. It got me more used to the idea of him being gone."

"We thought we'd drop by and see the captain," explained Randy.

"He and my dad knew each other forever, and it just seemed right to stop by." Bethany's right index finger was just settling on the up button.

"What do you mean by forever?" Monk asked. He shrugged his shoulders and cricked his neck. This seemed to be one of his long-shot hunches. "How long is forever?"

"Forever," explained the judge's daughter. "Since college, at least."

"Were they in the same fraternity?" asked Monk.

I won't say I had a clue at that moment, maybe half a clue. Maybe a quarter.

"I think so," said Bethany. "Is this important?"

"Maybe," he said. "We were looking for another connection between the captain and the judge. The fraternity is a connection. Did your father ever tell you stories about his college friends?"

She shook her head. "Dad wasn't much of a sharer."

Then Monk turned to me. "You remember the story about the whisky, the last frat brother drinking the whole bottle. Could they be the last two alive, the captain and Captain Thurman?"

It was a rhetorical question, but I didn't care. "Are you saying someone's killing off the frat brothers? Why would anyone do that? Revenge, maybe?"

"Maybe to drink the whisky," said Randy in that tone of voice that lets you know it's a joke.

Monk paused, not laughing. "Randy, you're right."

"I'm right? I'm never right."

"Randy's right," I agreed. "He's never right."

Monk ignored us and ticked off his points. "Stottlemeyer's father was a whisky expert. He brought back bottles from Inverness, the whisky Mecca. A lot can happen in forty years. Accidents happen. Things get rare."

"You're saying someone's killing people over whisky?" I almost snorted. "How rare can a bottle of whisky be?"

"Off the top of my head, I'd say one-point-four million. That was the price back in two thousand and ten. It may not even be the same whisky, but—"

"One-point-four million?" I gulped. "Dollars?"

"It was sold by Sotheby's, the auction house in New York."

"Sotheby's?" Hadn't I just heard that name? Someone had mentioned Sotheby's. Or I'd seen a Sotheby's catalog. Just last week. "Oh, my God," I said. "The Thurman house. On a chair by the bed."

"Room three forty-seven," shouted Monk. "Go, go, go!"

Randy Disher had spent enough years with us. He knew the shorthand. The ex-lieutenant was the first of us through the stairwell door, bounding up the flights of stairs. I was right behind him. "Right turn, left turn," I said toward his disappearing feet.

I was the second one at the captain's door. Randy was pulling at the knob while the officer on duty seemed torn between reaching for the key on his left side or his weapon on his right.

"Locked from inside," Randy shouted back at me.

"Give him the key," I ordered the patrolman. He was

young, with no memory of homicide lieutenant Randall Disher. But crazy Natalie he knew. "Give him the key!"

I got to the door myself just as the officer's key turned the dead bolt. Randy and I barged through, stumbling over each other. He recovered first and took in the scene. "Get the bag off him," he shouted.

The captain was in the bed sideways, just as we'd left him. But the sheets were a mess. A pillow was on the floor. And a plastic bag was over the captain's head, cinched at the throat with a drawstring. He wasn't moving, deathly white. But a tiny puff of air vibrated between the plastic and his open mouth.

I grabbed at the drawstring, trying to be fast but gentle. The bed rocked and jolted as a pair of wrestling men ricocheted off the walls. At some point, a plastic syringe scuttled across the white tile at my feet.

"Stop," screamed the patrolman, his sidearm nervously drawn and pointed into the melee. "Both of you." They stopped and his eyes finally focused and tried to take it all in—the barely breathing captain, the bag over his head, the syringe, the homicidal desperation on A.J.'s face.

"Lieutenant Thurman? Sir? What the hell? I mean, what the freaking hell?"

CHAPTER TWENTY-NINE

Mr. Monk and the Bottle

Not that I have to be fair to Lieutenant A.J. . . . . I mean, really! But to be fair to Lieutenant A.J., this had been his sister's plan from the start.

A.J.'s and Rebecca's interrogation statements were similar on all the major points.

They'd been unaware of the existence of the bottle of Aisla Dalmore until just a few months ago. That's when they were sitting by their father's bed, amid all the extravagantly expensive equipment designed to keep him alive. Rebecca brought out a photo album from the old days. Arny Senior perked up as he looked at the pictures and told his favorite stories, including the one about the whisky and their fraternity pledge. There were several yellowing snapshots of the boys posing around the large bottle, pretending to drink, embracing it like a lover, all of them impossibly happy and young and hopeful.

The story might have ended there, if not for the obituary column in the Sunday *Chronicle*. That's where Rebecca read about the death of Harrison Wheeler in a plane crash in Nova Scotia. He was the third of the six boys to die. She'd never considered her father that old. Yet here he was, third in line for a dusty bottle of single-malt whisky. It made her curious enough to go online and type in the words "Aisla Dalmore."

This, I have to point out, was not the same whisky that had gone on the auction block for 1.4 million. That was a 105-year-old Aisla T'Orten, which had been sitting undiscovered in someone's basement until 2010. But the Aisla Dalmore was in the same ballpark.

"It's hard to quote a value," the fine-spirits expert from Sotheby's had told Rebecca when she finally got him on the phone. "That whisky isn't supposed to exist. They were aging their best single malt in the storeroom of the Inverness distillery, saving it for the company's hundredth anniversary. Then came the storm of nineteen seventy-two. A lightning bolt hit the building and the place burned to the ground. One of the great tragedies in whisky history. If someone had managed to bribe or sweet-talk them out of a bottle before the fire, it would be the only one. Are you saying you have such a bottle, ma'am?"

Rebecca had hung up and told her brother everything.

Their first instinct was to steal the Aisla Dalmore. But the Mechanics Bank on Sansome Street in the business district had both keys and strict instructions not to open the safety-deposit box unless the requirements of the ghoulish agreement had been met.

All they could do was hope their father could outlive the two other heirs, even by a day. Then his inheritance would go to them. They could pay off the mortgages and finally have lives of their own.

Rebecca claimed the poison was her doing. She had

found umbrella stands on both the judge's and the captain's porch, which was what gave her the idea. Being an ER nurse, she was familiar with heavy-metal toxins. Two middle-aged men would die of natural causes on some rainy San Francisco day. Simple.

Their statements differed about when exactly A.J. was brought into the scheme. Both of them had visited Judge Oberlin in the hospital. Either one of them could have continued to poison him with the thallium. Rebecca blamed A.J. for this and A.J. blamed Rebecca. There was plenty of blame to go around.

At the judge's funeral, A.J. had done his best to humiliate Monk and avoid the possibility of an autopsy. That seemed clear. He was also the one who had written the seven-year note, hoping that this fake, anonymous motive would derail the investigation, which it almost had.

By the time he led the captain into the alley ambush, A.J. was certainly an active participant. Being hit in the leg by your own sister must have been galling. But they were in it together, with only one man standing in their way.

A.J. was the one responsible for the car bomb; he confessed to that one. He had lured Leland out of his sickbed. And he'd had plenty of time to plant it while we were inside the Tuscany Pines. He just hadn't counted on anyone else starting the car.

From then on, things got only more desperate. Arny Senior was requiring his daughter's constant skill to stay alive. Meanwhile, it was becoming more difficult for A.J. to get some valuable alone time with the captain. Their last chance would be in the hospital room.

Between a police lieutenant and a nurse, the Thurmans

knew what to do. The plastic bag would immobilize, not kill. Killing him would be left to the contents of the syringe. Succinylcholine, according to our forensics specialist, is a powerful muscle relaxant that paralyzes its victim and can mimic the signs of a heart attack within fifteen minutes.

Fourteen minutes after the injection, when the captain was breathing his last, his trusted lieutenant would unlock the door, race down the hall, and alert the hospital staff. But it would be too late.

Whiskey or whisky? "Do you spell it with an *e* or without?" Out of the five of us staring at the bottle, I was probably the only one concerned about the spelling.

"According to my pop, the Irish use the *e*, the Scots don't," said Captain Stottlemeyer. He kept staring at the simple, solid bottle with the black-and-white label—no *e* in "whisky"— and the two signatures and a seal verifying it as the real deal.

It was hard not to stare at thirty ounces of brown liquid with an auction value of perhaps 1.5 million. That was only the Sotheby's estimate. It could go higher.

"How could your dad afford it?" Randy asked.

"It wasn't quite that expensive," the captain explained, not for the first time. "But I'm sure he did some fancy talking and paid a pretty penny. I remember our trip to Scotland as a kid, how Mom and Pop fought. I thought they were arguing about the cost of the vacation. The amazing thing to me . . ." He choked up a bit and hid it with a cough.

"The amazing thing is that he cared so much about you and your friends," said Trudy, squeezing Leland's hand. "His best bottle by far and he never even tasted it."

"So when is the auction?" I asked, rubbing my hands together.

Captain Arny had died two days before, drifting off the same
night that his son and daughter were arrested on two counts of
felony murder and various other charges. The captain called us
that morning and asked us to come over and see what had been
dropped off at his bungalow in an armored car from Hamish
Stottlemeyer's safety-deposit box at the Mechanics Bank.

"If it happens in New York, Sharona and I can drive in to
celebrate." Randy seemed to share my auction fever, but the
others looked as if we'd just suggested shooting the family
dog. (Teddy, by the way, was in the backyard, happily gnaw-
ing a bone.)

"Leland made a sacred agreement," Monk said. "Does
that count for nothing in your world, Natalie?"

"You mean you're actually going to drink a priceless bottle of whisky?" I was dumbfounded. I turned to his wife.
"Trudy, you can't be in favor of this."

"Not the drinking part," Trudy said. "But honoring the
memory of his fraternity brothers? And his father? Leland
and I talked it out and I agree."

"You agree?" It was hard to find the words. "How could
you agree? It's a million and a half dollars versus a massive
hangover. Think what you could do with that money."

"We don't need that kind of money."

"Fine. Then give it to charity. You'll also be making a
whisky collector somewhere very happy. Or a museum or
whoever puts up that kind of dough."

"You have two sons," said Randy to the captain. "You can
leave the money to them. Or leave them the bottle."

"I'd rather leave them the story," said Leland. "How their dad kept his word to his dad and his pals. What do you think Nate Oberlin would say if I sold it? Or poor Arny? People are dead and his kids are in jail because they wanted to sell it."

"Okay," I argued. "Let's talk about Nate Oberlin. His daughter lost a father because of this bottle. Don't you think she deserves a say?"

"I talked with her this morning," said the captain. "I suppose that was last night in Thailand. She agrees with Trudy and me. To her it's blood money. 'You might as well drink a toast with it'—that's what she said."

"Wow," I said rather eloquently.

"What do you think is going to make the bigger impact on our lives?" said Trudy. "A new car or honoring Leland's friends? What if the whisky was worth a hundred dollars? Would you think it right for him to sell it then?"

"For a hundred bucks, no," said Randy. "But this is a million point five."

It had taken a little while to get my head around the idea. "Okay," I agreed. "I guess you're right. But you have to promise to save a few drops for your newer friends. I've never had a ten-thousand-dollar sip of anything. Deal?"

"I'm sure there'll be some left over," said the captain.

"Can we do it now?" asked Randy.

"Now?" Stottlemeyer laughed. "First you want to sell it, now you want to drink it for lunch?"

"Sorry. I'm just curious."

"No, I think I need to take my time before opening this baby. Maybe after Arny's funeral."

"Sorry," said Randy again. "The only reason I mentioned

it is because I'm heading back on the red-eye tonight. But you can tell me how it tastes."

This took us all back a step, not because it was un-expected—Randy had to go back to his life, we knew—but because the moment had been so perfect, the four of us to-gether and discussing a case, just like old times.

"You can't go back," said Monk. "I worked long and hard to put A.J. Thurman behind bars. I would have done it even if he was innocent."

"No, you wouldn't, Monk," said Randy.

"That's not my point. There's a vacancy at Leland's side. The planets are aligned. You obviously want to leave New Jersey and we want you back. You never have to speak about the past few years. In fact that's the way I prefer it. Like the disruption in our little universe never even happened."

"But it did happen," said Randy. "And it's not all bad. I'm a police chief in a town that needs me. Well, maybe doesn't need me—or want me. But I'm still their duly appointed chief by a majority vote of the city council. As of right now. Although they could vote at any time."

"I'd be glad to have you back," said the captain. "I can't lie. I mean, I understand about being the chief. That's im-portant, if it's important to you. But you're needed here, too. It won't be easy for me to trust a new lieutenant. Not after the last one."

Stottlemeyer had a point. He had done so much for Ar-nold Thurman Jr.—promoting him, defending him, entrust-ing him with his safety . . . and all the while it was the lieutenant who had been out to get him.

"Hell, Randy, you saved my life."

"I did not."

"Monk says you did."

Monk bobbed his head vigorously. "It's true. You're the one who got in there and grabbed the syringe. You're the one who joked about the priceless whisky. I never would have made that connection." I couldn't tell if Monk was exaggerating or not. "Never in a million years." All right, he was exaggerating.

Randy seemed to be warming to the notion. "Well, I knew it couldn't be connected to an old case. I mean, no one wanted me dead, right? That's just illogical."

"Absolutely," said Monk. "The captain would be lying dead and cold on the hospital room floor before I ever thought of the whisky."

"Adrian, please," said Trudy. She took a deep breath and shuddered. "That's enough."

"Well, you know what I mean. We need him."

CHAPTER THIRTY

Mr. Monk Aligns the Planets

Somehow, Randy had managed to survive his entire visit without renting a car. That was fine with me. It gave us a chance to spend some time together, just the two of us, as I drove him through light evening traffic to the airport.

"Are you texting Sharona?" I asked.

Randy glanced up from his phone, then rather guiltily placed it in the passenger-side cup holder. "Sorry. I guess I'm not very good company."

"No, go ahead. I assume she's picking you up at Newark."

"Hope so. I haven't been able to get in touch. With everything going on, I just bought my ticket this morning."

"When was the last time you talked to her?"

"Yesterday. She had some city meeting this morning and turned off her phone. She's relieved, of course, about Leland. And she's proud of me for helping."

"She should be proud."

"So Monk wasn't just saying that? To make me stay?"

"Not at all."

"Good. It gets harder and harder for her to be proud of me in Summit." He picked up his phone again and put it back down. "There's this weird snowball effect. People look at you a certain way and somehow you wind up being that way. I try to act nonplussed about it."

"Nonplussed?"

"You know, calm. I can't believe you don't know the word nonplussed."

"Nonplussed actually means the opposite of calm. It means confused. Unsettled."

"Really? Wow. It sounds like it should mean calm."

"I know. I used to say it that way. Adrian had to correct me."

He appreciated this. "At least you don't make me feel stupid. If I had used 'nonplussed' in Summit, can you imagine? The English teachers alone. Oh, God, I think I did use it, in a letter to the editor last month." He moaned and slumped into his seat.

"You really don't want to go back, do you?"

"I don't," he finally admitted. "I told myself it was impossible as long as A.J. was around. That was easy. But now he's not around."

"Look, Randy. I know I've been pushing you to go home and make the best of it, but if you'd really be happier . . . There's no shame. Honestly. Everyone here would love having you."

"But that would be running away from my problems."

"Hey." I had to smile. "A very wise man once told me you can run away from your problems."

"I think that was Monk."

"It was Monk."

"Right." He looked down to his phone again. "But I have to go back."

I tried thinking it through. "For Sharona?"

"There's a part of me that Sharona always admired, from back in the day when we were butting heads and working cases. I can bounce back. I can ignore criticism and keep going. It's a talent."

"And you don't want to disappoint Sharona."

He nodded and wriggled. "I guess that's what it boils down to."

I've never complained before about how close the airport is in San Francisco, how it's a straight sweep down the 101, and how traffic can be fairly light. It's never like that, almost never, except when you need a little longer with someone.

I dropped Randy at the curb and defied the printed warning—NO STANDING—by getting out and hugging him good-bye. I'm sure we said all the usual things about missing each other and staying in touch. Then he walked away.

It was getting late. But I had left Monk at the office and I wanted to swing by and make sure the place was safely closed and he found his way home. I was feeling sentimental and a little sad, as if I wanted to hold everyone and everything too close.

Monk and Teeger was still open, the lights still on. I parked in my usual spot, opened the door, and followed the squeaky sound of the clarinet.

My partner was sitting near the back of the shop, inches from the thin wall, playing the strangest of duets, his old clarinet harmonizing with the faint strums of the guitar from next door. He didn't stop when he saw me but finished out the song. Then he rapped on the wall. "Good night, hippies."

"Good night, Adrian," came Peter's voice.

I had to smile. " 'Where Have All the Flowers Gone?' That doesn't sound like you."

"I brought in my clarinet to annoy them," Monk said, looking a little embarrassed. "But we wound up knowing the same music."

"Good for you," I said.

He put on the mouthpiece cover and started breaking down his instrument, returning it to the old leather case. "So Randy is on his way."

"On his way," I confirmed. "And, for the record, I tried to talk him out of it." I could hear a car turning into the parking lot, probably Wendy in her van coming to pick up Peter, I thought.

"The planets were aligned," said Monk, each word a mournful moan. "It was perfect. How many more times do you think we can arrest a lieutenant for murder? I'll tell you how many. Very few."

"Adrian." I looked into his eyes. "We can't live in the past. A.J. is out of the way and there'll be someone new. Look, I can't promise everything will work out. But that's life. We have to be comfortable with life."

It was shaping up to be a good speech, if I have to say so. It would have been a lot longer, too, except for the fact that Sharona Fleming had just walked through the door. She didn't even pause to say hi.

"Where is he?" she shouted as she looked around. "Where's Randy?"

"Sharona?" I didn't know where to begin. "He's been trying to get in touch with you."

"I've been on a plane."

"Obviously," said Monk. "You should have called."

"As soon as I got out of that damn meeting, I went straight to the airport. I didn't know what else to do. I was so mad."

"Why didn't you call?"

"Because that would have freaked Randy out. He would have known something was wrong by the tone of my voice."

Her voice did have quite a tone to it, anxious and angry and ready to kill. "So what is wrong?" I had to ask.

"They fired him. The Summit city council fired Randy. After all he's done for them. Can you believe that?"

"Poor Randy," I said.

"I hate that town." Sharona took a breath, straightened her leopard-print top, and fluffed back her big, blond hair. "Hello, Natalie. Adrian. Sorry to be such a mess. Where's Randy?"

"The planets are aligned," said Monk, his eyes raised to the ceiling.

"What the hell is he talking about?"

"Nothing. But Randy isn't here. He's at the airport." I reached for my phone. "Don't worry. There's still an hour before the flight. Wouldn't that be annoying, crossing paths like that? Flying all the way here and then missing each other?"

"You're telling me?" I don't know who had dialed Randy's number first, Sharona or me. But one of us got through.

"Thank God for cell phones, huh?" I had to laugh. "I don't know what we would do—"

"Hold on." Sharona held up a red-lacquered fingernail and turned to face the open door. "Is that Randy's ringtone?"

It was Randy's ringtone.

And it was coming from the front passenger cup holder in my car.